NORTHERN
CRIME
one

**New crime stories
from northern writers**

MOTH
PUBLISHING

First published in 2015 by Moth Publishing, an imprint of
Business Education Publishers Limited, Chase House, Rainton Bridge,
Tyne and Wear, DH4 5RA

Cover design by Courage, UK
Printed and bound by Martins the Printers Ltd, UK

A CIP catalogue record for this book is available from the British Library

Paperback ISBN 1 909486 17 1
Ebook ISBN 978 1 909486 18 8

www.mothpublishing.com

CONTENTS

FACE VALUE   1
Nick Triplow

A LUCKY ESCAPE   19
Tom Moody

TOXIC AIR   29
Kathleen Mckay

QUID PRO QUO   39
Betty Weiner

APRIL FOOL   49
Basil Ransome-Davies

ALCATRAZ DIRTBAG   59
Ben Borland

THE COLD CALLING   69
Lynne M Blackwell

THE MILLIONAIRE'S WIFE   79
Karon Alderman

MEMENTO MORI   87
Pam Plumb

A DEAD MAN IN STRATFORD   103
Belinda Weir

A SMALL REBELLION   115
Alex Reece Abbott

TULPA   131
MJ Wesolowski

BADLANDS: A TALE OF FIVE PARTS   149
BLJ Langham

MAY TRICKS 165
Martin Robins

KEYS ON THE MANTELPIECE 177
Pat Black

FRAGMENTS 191
Michael Connon

POWER TRIP 199
Emma Oxley

INTRUDER 213
Danny Marshall

HONEYPOT 223
Sue Wilsea

DOG DAY AFTER LUNCH 233
Adrian Fayter

FACE VALUE

Nick Triplow

Bernice places the palms of her hands either side of Ronnie's face. There are two kinds of people on the estate, she says. Good people like Mrs Scott next door, Chloe at singing group and Reverend Gareth at St Marks. The sort who'll help if you forget your door key or need bus fare into town on Thursdays. Lee Symes and his mates who hang around Costcutter on Second Avenue, drinking cider and lighting fires in the boarded up houses on Bradley Street, they're bad people.

'That's why you never go down Bradley Street. Understand?'

Ronnie stares.

Bernice strokes his cheeks. She pulls out a chair and sits him at the table. She fetches the big pad and draws a picture of two faces. Round baby heads, one with squint eyes and a sneery mouth, the other with smiley eyes and a happy mouth. 'See what I mean?' she says. 'Two kinds of people. You stay away from the bad people and stick with the good people. Always.' She draws flowers, stars and butterflies around the good head and lightning and a black cloud raining on the bad head. She nods to Sergeant West, perched on the edge of the sofa. Ronnie calls her the lady police. It's the second time she's brought him home.

'S'all I can do,' says Bernice.

'I know, love. Just keep getting the message across and we'll do our best to keep an eye out.'

Ronnie says, 'Is she good or bad people?'

Sergeant West laughs.

'She's good.' Ronnie knows he's right.

'Just stay away from Bradley Street and Lee Symes an' that lot and you'll be fine. They're not your friends even if you think they are.'

He doesn't like how she says it. He never said they were his friends.

This is the first time in years Bernice has had to go away. Val Scott's taking time off work. Ronnie'll go there for breakfast and tea. Val will take him home and stay for evening telly, bedtime and overnight. The bus will pick him up from home and take him to work Monday, Tuesday and Wednesday. He'll take the double-decker to town on Thursday and collect his money from the centre, then come straight home. On Friday morning, Val will take him to singing group. Chloe will drive him home afterwards and make lunch. Val will come at four o'clock and stay until Bernice arrives home later that evening.

Bernice writes it all down. She draws a picture for each thing that's going to happen. Val Scott has curly hair. Chloe has long straight hair and her mouth is singing, which Ronnie says is wrong, because when she sings she ties her hair in a ponytail, but it's too late to change the picture. Bernice draws a box by each one. 'You tick these off when they've happened, then you'll know how far through the week you are.' She puts her arms around him. 'It's only a week. I promise.'

'Can I put the DVD on now?' he says.

On Thursday Ronnie takes the bus into town. He's early and spends time looking through nature DVDs in HMV. He likes the way jellyfish swarm and pulse through the water and would like to have another jellyfish DVD.

At the Centre he does Thursday exercise class. Lizzie keeps holding his hand when there's no need, which is annoying. He spends the rest of the time doing picture match on the computer until Judy brings the wage envelopes. He counts his money, folding one ten and one five pound note in his wallet, which goes in the inside zip pocket of his jacket. He puts four pounds sixty in coins in the button pocket of his cargoes. As he walks down Victoria Street towards the bus station he can smell McDonald's. When he's hungry the smell always makes him feel hungrier. Inside it's noisy with people. He already knows what he wants and orders a Big Mac Meal with a chocolate milkshake. He pays with the five pound note and carefully carries the tray to an empty table. He forgets to wait for his change, but the McDonald's lady calls him back and puts the coins on the tray.

Ronnie doesn't see Tanya and Becky when he sits down, but they sit at his table. 'Hiya, Ronnie.' Tanya has a good people face and very straight blonde hair like the picture of Chloe singing but not singing. She wears gold earrings, draws black lines around her eyes and colours in her eyelids pale blue. She smiles. 'That looks tasty.'

Ronnie finishes his mouthful and wipes his mouth with a napkin.

'Can I have a chip?' says Becky.

'One,' he says.

Becky's hand goes into the chip box and comes out with at least six chips which she stuffs in her mouth.

'That's more than one,' says Ronnie.

She opens her mouth and shows a chewed up mush. 'Want 'em back?'

'Where's your mum, Ronnie?' says Tanya.

He thinks for a moment. 'Away till Friday.'

'We heard she was in hospital,' says Becky.

His Big Mac will be cold if he doesn't finish it soon. He picks up the chip box and eats the chips one at a time, dipping each in ketchup until he runs out. There are always chips left over if he forgets to ask for extra ketchup.

Tanya says, 'You gettin' the bus home after?'

He nods.

'Aren't you a good boy,' says Becky.

'I'm not a boy.'

'Well you ain't exactly a man, are ya?' She does a weird head wobble.

He does a talk to the hand.

She says fuck off, scopey.

Tanya says, 'We'll come back on the bus, keep you company.' She smiles again, 'Won't we, Becks?'

Becky isn't listening. She's texting.

Ronnie wonders if he should tell them they've got off the bus one stop too soon for his house, but Lee Symes and Jason Ward are waiting. Lee puts an arm around his shoulder and asks did he have a good time in Maccy D's and does he want to get some sweets or a bottle of pop? He says he doesn't want any, because he is going to Mrs Scott's. He starts walking. Lee walks with him. He says, 'Just cos you don't want 'owt, don't mean we 'ave to go without, does it? Unless you're makin' the rules now, Ronnie?'

Because it isn't up to him to make the rules, they go back to the shop. Lee gives Ronnie the basket to carry and picks up a bottle of cider and some cans and puts them in. When they get to the till he asks for 10 Lamberts and blue Rizlas. It comes to twelve twenty-five.

'You got money, mate?' says Lee.

'Yes,' says Ronnie.

Lee holds out his hand. 'Gizzit then.'

Truth be told, Val can't wait for the week to be over. She doesn't mind helping Bernice out for a few hours now and then, but five days straight and she's exhausted. She watches Ronnie from the kitchen. He sits at the dining table, prods his fork at fish fingers, chips and peas, which he'd asked for but now doesn't want. He was quiet when he came in and looks peaky, but it's hard to tell. She asks if he's feeling OK. He says he feels sick and has a headache. The last thing she wants to do is fuss. They've nearly made it to Friday without any major hassles. She asks if he wants her to call Doctor Chalmers. He says he doesn't, but something's not right. He skips telly and goes to bed early. She tiptoes in later. Ronnie's sound asleep. When she picks up his cargoes and hoodie to put them in the wash, they smell of smoke.

Next morning he's right as rain. Dressed and ready to go to singing group after breakfast. They catch the bus together and Val carries on to work. Maureen's on till supervisor duty and puts her on the baskets-only checkout, which suits her fine and keeps her busy. She doesn't give Ronnie a second thought.

After the shift, she picks up a box of custard slices to take back as a sort of end-of-week celebration. It'll be a mess, but Ronnie loves his cakes. When she calls round, he isn't home. She assumes he must still be at singing group and phones Chloe, who says she left him watching a *Living Planet* DVD at two o'clock. She tries ringing Judy at the Centre, but she's gone for the weekend and they won't give a home number. The man she speaks to checks and confirms that Ronnie hasn't been there all day. Val thinks things through, then goes to St Marks and blubs an explanation to Reverend Gareth, who thinks they ought to call the police. She says, couldn't they look first themselves? They walk the estate until it begins to grow dark.

She blames herself for not calling the police sooner.

At 7.14pm Ronnie is officially listed as missing, a description circulated.

At 7.30pm Reverend Gareth phones Bernice.

At 7.42pm patrols commence a check of vacants on Bradley Street. The search ceases when, at 8.25pm, PCSOs stop three youths on Kennet Street who say they saw Ronnie Barrett earlier that afternoon. He was on his own, they say.

Going where?

'Down the docks.'

At 9.04pm Trish West is called to the dockside. The boss and DI McAlister stand, shoulders hunched, hands in pockets, debating whether to put men in the water. She knows the lad, what does she think?

'I can't see any reason he'd come down here. It's too far for a start. He'd never have had the energy to walk it, unless he was looking for Bernice, but he knows she's due home later.'

'So you're saying, Sergeant?'

West peers into black water. 'Wait until morning.'

The rescue team arrives at first light. Their dinghy bobs at its moorings. As they congregate on the jetty for McAlister's briefing, it begins to rain. 'We're looking for a 20-year-old white male. Last confirmed around 3pm yesterday afternoon heading this way, but no further sightings. Wearing grey jogging bottoms, green polo shirt and sweatshirt and a navy blue zip jacket. And he has learning difficulties. Right, who gets wet first?'

They swim from the jetty, paying out lines, diving and searching open water channels and sections between the hulls of boats, finding skeins of greasy rope and bits of net. An empty suitcase.

It's a long, cold, fruitless day. They call a halt as the light fails, trudging up the slipway and loading the gear back in the van as fans emptying Blundell Park jam up traffic and grab an eyeful. They haul the dinghy from the water onto the trailer and reverse the Land Rover to the water's edge to tow it back up.

Trish West has been there all day, helping out where she can, making on-the-hour calls to Bernice. She tells herself this is the job, no matter how hard it gets. Last week a pub fight outside the Bluestone: families and factions and a blind eye turned. Week before that a stabbing on Seaview Street. Before that a stash of stolen card details in a house on Wellington Street and beers after work. This week Ronnie Barrett: missing.

The call comes in shortly before nine on Saturday night; an anonymous tip-off from a payphone by the shops on Second Avenue. PCs Lawrence and Durford are first to respond. Lawrence tries to kick out what's left of the boards on the front door of 67 Bradley Street. Durford goes round the back, but the grills are bolted in place. He uses a tyre lever to wrench off a loose grill at the front and Lawrence follows him in. 'Watch where you're walking and for fucksake don't touch anything.'

67 is your classic junkie shithole with sharps and glass trodden in the carpet. They move through the rooms. When they find Ronnie Barrett upstairs on a sofa in the back bedroom, he screams.

Durford keeps his voice low. 'You're alright, mate. You're fine. We'll sort you out.'

Ronnie screams.

Durford steps back. 'OK, son. OK.'

Ronnie makes noises, moaning softly.

Lawrence calls it in. Says they've found him, but he won't let them near.

Durford goes outside to brief the paramedics. They chat to Ronnie from the doorway. Any closer and he screams again. It's almost dark in the room. A sickly light spills through a yellow bed sheet at the window. The place is rank with the smell of human waste, some of which comes off Ronnie. They try again to approach and Ronnie freaks. He cries and cries.

Lawrence steps outside and makes a call.

'Why the fuck wasn't I told sooner?'

In spite of the stink that hits as she crouches in the doorway, Trish West forces a smile. 'Hello, love, remember me? Lady Police. What you doing in 'ere, love?'

He takes thick, snotty breaths. Wheezes.

'Can I put my torch on? Promise I won't shine it at you.' She aims the beam at the corner of the room, then moves it around, bringing Ronnie into its periphery. At first she thinks there's blood smeared across his forehead, but as she brings the light to bear, she sees it's the word *MENTAL* in red marker. She asks Ronnie if he remembers the pictures Bernice drew of good people and bad people.

He says he does.

'You remember what you said I was?'

'Good people.'

'And you, you're good, right?'

Ronnie is silent for a long time. 'I'm bad now.'

'I don't think you're bad, mate. I think you're not very well and that's different. Now listen, Bernice is on her way. She'll be here soon, but I need your help, because we don't want her to see you in a dirty place like this, do we?'

Ronnie's long sigh carries a world more hurt than West can bear. She steadies herself against the door frame. 'I want you to meet these friends of mine, all good people, I promise. They'll make you feel better.' She stands, uncramps her legs and takes a step into the room.

'I can't get up,' he says. 'I've made a mess.'

'D'you want me to help?' She holds out her hand. When Ronnie reaches up she sees cigarette burns on his forearms.

In the early hours of Sunday morning Lee Symes and Jason Ward are taken into custody. Jason paces his cell and every so often presses his face against the cracked observation window to call PC Lawrence a cunt. Lawrence keeps tabs and says nothing. Tanya and Becky are in another room, pissed up and underage. Becky is mouthy and belligerent. When West calls her parents, Mr and Mrs Mawson are reluctant to leave the social club, until she offers to come down and drag them out. They're on their way. She leaves a message on Tanya's mum's voicemail.

While she waits for news from the hospital she tops up the coffee perc, takes one down to Lawrence and brings another to Brooks on the desk. 'Hot and strong, Dave.' The smile has a worn-out feel. 'How's it been?' she says.

'Saturday night. Pissed-up dickheads or dicked-up pissheads, take your pick. My personal highlight so far is a stag party knocking lumps out of each other in *Casablanca's*. The bastards turned on PC Wilson and Mick Marham. I sent DS Collier's mob in for back up.'

'*That* heavy?'

'They nicked the groom, best man and ushers. Get this, all of 'em in fancy dress. We 'ad Tinky Winky, Darth Vader, Batman, a pink rabbit and fuckin' Spongebob in 'ere. Apparently the bride's honour had been at stake.'

'Lucky girl.'

'Trust me, that horse has bolted. I know the family.'

'You charged 'em?'

'Too right. They're sleeping it off in paper suits downstairs.'

She sips her coffee. It burns her lips. 'They found Ronnie Barrett in a squat on Bradley Street. Frightened out of his life.'

'How'd he get down there?'

'I think – actually, I'm certain – Lee, Jason, Becky and that Tanya enticed him. They beat him up and took his money. I don't want to think about what else.'

'Anyone told Lee's dad?'

'Not yet.'

West ignores Brooks' raised eyebrow. 'There's fag burns on his arms and stuff's gone from Bernice's place. Telly, DVD. She kept a few quid rainy day money in a tin and that's gone. Only her and Ronnie knew where it was.'

'They nicked the stuff and took Ronnie with 'em.'

'He didn't find his own way down Bradley Street, did he?'

'You got evidence?'

'Probably not. CCTVs are knacked up that end. Durford said he'd see if we can get something on Second Avenue by the payphone. He reckons there might be something from one of the shop cameras.'

The coffee's right for drinking. She thinks about giving it another go with the girls. Not that there was much to be had out of a session with Becky Mawson in attack mode. Tanya hadn't said a word. West suspected it was the first time she'd been banged up. Jason was walking up the walls, and Lee was Lee. Poison.

Brooks takes a call; Tanya's mum's on her way.

'Should have seen 'im in that shithole, Dave. It was 'orrible. You know they'll walk. We'll have a possession charge on Jason, but that's it.'

'Any witnesses?'

'None, apart from whoever phoned it in.'

'What about Ronnie?'

'Assuming he's in any fit state to give a statement, and if he remembers and has the words to explain what happened, well then we've just got the CPS to convince he's a reliable enough witness to overcome a defence with a readymade discredit argument.'

Before Brooks can respond, a bleary-eyed woman arrives at the desk followed by an unkempt bloke in tracky bottoms and London 2012 T-shirt. 'We come to take Becky Mawson 'ome.'

West signs them in. She hears herself thank them for coming. 'I'd like a word with you first. Then with you both and Becky together.'

The man yawns. 'Fucksake, can't we just take 'er? We've got a cab waitin'.'

The Mawsons are as adept at playing the game as their daughter. No proof, no crime, and she's a minor. Not that West expected the light to shine down and make them tell the truth, but a glimmer of sympathy would help. The Mawsons stand behind Becky in the interview room. She's Lee Symes' girl and she'll stick by him. West asks, will she tell them what happened to Ronnie? Were there drugs? Was it sexual? Becky laughs. West has no choice but to let her go.

She leaves Tanya on her own for a few minutes and then takes her a cup of tea. 'Quieter without your mate.'

Tanya's panda-eyed, still a bit teary. 'When can I go 'ome?'

'When your mum gets here and when I'm satisfied you've told me all you know about what happened to Ronnie Barrett.'

Tanya wipes her nose on her sleeve. 'You got a tissue?'

Brooks buzzes through to say Tanya's mum's in reception.

The mother and daughter reunion is quiet and for the most part wordless. West senses conversations had and warnings unheeded. She lays it on thick with the mother, hoping she'll talk sense to the girl.

'I know you're frightened, Tanya. But you're bright enough to know when something is wrong. What happened to Ronnie *is* wrong, isn't it?'

Tanya's mum squeezes her hand.

Tanya looks up. 'I dunno. What happened to Ronnie?'

The girl can't hide the speck of shame in her eyes. West takes a punt. 'You tell me, Tanya. You rang in the 999.'

'It weren't me.'

'We can have it checked. You want me to fetch the recording?'

'It fuckin' weren't me.'

Tanya's mum picks up her bag. 'Anything else?'

Brooks is back from a chat with Lee Symes. 'That twat wouldn't recognise shame unless it rolled him a spliff,' he says, 'You'd reckon he 'ad a face only a mother could love, only I've met her and she hates 'im an all.' Brooks has had a tenner on Symes as 'the boy most likely' in the station sweepstake. Nothing less than a five-stretch wins the kitty, which narrows down the offence potential, but he's well on the way.

West takes a call from the A&E doctor, who confirms that, in her opinion, the burns on Ronnie's wrists, some bruising on his upper arms and cheek, and the pen marking on his face suggest he has been… she struggles for a word and lands on 'tortured'. More worrying, she continues, are needle marks on his arms and torso. Given where he was found, these could have been accidental or, considering Ronnie's state of mind, they might have been self-inflicted. She realises it's idiotic, but if she doesn't consider it, someone else will. West knows the wounds are a result of the same disgusting game as the other injuries. The doctor also believes Ronnie's ingested a substance, possibly ketamine, within the last 24 hours. Initial tests are inconclusive and more detailed results won't be available until the lab opens in the morning.

'It is morning,' says West.

'Is it?' The doc rings off.

West relays the news to Brooks.

He says, 'So what do you want to do?'

'I'm hoping one of them will turn, Tanya maybe. I'll see her at home tomorrow and speak to Jason when he's calmed down.'

'If it's none of the above?'

There's a weight in Brooks' question which makes her think

before answering. 'Then Lee Symes and his mates walk out and we'll live with it.'

'You're sure?'

'There is no other way.'

Brooks nods. 'Fair enough.'

She spends the last hour of the shift wearing out the office lino. Her face is sore, the skin dry from the day on the docks. The clock ticks round and she stays when she should go home. Brooks suggests she takes a drive to the hospital. Ronnie might give her some scrap of information. If not, she'll be company for Bernice.

'You want 'er to 'ave *company*, get her a fucking dog. I'm trying to do a job.'

Brooks looks over his glasses. 'You know that's not what I meant.'

'Would I be this pissed off if I did? You want me out the way.'

'Yes – please.'

'Don't fuck around, Dave. This is too important.'

West finds Val Scott in the A&E waiting area. She's been crying. 'Those people are animals. You gonna lock 'em up?'

'We'll do everything we can.'

She nods. 'You sound like that doctor.'

Bernice comes through. 'He's calmer now. They gev him something that'll help him rest.'

Val Scott's face is pinched and pale. She looks as though she's ready to cry again. Bernice puts a hand on her shoulder. 'You go. I'll pop in later once we know more.'

West says, 'I'll be here for a while, Mrs Scott.'

The log book records that PC Lawrence is withdrawn from observation at 3.35am with Jason Ward sleeping. Shortly afterwards, Sergeant Brooks requests a doctor's visit. Twenty minutes later Ward is compliant when they bring him to the ground floor medical room. The doctor asks for the CCTV to be turned off to protect his patient's privacy. It takes him a little over five minutes to decide that, aside from the effects of excess alcohol and cannabis, there's nothing wrong with Ward beyond the inherently unhealthy constitution of a habitual drink and drug user. The doctor annotates the custody record and hands the clipboard back to Brooks. 'Next time, make sure there's a bloody reason to get me out of bed.'

A few minutes later, Jason Ward is dozing with his head on the medical room table when the giant Pink Rabbit enters and closes the door behind him. The voice is gentle. 'Jason, wake up. I want to talk to you.'

Ward peers through the murk and sees what he thinks is a fluffy pink bunny large as life sat across the table with a plastic smile moulded across his face. 'What the fuck are you?'

'I'm Pink Rabbit, me.'

Ward drops his head and issues a muffled, 'Fuck off, Pink Rabbit.'

'Where were you earlier this evening?'

'Nowhere.'

'Everybody's got to be somewhere, son. I was in my hole mindin' my own business when the bunny signal went up, so where was you?'

'Here.'

'Before that?'

'In a cell.'

'And before that?'

He stalls.

'Don't make me ask again, Jason.'

As Ward lifts his head, a big pink pad comes across the table and cuffs him around the ear. 'Tell me what happened to Ronnie Barrett.'

Jason sits up, the haze clearing. 'You can't interview me without a lawyer.'

Pink Rabbit leans forward. '*Ronnie Barrett.*'

'Fuck off. I aren't sayin' fuck all.'

Pink Rabbit walks to the door, shaking his head. He pauses,

twisting one of his long pink bunny ears. He turns and makes two bunny hops that put him in Jason's face. His pad hands cuff Jason around the head, softly, with a rhythm, 'What did you do to Ronnie?'

'I din't do nothing.'

He cuffs harder and sing-songs louder, 'What – did – you – do – to – Ronnie?'

'It weren't me.'

'Who then?' Pink Rabbit stops cuffing, all friendly again. 'Come on, you can tell me, I'm a fluffy fucker.'

'I can't.'

'I'll rip your fucking ears off. Who hurt him? Who burned him? Who made him sit in his own shit?'

'I – I can't.'

'Y'can.'

Pink Rabbit twists Jason's ears.

'Ow fuck!'

'What was it, some kind of sex game? You get off on it?' Pink Rabbit wanks his invisible fluffy pink cock.

'*No.*'

'Your idea?'

'No.'

'Tanya's?'

'No.'

'Becky Mawson?'

Jason hesitates. A flicker.

'Becky then. What about Lee?'

Jason knocks Pink Rabbit's hands away. 'You don't understand.'

'That you're frightened of Lee Symes and his old man? Tell you what, son, I'll bounce you round this room and we'll see if you're more frightened of them than me. They ain't fuckin' 'ere. I am.' He drags Jason up and shoves him back against the wall. 'You want out, Jason. I know you do, it's natural. You're probably gettin' the message, thinking I might do to you what you did to Ronnie. But you definitely want out. So tell me, what did you and them bastards do to Ronnie?'

West is stirring vending machine tea with a biro when the text comes in from Brooks: Jason Ward has had a change of heart and wants to make a formal statement.

PC Lawrence is standing guard in the interview room when she arrives. Ward sits with the duty solicitor, a man called Whitley. The pair of them bleary-eyed and bored. 'My client wishes to give a statement. He realises, under the circumstances, it's the correct thing to do and he would like this to be taken into consideration.'

'Duly noted,' says West. 'How are you feeling now, Jason?'

He shrugs.

'I need to know you're giving this interview willingly.'

'S'pose.' Jason glances towards PC Lawrence standing at the door. Lawrence touches his ear.

'Are you or aren't you?'

'*Yes.*'

Trish starts the recorder. 'Sergeant Patricia West interviewing Jason Ward. Also present are PC Lawrence and… '

'Duty solicitor Christopher Whitley.'

'Let's start from the off, Jason. Whose idea was it to pick up Ronnie Barrett?'

'Lee's.'

'Lee who?'

'Lee Symes.'

Whitley looks miserable when a whistling Dave Brooks signs him out an hour later. 'You always this cheerful at six on a Sunday morning, Sergeant Brooks?'

'End of shift in sight, mate. Home to a full English. Sunday papers, warm bed. I'm happy as Larry.'

Whitley has been alone with Jason Ward for 15 minutes while West completes the paperwork. She buzzes open the security door for him to leave and thanks him for coming in. He pauses. 'For what it's worth, Sergeant West, no court will accept that statement. Ward claims he was forced into giving a confession and we'll be registering a complaint.'

'Who forced a confession from him?'

'We don't know.'

'He just told us it was given of his own free will. You heard him.'

Whitley glances behind as if he expects someone to be listening. His voice is barely more than a whisper, 'He says someone dressed as a pink rabbit assaulted him and threatened further violence if he didn't tell you what you wanted to hear.'

West studies his face for signs that he's joking. 'Come again.'

'Even if it didn't actually happen, and I'm not saying it absolutely did, there must be a case for him being under the influence.'

Brooks slides a form across the desk. 'Sorry to interrupt. I couldn't help overhearing. We had the doc check him out earlier. Said he was fine. You can keep that, it's a copy.'

West watches Whitley go as a grey dawn struggles to lift itself above Kwik Fit. 'I don't know what just happened...'

Brooks chips in, 'Been a long night, Trish. You want me to charge Lee Symes or will you?'

'You do it. I'm going home.'

Later, they'll bring Becky in and work through Jason's story. If she's any sense, she'll say what needs saying. After that, a home visit with Tanya. Some home truths needed there. West stops at McDonald's drive-thru for coffee.

Bernice has been sitting by Ronnie's bed for an hour, stroking his cheek and talking about jellyfish. There's a faint trace of red marker on his forehead. He looks at her, through her. She can't tell if he's listening. She tries to find a smile from her repertoire, but there isn't one. She rests her hand on his head, like an act of faith. She tells him they'll be OK.

A LUCKY ESCAPE

Tom Moody

He picked his way across the yard. Iron-hard ridges of mud were
held fast by a frost that hadn't eased all day. He didn't want to turn
an ankle when he had things to do. He stopped to look up at the fell.
The light snow-fall had turned the hills white. He knew there was
more to come, so today might just be the day. But for now, he felt
warm enough in his old overcoat. He threw hay-bales down from the
loft and cut the rough hessian twine. Breaking the bales into sections
he scattered them along the worn, wooden mangers. The shaggy
black Galloways jostled to pull the fodder through the bars. The
smell of summer meadows rose up from the dried grasses. He fed
the beasts automatically, his mind shuffling possible futures. Leaving
the gloom of the barn, his careful steps took him back to the garden
gate. The air was so still he could hear the thrum of the small birds'
wings as they worked to clear the bird table.

In the kitchen, his collie, Meg, fussed around his feet. He
balanced on the sheets of newspaper that were always laid inside
the door and pulled off his black rubber boots. Then shrugging off
his overcoat and jacket he crossed to the sink, turned on the tap and
looked into the brown spotted mirror. He snorted, 'Yer beginin' to
look yer age, Jack Lazarus; even if you still feel like a young un.' At
69, working in all weathers, his skin had tanned like brown leather
and it stretched over angular cheekbones. A few burst veins showed
as red threads in his cheeks. His chin bristled with frosted stubble,
like an autumn field. Under spikey eyebrows, his eyes were seamed at
the edges, their blue as pale as the ice on the water butt. He'd always
been a skinny beggar; years of wresting a living from this small-
holding had seen to that. He filled the kettle, waited for it to boil,
and massed a pot of tea. He sat at the scrubbed pine table and looked
around. The place was tidy but it lacked a woman's touch. He'd

propped his old 410 single-barrel behind the door. Mary would have had something to say about that, if she'd still been here. His brow creased; she wasn't here though, and that was the rub.

He couldn't remember exactly when he'd bought the gun. Originally it was to keep down rabbits and other vermin. He'd not been above a bit of poaching in the early days, when money was scarce. But he hadn't shot for years. Mary had never discussed it with him, never criticised, but she would run her fingers through fur or feathers and admire their beauty. Then, one day, he'd shot a hare for the pot, up in the top meadow. It's big, amber eyes had looked at him, shocked and puzzled, as though to say, '*What did you do that for, man?*' Then the light behind them went out. He remembered now, the feeling of shame that came over him. He'd tried to explain to Mary, tried to put his feelings into words. She had just held him tight, cuddled him like he was a babby and said, '*I'm glad, Jack.*' Nothing more was said. He'd locked the gun away for good, or so he'd thought.

The dull ache was back in his belly. It always came on when he thought of his wife. She had gone and that was Mortimer's fault. In the past he'd met setbacks head-on. His strength, aye and his stubbornness, had always seen him through, but he couldn't fight illness. Not in another person, no matter how much he wanted to. Mary had gone downhill as her memory got worse. One rainy day he'd come back to find her in the yard, wearing her nightgown, confused and soaking wet. He'd known then that she couldn't be left on her own. That was when the doctor had persuaded him that Mortimer's care home was the only choice.

He always thought of Mortimer as greasy. His manner was oily and slick. He was fat and bald. His few remaining hairs were always plastered to his scalp. The under-arms of his shirts were always dark with sweat. Mortimer, like his care home, had an overpowering, sickly-sweet smell. Jack hated the way his piggy eyes would never hold his gaze. Sliding away, usually coming to rest on one of the younger care assistants. He'd bought a hotel in the village and then changed it into a care home that looked so modern it hit you in the eye. Then Mortimer snapped up a hill farm, causing much resentment among the hill farmers. Turning it into an American-style ranch house put him beyond the pale. On most days his coffee-and-cream Jeep squatted like an ugly toad in the square. Letting everyone know Mortimer was in town.

Jack realised that it had been a mistake to put Mary in Mortimer's hands. The home smelled worse than his byre most days. At least the smell of his cow's muck wasn't mixed with cheap air-freshener. It was always too hot in the lounge and too cold in the bedrooms. He was glad to get into the fresh air after visiting, but he hated leaving Mary behind. The staff spoke to the old folk as though they were children. Jack knew that most of the residents, like Mary, couldn't understand or didn't care. But it still wasn't right. He'd brooded over what might happen when the visitors had all gone home. He didn't blame the staff so much. Mortimer paid only the bare minimum wage so anyone with any gumption soon left. It was the owner he blamed.

He had complained, but Mortimer always had a plausible answer. It was like swatting midges. The slippery swine always had a glib line of patter that left Jack feeling helpless and frustrated. He'd had to watch as Mary slipped into apathy; and then she was gone. She just lost any reason to stay alive. He knew Mortimer was to blame.

He had tried to bite back his burning anger. At first he'd complained to Social Services. After a few weeks a letter had come back full of fancy phrases: no proof any misconduct, no evidence, and no corroboration. They had obviously had full measure of Mortimer's evasions.

Then other rumours began to circulate around the dale. About Mortimer's meetings, late at night, with men wearing sunglasses and dark suits. Men with minders, who'd arrive in a black limousine, carrying a metal briefcase. Jack found such rumours all too easy to believe.

He'd spent a lot of time thinking about Mortimer. He knew every yard of his route across the high road. He'd watched him going to work and marked the time when he returned. Jack had watched him drive by, with his eyes fixed on the road, but he doubted if Mortimer ever noticed a nondescript shepherd and his dog.

Jack had hatched his plan. He knew what the weather would be like when the time came. He had felt the sting of wind-blown ice on his face. He had felt air so cold that it made the lungs and throat ache, made the breath freeze onto the face. It was not new to him but it would be a surprise for Mortimer.

A clanking came from outside as a bucket blew over and went rolling across the yard. He looked out of the window. Snow was tumbling out of the darkening sky. He finished the dregs in his cup, stood up and then lifted his green waterproofs off the hook behind the door. His collie cocked her head to one side. He bent down and ruffled her ears, 'I'll be back soon enough, owld lass; and if a'm not… well the neighbours will come round to see t' ye.'

His old Landrover started first time, in spite of the cold. The wipers ticked back and forth, leaving him a narrow view through the cleared wedges of glass. He turned left onto the road that wound up the side of the fell. The wind was already licking the snow into dunes that were creeping out of gates and across the white ribbon of road. After just over two miles, he braked to a slow stop and then reversed into the little hollow quarried out of the hillside. He could wait here and have a good view of the road without his vehicle being noticed. There'd be little traffic today. Locals would stay at home, or choose lower routes, but Mortimer would come this way. He'd come battering through the drifts. He had horsepower to spare, but he wouldn't know that the verge here ended abruptly in a drop of three or four feet.

Jack felt a prickle of anticipation when the glow of lights shone through the storm. Mortimer must have left early, but it was certainly him. No other vehicle was as wide and had so many driving lamps. Jack wound an old jumper around his head, turban-style. All the local shepherds did this as protection against the driving snow. The fact that it disguised him, and would give him the air of a terrorist, was a bonus. He pressed down on the accelerator and edged out onto the road. The lights were approaching fast. As they drew close, he veered towards them, flicking his lights to full beam. The Jeep slewed hard to the right. Jack braked and glanced up at his mirror. He saw the back of the other vehicle rear up, as the front dropped off the road, burying its nose in the bank below. As the muffled crunch reached his ears, he changed gear and reversed back to the crash scene. Clutching his gun, he jogged across the road and plunged through the snow to the wreck. Mortimer was sitting rigid in his seat, his hands locked onto the wheel. As the door came open he yelped. The gun thrust under his nose stopped him short. 'Out,' barked Jack. The fat man slid out into the deep snow His eyes were wide with fear and he was trembling even before the cold had time to hit him. 'What do you want? I've got money in my wallet, take it!'

'Shut up! We're going for a walk. No! Leave the coat.'

Jack gestured downhill and followed Mortimer as he trudged, slipped and stumbled down the slope.

'What's this all about? It's a joke, isn't it? A joke, right? Look, who sent you? Is it Nicholson? It is Nicholson, isn't it? Look, I'll pay you double what he's paying you. No, OK, triple what you're getting from him. I'll square it with him, honest. Come on, how much do you want? I'll pay, name your price, what do you say? Please, just let me go,' he wailed, looking back over his shoulder, 'I'm going to freeze to death out here.'

'Aye,' Jack confirmed, scarcely audible above the wind noise.

They had only gone a few hundred yards but the road had quickly vanished behind the swirling wreaths of snow. Mortimer was stumbling, his teeth chattered, he was crying now, begging, and pleading. The fat man fell onto his hands and knees. 'Why are you doing this, what have I ever done to you?'

Jack stopped. Standing over Mortimer he howled above the gale, 'You really don't know, do you? You great big blubbering bag of guts, I hate you for what you are, who you are, and what you've done. The whole Dale hates you. Not just people. Not just the young lasses that you ogle, or their boyfriends or husbands. Not just the old folks and their relatives. The whole bloody land hates you, the hills themselves. There's a hush down there, a deep gulley in the hillside. That's where you're bound for. This weather will see you off.' Jack caught his breath. He looked at Mortimer grovelling in the snow like a big revolting slug, and the slug was pleading again, 'Look, I don't know who you are. I don't know what I've done to deserve this. Please don't leave me out here, I've got a wife.'

'Aye, I had a wife an' all. Not a floozy like that painted tart you're living with. A decent lass; she was good, she was kind. She never said a bad word about anyone. She never harmed a soul in her whole life, not even a fly, or a snail, or a…'

Jack felt his anger ebb as he looked at the pathetic creature cringing at his feet.

'Arrgh, damn blast! Why am I wasting my time on shite like you? Listen to me, you slimy sod, I'm off! But if you don't find your car, it's likely this snow will do for you anyway. Think on; you've made plenty of enemies out here. Remember this moment, you greasy bastard, remember how easy it was to do this. You're an incomer, you don't belong. You won't survive out here. Next time it'll be somebody harder than me, someone who won't have second thoughts. Away t' Hell wi' ye!'

A boot on Mortimer's ample backside sent the fat man sprawling. Then Jack turned and waded back uphill towards the road. Back at his Landrover he stowed the gun under some old feed sacks in the back. Then he threw his headgear in after the gun and stepped around to the driver's door. With a sinking heart, he saw the glow of headlights approaching. When the roof of the oncoming vehicle began to pulse with blue lights, he groaned aloud. 'Would you credit it! Just when I've decided to let that fat bastard off the hook, the polis' turns up. Well this just about puts the tin-hat on it.' Above the howling wind he heard doors slamming. Then two bulky figures, in fluorescent green jackets and shining powerful torches, loomed out of the blizzard.

'Is that you, Jack Lazarus? What's happening here then?'

Jack was just putting away his lunchtime crockery when a heavy knock sounded on the door. He had been expecting a visit from the local bobbies for the last two days so he was not greatly surprised to see plain-clothes men on his doorstep. The smaller detective showed his warrant card. 'I'm Detective Inspector Alder, this is Detective Sergeant Armstrong. May we come in?'

Jack stood aside to let them pass. Alder was slim and dark haired, Jack judged that he would just about make the regulation height. The other bugger was like a house-end, sandy-haired and hard-looking. Jack waved towards the kitchen chairs, 'Sit down, lads, are the roads still bad?

'We managed. We wanted to have an informal chat, Mr Lazarus. It's not an official interview.'

A rumble came from Armstrong, 'Unless you say anything incriminating, in which case we'll have to caution you.'

Jack saw Alder shoot a glance at his Sergeant, 'I'm sure that won't be necessary. I'd like you to help clear some things up for us, Mr Lazarus. Or can I call you Jack?'

'If you like, don't stand on ceremony.'

Alder rummaged inside his red designer windproof and brought out his notebook. 'OK, Jack. Why were you up on the high road two nights ago? The night Mr Mortimer had his... accident.'

Jack noticed the hesitation, but gave no sign of noticing. 'There were one or two yows I'd missed when I'd gathered the sheep last October. I thought the wind might push them over that way so I went up to tek a quick look.'

'When you arrived at the crash scene, did you see any sign of another vehicle?'

'Nowt, 'ceptin' the Jeep. Allan Price would likely tell you that.'

Alder frowned, 'Sergeant Price told me that you pointed out some footprints that were almost covered by the snow. Lucky you've got such sharp eyes, Jack. The Sergeant said that you helped them find Mr Mortimer. I've read his report, and PC Parker's, but they were short on detail. It's unlike either of them to be so... reticent. I'd like to fill in some of the gaps. I don't like loose ends,' he leaned forward, resting his forearms on the table, 'and I don't like gun-toting vigilantes on my patch.'

Jack met his gaze squarely, his face and eyes blank, 'What's that mean, Mr Alder?'

'Mr Mortimer complained that someone had driven him off the road and dragged him off into the snow at gunpoint. He described his assailant as big, masked, and heavily armed. Sergeant Price said you were the only person at the scene when he arrived.' As Alder sat back, his voice lost its hard edge, 'But you don't fit that description, do you, Jack?'

Jack gave slow shake of his head, 'Yer right there, lad. Doesn't sound like me at all.'

Alder raised one eyebrow, 'You told Sergeant Price that you saw no other vehicle when you came from the east side. Sergeant Price came up from the west. He didn't see anything going that way. A bit of a mystery, don't you think?'

'Aye, it seems a bit of a poser, Mr Alder, but there's side roads, farm tracks and such like.'

Alder nodded, as if considering this for the first time, 'Of course there are. In his report Sergeant Price also noted that Mr Mortimer was suffering from exposure. He stated that he was confused and incoherent. Our police surgeon confirmed that this was indeed a possibility.'

'Sounds likely. Mebbe he'd had a knock on the head and all, when his Jeep went over the edge. It can be tricky, driving in the dark, in that sort of storm.'

'I'm well aware of that, Jack. Nevertheless, Mr Mortimer has been making a lot of fuss about this. Our boss told us to investigate this alleged abduction. We've been to see Mr Mortimer. We told him that we'd need to look for a motive for the attack. We'd need to run a careful check of his records: staffing, complaints, financial transactions and so on. That was when he seemed to reconsider. He said he *had* been confused and that we should drop the investigation. In fact he *insisted* we drop it. Odd, don't you think?' The question hung in the air. Jack didn't even blink. Alder went on, 'I did notice that your name cropped up in the list of complainants.'

'Aye, and a fair few others, I dare say.'

The inspector gave a tight smile, as if to concede the point, then his face became serious again. 'Jack, our records show you used to own a shotgun at one time but you haven't got a current licence.'

Jack calmly met the detective's gaze. 'I've never fired a gun in years, Mr Alder. You can search the place if you like. It's long gone.'

'Really? Well that is… reassuring. As you say, I don't think a search would turn anything up now, after all this time, eh? Oh, just one more thing before we go, Jack. I thought you might be interested, you having helped save the victim of the… accident. Mortimer has told us he's decided to sell up. He said he thought it was time to move on.'

Jack nodded slightly, 'I'd say he was right. He's had a lucky escape. Who'd want to risk another accident like that, eh? Most locals won't be sorry, and maybe some others, not so far from here?'

Alder's eyes narrowed, 'Tell me, do you play much poker, Jack?'

'Dominoes, lad, that's my game. But you still give nowt away by yer face. No matter what hand ye've picked up.'

There was a sudden scraping of chair legs on the stone flags, as Alder rose abruptly. 'Sergeant, if we ever see Mr Lazarus in a pub, remind me not to play him at dominoes.' He turned to leave, closely followed by the big Sergeant, who suffered a sudden twitch in one eye as he nodded his goodbye from the kitchen doorway.

TOXIC AIR

Kathleen Mckay

I woke before the sun rose, to gaze out at the flat, cold garden. The dead blackbird underneath the rowan tree looked like a broken umbrella at first. People were always throwing rubbish over the wall into our small back garden: cigarette packets, coke bottles, condoms, and chocolate wrappers. I don't like the feeling of being closed in, and had held off getting a tall fence, unlike most of the neighbours. Better to see what's going on in the world. But rubbish lowers your spirits and only after two cups of tea did I feel awake enough to venture out. It was only 5am.

The bird was stiff already, surrounded by twigs and leaves from the mountain ash. It could have been there for days, as the weather had stayed wet. There were no obvious maggots, but I didn't want to peer too closely. With my head turned away, I shovelled the bird onto newspaper and wrapped it in two plastic bags. You could still see the rigid outline of its beak through the plastic when I threw it in the bin.

I was tired that day after such an early start. Cataloguing books usually made me happy, as did following up enquiries. I normally loved my job, with its sense of order and control. I'd worked in libraries for years; since my daughter was a teenager, and had developed a librarian's hunched-over stance. The smell of books, their feel, the covers, the library stamps, the way we arranged books on the shelves, the neat order of the spines – everything about books appealed. When my daughter left home, books were what saved me. I'd read through my tears and the ache of missing her. Nowadays, reading almost came second.

Today I felt lacklustre and lethargic, aware of the low hum of voices, but instead of picking up on what they were saying, I kept my head down cataloguing, and screened the voices out. After work I went straight to bed.

So it wasn't until the next morning, after the police had taped off the house on the corner, and two portly policemen were self-consciously riding up and down on mountain bikes, that I found out from Sal, a neighbour, about a boy up the road who had died. I'd known Sal for ages. We'd lived close by for years, and watched the area change. When I moved into a smaller place she stayed put, her children still at home. She's slight and dark haired, with nervous quick movements.

'Might be suspicious.'

I tried to digest the news. A good looking boy, rather shy. The mother was a local GP, the father did something that took him out each morning in a suit. I hadn't seen them around recently.

'They were away,' said Sal, reading my mind. 'They left him at home, alone. God, imagine getting that phone call.'

Her next words penetrated.

'I saw someone.'

'What?'

'I saw someone in the early hours of the morning.'

'What do you mean?'

I didn't know what she was talking about. I was trying to get the fact that the boy was dead to sink in. How could someone so young and alive be dead?

'I was up half the night arranging clothes. I've got a big order.'

Sal had a network of people who passed on things cheap, which she resold. It used to be in markets and car boot sales, but she's graduated to eBay. Says it's the future, and she'll be able to earn a decent living. Ends of lines, and discontinued stock, mainly baby and toddler clothes. She'd also branched out into equipment. Again, baby and toddler stuff, although she was getting disabled equipment as well. Commodes and hoists, pill dispensers, easy open tin openers.

Once it was all young families round here. But then they grew up, and by that summer there were more grandchildren and great grandchildren around, and the older people were starting to need their places adapted. Our area was still scruffy, but on the cusp of coming up, with the middle classes moving in. The local shops had begun to sell olive oil and decent bread. That suited me, as I'd grown up with a grandfather in love with everything Italian. He'd even persuaded my parents to call us by Italian names: Estella, Gioia and Deola. Funny thing was, when I was a kid, people did think we were Italian, with our olive skin and dark hair.

I focused back on Sal.

'What did you see? The poor mother, I can hardly believe it.'

'I know. The police had to bring the family back. You should have seen the sister this morning. Remember when they were kids and I used to baby-sit and clean for them? He was only seventeen for Christ's sake. Just finished his AS levels.'

'Poor kid, I heard he was heading for law at Oxford.'

'Was he? He was supposed to have been a brilliant student. God, he was always a clever little thing. Used to make up these plays. Really dramatic, with lots of blood and gore.'

She stopped herself, and wiped away a tear. I pictured his skinny figure. Sometimes in the summer, after a late shift at the library, I'd see him pounding the streets, his incongruously skinny legs perched on his clumpy trainers. Or playing cricket in the park, long and lanky as he ran during his innings.

'I wonder how he died? They haven't said.'

I flinched, and switched the TV on. The local channels were full of speculation. A reporter said that the police were treating the death as suspicious.

'The family had left Paul alone for the weekend. They'd gone to a poetry festival.' The reporter made a moue of disgust, as if she had stepped in shit.

'At present police are not looking for any other person.'

Sal stared at the screen. We drank our coffee, an own blend I get from a place in town, in silence.

At one point she'd known the family well. At secondary all that changed, when her sons went the local comp, and the boy and his sister travelled across the city to school.

Sal started wittering about her new anti-allergy line 'especially for asthmatics'.

'Business must be good. But what did you see?' I asked again.

I drained my coffee cup, refilled both, and dunked an amaretto. In the afternoon sun, the redbrick roofs took on an orange glow. If you half-closed your eyes, you could be in Italy. Yet there was a quickening in the air, a scent of danger. The sun was bright and warm, but tonight would be chilly. This death would send its ripples wide. The air we breathed felt unsafe.

'What?'

Sal leant back, wiping coffee off her mouth. She nibbled at a biscuit, sawing round the edges with her pointy teeth.

'Rumours are flying round.'

'Like what?'

'One story is that two black guys were seen running away. Marcus has been taken down the station. He was caught burgling the house two doors up.'

Marcus was a lousy burglar. Other kids put him up to things, getting him to climb in through tight windows they couldn't fit through. He was usually the one caught. You'd watch him posturing around bigger kids, trying to ape their walk, inexpertly smoking.

'His mother's beside herself,' added Sal.

The TV camera honed in on a billboard headline.

'Yardie link boy death?'

Sal stood up to go.

'So what did you see?'

'Probably nothing.'

'Tell me.'

She sighed and sat down again.

'I saw another lad leave a bike outside and go into Paul's house.'

'Are you sure?'

'I couldn't sleep and had got up to make a drink.'

'When? What time are you talking about?'

'Middle of the night. About two thirty in the morning.'

'Didn't you think it was odd someone coming that hour?'

'I thought it was a bit late, but you know, I'd seen that kid before, and it wasn't like he was breaking down the door or anything. The door opened straight away, as if he was expected. None of my business.'

'Where had you seen him before?'

'Once, on the train to Manchester, I saw them sitting right next to each other. I mean, right next to each other. Close. They pretended not to see me.'

'He could be a murderer.'

Sal's face paled.

'Or an accessory,' I went on.

Sal got that stubborn look on her face she gets:

'They haven't said it was murder.'

'They haven't said it's not.'

'He was only a boy.'

She kept talking nervously.

'It was one of those thin, modern, aluminium type bikes. A racer.'

'Didn't the police talk to you?'

'I was out.'

'You have to go and see them. You have to.'

'I know.'

'Do you remember anything else?'

'His hair. He had a floppy hairstyle. They looked like each other, that's what struck me that time on the train. They were like twins.'

'You've got to tell the police.'

'I know.' She stood still. 'It's his sister I feel sorry for. She found him, poor pet. Anyway, I've got to go. A man's coming round for a hoist for his wife. They've let her out of hospital after a stroke.'

'Tell the police. This morning.'

'Yeah.'

Over the next few days, the atmosphere grew tense. There were rumours that the boy was the victim of a gangland murder. Houses were raided, and the neighbourhood group for community cohesion claimed that a disproportionate number of black kids had been targeted. Experts in the paper talked of feral children.

People became edgy, and suspicious of each other. Parents told their children not to walk even short distances, and drove them instead, filling the streets with toxic air. Someone shouted 'White bitch' at me as I walked home one day.

Then the temperature dropped, tension eased, schools started back, and people slipped back into indifference. We kept going to the shops, getting on the same bus, taking kids to the same school.

When I saw Sal again, I asked her about the police.

'They took all my details, but kept asking whether I could have confused the nights. Kept trying to trick me by asking what was on the telly earlier on. I must admit I did get confused. With this Freeview I never know what day it is, whether it's a repeat I'm watching, or the first showing. And they said there were no track marks from a bike. "*If* there was a bike," they said. And no one else's footprints. But it had been raining, that would have washed away the tracks. And he could have taken his shoes off, couldn't he? I always take my shoes off when I go into someone else's house, don't you?'

I murmured something non-committal.

Sal was on a roll:

'I felt like they had already made their mind up about what had happened. "Thank you for coming, Mrs Graham," they said. "It's very important that citizens get involved, Mrs Graham." I told them I wasn't a Mrs but they just looked at me. They kept implying I was mistaken.'

Next day the police arrested four lads, but in the end only charged them with possession of cannabis and theft from an all-night garage. A giant packet of prawn cocktail crisps to be exact, one reporter noted.

Theories abounded about the boy's death. 'Robbery gone haywire,' said some. But anyone knows that a robber is not usually a killer, and if it's a robbery gone wrong, it's messy, inconsistent, the killer leaves all kinds of clues.

Other rumours were that the boy's death was connected to a police operation, that the boy's mother had done it, or his father. A woman whose granddaughter had an abortion sent a letter to the dead boy's mother, calling her a baby murderer, because she'd signed a petition against curbing abortion rights. The letter writer was arrested for wasting police time.

A notice appeared at the surgery. 'Doctor Roberts is on extended sick leave.' We were torn between sympathy and blame. Bad luck might be catching, we thought. Yet there was homemade food left on the family's step, flowers.

When the funeral finally took place several weeks later, people lined the streets. Lots of the local secondary school pupils turned up, as well as the boy's friends from across the city, spilling out from the church. Most of the young ones, including the boys, were dressed theatrically in black, with thick eyeliner, and sported complicated, distressed hair. The boy's family wore colour.

A floppy-haired kid hung back from the main group. I thought about the lad Sal had described. Was this him? He sported a *Brideshead Revisited* type of look. Sal's youngest had come out in spots, so she wasn't there to check with. I kept my eye on the lad. He greeted a few people, then went off by himself. I didn't see him at the sandwiches and coke, beer and spirits thing afterwards, when some of the kids got really drunk, and began wailing dramatically. When one produced a guitar, I left.

It's the way teens close against you, that's what I remember about that time. Loads of them would have known what state the dead lad Paul had been in. But the police came up against a brick wall.

A few weeks later they said they weren't looking for anyone else, and everything went quiet. The verdict at the inquest was suicide. Paul had taken pills and then cut his wrists.

No one else was implicated.

One of my jobs was dealing with inter-library loans, and fines. We rarely took people to court for non-return of books: we used to threaten it, but it was much easier if people paid up. There were a number of sanctions: relinquish your library ticket for a length of time, pay for the book at the retail price, or give a donation to the Library Fund.

October, and the town streets were already full of bangs and flashes. I didn't normally phone up the actual borrower, but the Manchester office had been busy all morning, so I thought I might as well go straight to the horse's mouth. The book, *The Bicycle Maintenance Handbook*, came up as checked out on 11 May. It had been renewed several times.

The woman who answered sounded tired and distracted. I got the feeling that she'd been waiting.

'Yes, of course, that must be my son Louis's. You know what these young people are like. He's not here at the moment. He's away at university. Got into Cambridge.'

I grunted.

'Studying psychology. Wants to go into research. Yes, of course I'll send it back. I'm off to the post office this afternoon. I'm due to see him tomorrow. I'll pop it in the post. You should get it soon.'

People who said 'pop' lived in nice worlds, where nothing ever happened. Pop on that chair, pop that gown on, I'll just pop this needle in. I took her for a nurse.

'I'll tell him I sent it,' she added.

A rash of bangers started up. Ra ta ra ta. Crack. Crack. As soon as it was dark, the men working in the halal butchers would fall upon slices of meat, shoving it into their mouths to break their fast.

'Is that all? Is there anything else I can help you with?'

She sounded like a bank worker. I was just about to put
the phone down. A simple administrative problem solved. But
something had been troubling me for a while. I like mysteries solved,
ends tied up. The question shot out, surprising me.

'Does your son have a bike?'

'Why do you ask?' There was fear in her voice.

I didn't answer. She filled the silence.

'Oh, obvious really, I'd forgotten what the book was called. Yes, as
a matter of fact he does. He's taken his bike to Cambridge. It's a good
place for cycling.'

I agreed.

'He's such a keen cyclist, once he even rode from your side of the
Pennines all the way back to Manchester when he missed the last
train and it was too long to wait until the next one. Over the back
roads of course, past Rochdale.'

'That's a long way. Do you remember when that was?' I was
getting excited.

She was on a roll, wanting to talk, and didn't seem to notice the
oddness of the question.

'Sometime early summer. I don't remember exactly. I do
remember he stayed in bed the next day. I had to get up early for
work. The CAB.'

'Oh.'

'I only volunteer there one day a week. Makes a change from
school nursing.'

'I'm sure.'

I saw him riding away, speeding to the station, finding the next train
wasn't due for two hours, continuing his ride. And keeping going.
Over the Pennines, through sleepy villages and past all night garages,
putting the distance between them. He probably had blood on him.
Paul was alive when Louis first got to the house. Sal saw them. What
happened? Had Paul already taken the pills? And then waited for his

friend to arrive before he slit his wrists? Or did something happen between them to make Paul take them? Did Louis try to stop him? Or stand by? Why didn't he phone for help?

When she next spoke, the woman's voice had lost its quavery, underwater quality, and she was decisive and crisp.

'I have to go. Nice speaking to you. I'll pop the book in the post.'

'Thank you.'

A slight tremor in her voice.

'He's a sensitive lad, my boy. He's been a bit upset these last few weeks. Lost a good friend in an accident. Won't tell me anything about it, but he's been on tablets. I'm hoping he'll settle down, put it all behind him.'

When the book arrived, next day, several of the pages were stuck together with dried blood.

I liked my job back then: cataloguing, arranging shelves, answering queries, putting books in categories. Romance. History. Crime. The book fitted into Leisure Activities. But the story didn't fit neatly into any category.

I imagined the boy cycling round university squares, his scarf trailing in the autumn sun. And all the time the ripples of Paul's death were seeping into every corner of his life. In pain, people act blindly. Had Paul? Was it revenge? Or love? Or hate?

I filled in a report for Damaged Goods, and filed the report under Extinct Stock. I wrapped the book inside two plastic bags. You could still see its rigid outline through the plastic when I threw it in the bin.

QUID PRO QUO

Betty Weiner

Elaine always makes a big show of being protective of her older sister. She'll tell me she can't understand the attraction of getting undressed in public after you've gone to the trouble of getting dressed at home. And especially not of getting wet and overheated in a local authority basement. 'It'll kill Freda,' she once said to me, 'that heat. Is that what you want?'

'Sorry I'm late,' Freda pants, as she gets to the top of the steps, gear in one hand, the other gripping the metal handrail.

'You're not,' I say. 'Don't rush.'

'Can't,' she says, and takes three slow, heavy breaths. 'It's getting worse.'

I keep telling her to see her GP. She says she already rattles like a kid in a Smartie factory: 'Pills! Pills! Pills!' she'll say.

I slide a note under the glass barrier and ask for the 'Pensioners Turkish, please'. The attendant gives me a ticket and my change. Freda does the same but doesn't see her 20p on the counter. I pass it to her.

We head for the basement where the Turkish and Sauna Suites are, down a curve of stone steps. A chirpy girl in a mini skirt and bikini top takes our tickets and slides the signing-in book along. Health and Safety. We sign our names: 'Freda', 'Charlotte'. The chirpy girl leads us through the sofa area to a double cubicle with two narrow beds behind a heavy curtain. Before we've even decided who's having which bed Freda is sounding off about Elaine.

There never were two sisters more unalike. For great swathes of their adult lives they hardly kept in touch. Yet after Elaine's divorce they chose to live together. As though they'd forgotten how much they'd hated each other as children and how little they knew of each other as adults. Now they've been together again for ten years in the house they both grew up in, left to Freda when their parents died.

Holly Villa. Freda's retired, Elaine still works part-time.

Neither of them had children but Elaine compensated with dogs. Brought one with her into the new ménage. That was then. Now Freda won't have a dog in the house any more and Elaine is so resentful it's scary. 'I'll get you locked up, you dementing old bag!' I once heard her yell at her sister.

'What am I going to do, Charlie?' she asks. Each of the beds has a white pillow on it and a little locker on the wall above. We're sitting facing each other, our knees almost touching.

'She says the house is as much hers as mine. She won't let me change it.'

'Don't be silly,' I say. 'It's your property and your will.'

I know what this is about. Freda wants to change her will and leave less to Elaine and more to the children of a cousin.

For years Freda looked after her ageing parents in the family home. Elaine was married to Quiet Eric and a yappy little dog called Nero. Eric was a pharmacist and Elaine worked in the shop. In her spare time she went to dog shows and watched dogs on television. Her connubial feelings regarding Eric were semi-detached, at best (according to Freda), but she had a symbiotic relationship with Nero, the little yap: kissed on the lips and slept together. Eventually Quiet Eric saw the light and left. The business and house had to be sold. Elaine claimed to be homeless. Freda, now on her own in Holly Villa, could sleep in a different room every night if she so chose. Elaine's move back to the family home seemed to make sense.

They failed to discuss how little they knew of each other, assumed two adult sisters could live together, argued only about keeping a dog. Freda didn't want a dog in the house. Elaine had tantrums. Then she threw the knee thing at Freda. So then Freda gave way. Elaine kept her dog and found herself a part-time job in a hospital pharmacy. Then the dog died.

'She said I'd killed it! Can you believe that? She really thinks I did.

She'll get her own back, Charlie, you'll see… ' Freda telling me this in a Turkish cubicle soon after the dog's death. 'She's into revenge. Wrote the book!'

Elaine has named several animal charities in her will but she doesn't seem to feel she has enough to leave them. Freda now wants her solicitor to change her will so that half of the value of the house would go straight to the young relatives.

'Elaine doesn't need a big house. She'll have to sell the Villa when I've gone, get a little place with her share of the proceeds and give Maisie's kids the rest. Mum and Dad didn't leave it for bloody kennels.'

Elaine is furious. It would mean lots of noughts less for the Cat and Dog Home. No wonder she's trying to stop Freda going to her solicitor.

Freda looks near to tears going over it yet again. 'I've written to the solicitor about it. You know what Elaine will do? She'll make out I've lost my marbles…'

'Oh, come on…'

'Why did I ever agree to live with her?'

There's nothing we can say about this that hasn't been said a hundred times already.

We sling our towels round our shoulders and make our way up to the swimming pool which is on the entrance level where we came in. The water feels cold to start with but we warm up quite soon. When we first retired we'd swim ten or twelve lengths. We haven't done that for quite a while. Today Freda's barely got there and back the once and she's exhausted. 'I'm done,' she says, holding on at the steps, water lapping at her chest. 'You stay.' But I decide to go out of the water with her. It's not much fun in the pool on your own and the steps can be wet and slippery and Freda's vision is so poor.

Back in the sauna area we spread our towels over two deck chairs. I've been saying to Freda for some time that the heat cannot be good for her. Elaine is right, actually. Why doesn't she just do Jacuzzi and gossip and maybe a short swim when she feels up to it? This time she agrees. It's sweltering and after two minutes she heads back to the cubicle. 'I'll lie down for a bit,' she says. 'Don't you rush.' I stay for ten minutes and sweat a lot. Then I have a shower. Then I get two instant coffees from the chirpy girl in the bikini top and we drink them lounging on our beds in the cubicle with the curtain closed.

'She always holds it against me,' Freda complains, as though our conversation hadn't been interrupted at all, 'like it's my fault she didn't become an Olympic runner. My fault she can't climb Everest. My fault she married Eric instead of Prince Rainier...'

'Did you really push her down the stairs?'

'I believe I did,' Freda answers.

'Your parents called it an accident?'

'They didn't want to believe...'

'How old was she?'

'Oh, I don't know. Four, perhaps. I was thirteen.'

'Jealous?'

'Of course. I never was one of those maternal teenagers.'

'Can you remember? What it was about?'

'No. But Elaine claims to remember every detail – her shoe getting caught, my pushing her down the stairs. The hospital. The operation. Waking up and not knowing where she was and all alone, all alone...' Freda rolls her eyes and stares up to where the lockers are and says, 'Phoo! There'll have been a whole agony of nurses holding her hands.' She looks at me again. 'The twisted knee. Her zero life chances. Parents ashamed of a limping daughter...'

'It's hardly noticeable!'

'Didn't even like her...'

'What? Your mum and dad didn't?'

'Why would they, disagreeable little runt – when they had an angel like me?'

'Oh, yeah, yeah!'

Then Freda lies down on her bed and says she needs to rest.

'Did you go to the doctor?' I ask.

'Does it ever help? Yes, I'll have to go again…' And she sighs.

'OK. I'll go for a steam,' I say, 'and collect you for the Jacuzzi.'

And that's what I do: more sweating, another shower. Then I go back to the cubicle for Freda. I find her lying on her back, the foam pillow cushioning her head. 'Jacuzzi?' I suggest. She opens her eyes slowly and nods. She picks her towel up from the bottom of the bed.

We stand for a few minutes waiting for the bubbles to begin again. They're on a ten minute cycle. Freda's leaning against the rails. I give her a questioning look – You OK?

The bubbles begin and we climb in. The water is soothingly warm. We slither on our bums from the top step to the middle one and then to the lowest one. I wriggle to get a jet massaging my ankles. Freda, with closed eyes, is enjoying the sensation of weightlessness.

I shuffle round to make space for a big woman backing down the steps into the water. She's in a red swimsuit and for a moment it's like two balloons descending. I want to smile. I turn to Freda just as her feet come up and her head goes under. She hasn't done her floppy-doll imitation for ages. And she's not doing it now. She's unconscious.

For a stunned second I stare at her. The other woman sweeps over and pulls Freda's shoulders up out of the water. 'Freda!' I scream and grab her arms. The woman is holding Freda in a life-saving position, Freda's head against her red breasts.

Other women are watching, shocked. The attendant girl appears – someone must have dashed to find her. She says the manager will be straight down. I can't do anything but hold Freda's hands, talk to her, try and get some response. Her eyes stay closed. The manager arrives with two male attendants in vests and shorts. They lift Freda out of the jacuzzi and take her through to the lounge area. They lie her down on one of the sofas and I cover her with both our towels.

The manager says an ambulance is on its way. I'm still holding Freda's hands. Two paramedics appear; they feel pulses, lift eyelids. Look at each other. There doesn't seem to be anything else they can do on the spot. They take her up to the ambulance. I rush to our cubicle to get my shoes and throw a jacket on over my swim suit. I race upstairs to the street. 'Where to?' I shout as they set off. 'Royal Victoria,' the driver calls back.

But it's too late. By the time I've got to the infirmary and waited an hour for someone to tell me what's happening, Freda is dead. It seems she died straight off, perhaps even in the jacuzzi.

By the time of the burial a little of the shock has worn off, though not much. It was five days before I was able to look into my swimming bag again. I'd never want to use that same stuff again, the shampoo and the body wash and the lotion, so I put it all in the bin and then I cried.

Some days later, I get a call from a voice I can't place. It turns out to be Quiet Eric and he's ringing from Holly Villa. He couldn't get to the funeral but he was always fond of Freda and it seems Elaine did contact him. I didn't know they were still in touch. He'd come to see if she was alright, having lost her sister so suddenly. He saw her yesterday but today she was away dog-sitting for a friend. She asked him to ring me: would I collect my towel which she had recovered from the hospital and also anything else of mine at Holly Villa.

'How's Elaine?' I ask. There's a little pause. Then he says, 'Champion. Yes, she's champion.'

I ring the bell and Eric opens the door. He has curly grey hair with little strands of ginger. He smiles and says, 'Charlotte – have we met before?' He leads me in and I see my towel neatly folded on the hall table on top of some telephone directories. We talk about Freda, about how it happens like this sometimes, suddenly, unexpectedly. I describe what happened at the pool. Then Eric comes up with me to Freda's bedroom. I know some of my books will be on her bookcase there. I find my Sue Grafton and *Ukrainian Tractors*. Eric is studying a mass of white packages on the bed.

'Poor Freda – all this medication,' he says and then, by way of explanation, 'The drawer was open.'

'She always said she could compete with a rattlesnake,' I tell him. Then I ask, 'Could some of them go back? The ones that aren't open?'

But Eric doesn't seem to hear me. He's examining cartons, reading labels. I assume he's looking for blister packs that haven't been started. 'It's such a waste, isn't it?' I say.

But Eric doesn't hear me. He's breaking into the foil of a blister pack and sliding pills out with his thumb. Then another pack and another one. I stand by the bookcase, holding my books, watching him. Soon there are little mounds of pills all over the bed. What's he doing? He crumbles a big tablet between his fingers, then a small one, then tastes something with the tip of his tongue. Then he opens up a capsule and spills tiny blue and white globules onto his palm.

'Did she take her pills regularly?'

'Of course,' I say. 'Like clockwork.'

'I wonder how long this has been going on?'

I don't know what he's talking about.

'She didn't see at all well,' I tell him, 'but she always knew what she was taking.'

'I don't think she did,' he replies.

I feel my face getting cold. What's he on about?

'D'you know what these are?'

Freda was always chuntering about her endless pills but I didn't know what she was taking. I tell Eric she took masses of pills and had recently been complaining a lot about her health.

'These,' Eric says, pointing to two little mounds, 'these are ordinary, mild pain killers. Some of these others are vitamin pills. Most of them…' and he waves his hand over the rest… 'just sugar. Nothing to do with what it says on the label. These long ones here – like those little orange ones – well, probably from a health shop.

Plenty of chalk mixed in. Not a thing that would help with your blood pressure or...'

'She'd have noticed, surely?' I insist.

'Where did she get them – which chemist?'

'No,' I answer, 'Elaine was getting them for her from the pharmacy where she worked.'

Elaine used to say it was the least she could do for Freda, picking her pills up for her. Eric is staring at me now. What's been going on? My brain's beginning to feel like popcorn in the micro. I know that the print on pharmacy labels can be hard to read. I pick up a white box from the bed. Elaine has replaced the pharmacy label with a bigger, hand-written one so Freda could read it. Except what she's put on the label wasn't what was in the box. That seemed to be what Eric was saying.

'Freda wouldn't know,' Eric says, shaking his head. 'She must have been taking these for months.'

Freda never feeling better, her doctor prescribing more and more tablets, Elaine bringing home junk and changing the labels. After a minute Eric says quietly, 'Elaine...' but then he stops. Whatever he was going to say to me about his ex-wife he's thought better of it. Then he says he'll make some tea.

We go back downstairs and Eric makes a pot of tea. He brings a couple of mugs over in slow motion. I feel a bit sick. When did Elaine invent lying labels and start giving Freda chalk and vitamins instead of her heart pills? It couldn't go back to when the dog died, could it, surely not? We don't speak. I refuse a second cup, I just want to go home.

I pick up my towel and the books. Eric just about manages a smile as he opens the front door for me. I have to ask – 'So – what about the...?'

And Quiet Eric says, 'You go on home. I'll think about it.' Then he says, 'There's a telephone directory here somewhere, isn't there? Yes – it's on the hall table. I'll look at the pills again and then I might just ring the...'

46

I think he's going to say 'the pharmacist' or 'the surgery' or even 'Elaine', since she must have left him a number. But his lips are forming the words – 'the Police'.

I go down one step and turn back.

'Elaine…?' I say faintly.

'Take care of yourself, Charlotte,' he says, and closes the front door.

APRIL FOOL

Basil Ransome-Davies

The modern world has no time for the free and easy. We're chained to each other by mobile phones, it's as hard to be remote as it is to be unknown. Then when you lose a cheap old clamshell, panic stations.

We were almost at the Passat before I realised. I gave Eunice the keys and set off back to the restaurant. I was half-cut from lunch and getting lower-back twinges, irritated at my own carelessness. The late afternoon sun made the quiet bay sparkle but the pleasant day had been hijacked by an unthinking lapse.

At the restaurant I found no one but a black guy in a green polo shirt doing some plastering around a light switch. I couldn't follow his Spanish or summon enough of my own, so I took a card from the little rack on the bar and headed for the car again.

The rather belated idea was to use Eunice's mobile to contact the restaurant. Only there was a dusty space under the palm tree where the car had been and no sign of her.

It was a time for self-control. I sat on a bench and watched the small craft floating like ducks in the harbour and lit a smoke and mentally replayed the last six hours. What I was trying to pinpoint was how I might have pissed Eunice off. Not getting her own way could turn her into a sulky, accusing adolescent. Even at 50 she thought that female beauty trumped everything. She wasn't wrong either. A distressed phone call had brought me to Santander within 24 hours.

But a sudden disappearance? It didn't fit. Firstly, given her disturbed emotions I had walked on eggs, nodded sympathetically, accepted her agenda for the outing (lobster, mainly, at a restaurant of her choosing). More importantly, if you upset Eunice she didn't silently vanish. She stood there letting you know it. So was this a new level of unpredictability? I disliked the thought, though not as much as some of the alternatives. True, she had been a shade subdued and distant during the 40-minute drive along the coast, but she'd devoured the expensive lunch with gusto.

There were those questions, and there was the phone, or what was in the phone's memory. And a bloody hire car. I'd no means of transport or communication. Fortunately I did have money. The timetable at the bus station told me there was a coach to Santander in two hours that would take another hour to arrive. Business in the little port was just resuming after the lunchtime lull so I went looking for a taxi.

At the hotel I got my smartphone out of the strongbox in the wardrobe and called the clamshell's number. A rather abrupt voice answered – my own, I realised – and told me to leave a message. I tried something in English and Spanish and left the name and number of the hotel. Then I called Eunice's apartment and mobile and both times heard her recorded voice.

We were adrift in the ether, out of reach. There was a cafe opposite the hotel and I went there for a *cortado* and a brandy, sitting outside to smoke and evade a thunderous fruit machine. A warm April evening in Santander had brought out the promenaders. I watched the strolling couples under the palms in the nearby public gardens, their relaxed movements, their casual purpose.

Eunice and I shared a history that always looked like unfinished business though we had tacitly agreed it wasn't. As a result, I'd become her confidant. That often meant listening while she lengthily berated the men in her life, men who were getting what I wasn't. I was never sure why I accepted the role, only that I'd tolerate it from no one else.

But the call from Santander, where she was a TEFL teacher, had struck me as more than a litany of complaint. Her voice had the urgency of someone seeking immediate support. She was angry and troubled. There was a man, or men, in it. I blinked at an onslaught of concerns rather low on detail. I wondered how many others she had called first, but I said yes. Then I'd dug out my passport and made cat-minding arrangements.

By the time I'd finished my drinks I understood that I needed to be active, do legwork. The first stops were the language school and Eunice's apartment.

Lapworth I knew from other visits, a fat Englishman in his fifties, a commercial success because he staffed his school with qualified people, a delegator supreme. The school wasn't his sole source of profit.

Santander is a hilly town. The Escuela Inglés, also Lapworth's residence, was a semi-grand old building among newer blocks on the crest behind the shopping area. It looked over the bay to a horizon of snowy peaks. Below it, an ascending street became an escalator, then a small funicular. My back and knees were grateful. I found Lapworth in his office watching a DVD of some golf tournament. He was drinking Johnny Walker and invited me. I shook my head.

'Have you seen Eunice today?' I asked him.

'Thought she was with you. Gone AWOL, has she?'

'She's been very upset. You know that.'

'Not my doing, old thing. Don't expect a mea culpa from me.'

I sometimes thought he used dated idioms to annoy me. For all the fruity manner he was a 21st century shark, amassing it while Spain bled economically.

'But you know about it, yes?'

'I know it's boyfriend trouble. What else could it be with Eunice? She's bloody fond of cock.' He waved the remote airily. 'Takes on all comers. Toyboys, waiters...'

The oafish remark recalled what Eunice had once said to me when she wanted a bit of distance: 'You can't get all you want from one person.' She was probably right, but she might have touched my weakness. Though not promiscuous, she loved to play.

Lapworth snorted and swore at a badly missed putt.

I said, 'It's more than that. She's talked of violence.'

'Really? Seen any bruises?'

'Threats of violence, then.' Some of what she had incoherently poured out could be interpreted that way. 'Why the hard heart? She works well for you, doesn't she?'

'She's the best, professionally. Never doubted it. That's why I want to retain her. Her private life is off my patch.'

'And doesn't she keep it that way?'

'She has done. Now she's on the verge of a wobbler. Wasn't that the point of you taking her out? To calm her down, reassure her. The father-figure of them all.'

'Fuck you,' I told him. I was ten years older than Eunice. And Lapworth had no cause to be surly if Eunice was doing her job well. Maybe he was getting harassed by his truculent German wife, the ironclad Ingrid. I left him refilling his crystal tumbler.

I hadn't reported the phone lost or notified the police of Eunice's disappearance. Those were two basic precautions, but they could wait 24 hours at least, especially the second. I was a grey-economy man. On retiring from a travel agency I'd used my European contacts to build up an informal import-export trade. Some of it was borderline legal and most was off the books. I wasn't big-time, just one of thousands making an independent living below the radar of HMRC, but it would be costly if the facts emerged. Once they get you, the law are worse than crabs for hanging on.

Curdled thoughts. I counted concrete steps to subdue panic as I dropped down the far side of the rise and climbed another to reach Eunice's. It was in a neighbourhood with schools and shops, where buildings and all-weather sports pitches were illuminated as daylight faded.

In the smoked-glass twilight I began to imagine what Eunice's stratagem might be. She wasn't impetuous but she was wilful. Another of her sayings: 'You can't live your life and understand it at the same time.' It might be true; she seemed to give it the status of an alibi. A mature, intelligent female with the ego of a headstrong child.

In the next second I pictured myself arriving, pressing her bell, not being admitted, retreating with a mental vision of Eunice and her latest love slave sitting up in bed laughing. For some reason I had made him a *louche* Mediterranean type.

An ugly, idiotic projection. It made me keener to surprise her, to round out the plot her trick had started,

She had a fifth-floor one-bedroom apartment in a reddish modern block. The elevation afforded dominating views, and her décor made the interior both warm and efficient. We'd shared more than a bottle and some tapas there the previous night. The living/dining room with its wide glazed balcony featured a print of Cézanne's 'Still Life with Skull'. Eunice said she found it amusing.

I hadn't a key but there was a party entering by the main door and a man coming out and I glided through among them. I shared the lift with a young couple and somebody's granny, courteous nods and smiles all round. On the fifth floor I stepped out alone.

The hallway was empty. I was hesitant. I wanted a smoke but it was forbidden. I found some gum in my pocket and chewed it looking out of a window. Town lights, sea lights reflected in the invisible water, a luminous constellation. If I'd had a better day, if Eunice hadn't played me for a fool, it would be a welcome, even romantic, sight.

I didn't use the bell. I banged the door angrily with a firm palm, and it stirred inwards, exposing the narrow hallway.

That was unexpected, but if Eunice had just got in with an armful of shopping she might have kicked the door lightly behind her.

There was no sound from inside.

I called her name. Nothing.

I was on the threshold, stuck, an unhappily apt metaphor for my relationship with Eunice, and at that point I didn't want to go in. In the same moment whatever I wanted became immaterial. Compulsion took over.

I went into the living room first. The skull in the picture stared back at me from its garland of assorted fruit but nothing was out of place. The kitchen too was in apple-pie order. Eunice hardly cooked and her main investment was in labour-saving appliances. She paid a woman to clean.

That left the bedroom and bathroom, the intimate haunts. The first was as chaotic as the kitchen had been neat. Eunice had plenty of clothes and was not tidy. A fight might have taken place there, you couldn't tell.

The bathroom was different. I caught the sickly odour as I approached it, noticed the slender line of light under the door. There was even a faint, repeated patter of water dripping.

She was in the shower, or her torso was. Her legs protruded, ankles resting on the floor tiles. The glass shower door, fogged with condensation, trapped her at the hip. The drip was from a leaking chrome hose. I couldn't see Eunice's face. I had to see it.

I nudged the curved door with my arm and it slid a few inches along its track. Her body rolled slightly. I pushed the door further, she slumped into the tray. Then I did see her face, and wished I hadn't.

An obscene caricature. The swollen discoloration, a pyjama-cord ligature sunk so deeply into her flesh it was barely visible. Someone's violent, unimaginable climax of passion. Its impact was like a brutal kick in the stomach.

I jacknifed helplessly over the bidet, vomiting a grey wad of gum along with the flaccid, half-digested remains of lobster and molluscs. I turned on the cold flow, splashing water on my face as my stomach erupted again. That exhausted me. I knelt, trying to hang on to consciousness while the water trickled away. I was certain she was dead, no one could have survived what I'd seen, a fact like an iron barricade that blocked any other thought till I realised I had left the apartment door ajar. When I'd shut it and wiped myself down I had no thought but to get away from the horror.

I cleaned up traces of my sickness without moving anything and went, leaving nothing but my prints and DNA, innocent presences from my previous visit. I hadn't touched the body. I shut the apartment door firmly, then stood in the lift with the scene I was deserting scorched into my brain. Every repellent detail.

It was the first time I had seen Eunice naked.

In my hotel room I poured a brandy and smoked out of the window. Lively music and chatter from a local bar meant no more than the empty night sky. I would not have Eunice in my life again, ever. She would be purely a figment of memory, a permanent vision, unchangeable. Our future history could only be lived by me, in retrospective wish-fulfilment.

Of course on that level I would always possess her.

I shut the window and went for the brandy bottle. Though I hadn't killed her I was acting as though I had. It was an awkward necessity, because I realised I would have to face the police.

Some pretence aside, the truth was my friend there. Nearly all my movements could be verified. At the restaurant I pointedly hadn't tipped the waiter, a snotty youth. He'd remember me. He'd certainly remember Eunice. For most of the time after that I had eye-witnesses – a cab driver, people on the cafe terrace, Lapworth, maybe some of those I'd encountered at the apartment block. I wouldn't even have to deny calling on Eunice. My story would be that I rang the bell, got no answer and went away.

And that's what I told the police when they interrupted my breakfast the next day. A pair of them in near-identical brown suits. Smart cops, and civilised too. No pressure, no mind games. They listened politely and made notes and that was the last I saw of them. It helped me that they already had a promising suspect.

I learned about him when the news broke. Carlos. He was the waiter, the boy whose attitude had annoyed me. According to him he'd picked up the clamshell, then seen me heading back to the restaurant as he went off duty, so he hurried to the car park and talked Eunice into taking a joyride in the Passat.

If so, he must have caught her in the mood for April folly. The rest of the tale involved a stop by her flat, then an abortive trip to return the car. He'd run out of fuel, left it on a country road and walked the four kilometres miles home.

He was her lover, of course. I recalled Lapworth's comment about toyboys and waiters, which I'd taken as an offhand put-down that said more about him than her. Small wonder Eunice had been so positive about going to that restaurant.

I didn't want to believe the kid, but I did. In media photos he had the pale, frightened face of a mother's boy; Eunice was probably his mother's age. I got the picture: she'd had a bust-up with Carlos, used me to mend their fences, taken off with him.

Fooled again.

There was soon more breaking news. It came after I'd spent too much time with the brandy bottle and some weed I'd bought in a bar near the beach, but two items on the local TV channel, suggestively presented in tandem, quickly sobered me up. One showed the release of Carlos from custody, still with a fearful expression. The next, shockingly direct, announced Robin Lapworth's death. No cause given though the commentary hinted at suicide. There was a photo, taken some years before, probably obtained from a bribed acquaintance. He was wearing a blazer with an elaborate crest and looked as pompous as ever.

It appeared I had to think my way through mysteries as twisted as a problem in algebra. Lapworth, of all people. Why? I swilled down my evening pill, took a shower and went out for a *cortado* where I could smoke and start joining the dots.

Coffee and night air brought clarity of perception. Lapworth's harsh, contemptuous view of Eunice's personal life and feelings had struck me as odd, not pathological, mainly a facet of his self-centred worldliness. But if his hostility ran deep, if he felt that her behaviour might jeopardise the school, if his bluff manner gave way to rage and panic, if she laughed at his conceit– who knew? What was eye-witness certain was that she had been attacked in a savage, unrestrained frenzy you could only call an outrage.

Whatever had burst his self-control had taken him over the edge. And when he had to confront himself as a murderer he saw only one exit. You could say that killing Eunice was the postponement of his own death wish.

Now I had the answer I could call Ingrid to offer condolences. I paid the waiter and took my phone into the gardens, where the darkness was punctured by light. Solar globes on metal stalks glowed among the palm trees. At a distance were the illuminated portholes of a moored ferry. There was a faint cannabis scent on the breeze, and the headlamps of a bus as it veered to manage a sharp corner lit the ghostly, vacant eyes of a cat crouched in the grass. The LEDs of my keypad danced.

Someone was picking up the phone for her, screening calls, but Ingrid came on the line when she heard my name.

The first thing she said was, 'He took caustic soda.'

'What?'

'Caustic soda. For unblocking drains, you know? It burns its way through anything you can imagine. What it does to flesh you could not imagine.'

She was making it hard.

'God, Ingrid, that's awful.' It sounded too little to say, so I went on. 'I suppose he couldn't live with himself after…'

'After what?'

'Knowing what he'd done, I mean.'

She seemed to dwell on that before she spoke again.

'What he'd done? What do you think he did? Murdered Eunice? You cannot mean that. Of course he didn't kill her. Inconceivable. He would never have done such a thing. He loved her. But not she him. Without her he did not wish to live. Although he did not have the faintest chance ever. Love that is never returned, that lives in such a

57

hopeless vacuum, don't you know how that screws people up? You insane bloody fool, how many dead people do you want? Do you feed on corpses?'

A sad, bitter, drunken woman, and afraid of the truth. Not that it mattered any more. I left for Bilbao before the funerals. I had business in hand. I also had my clamshell, personally delivered by a uniformed junior policeman. The Passat had been vandalised and the car hire firm tried to get sticky about it, but after what I'd been through I wasn't taking any crap from them.

ALCATRAZ DIRTBAG

Ben Borland

The bedroom had changed since the first time he came here. It was no longer the domain of a teenage girl, the posters – Pulp, Elastica, Luke Perry from *Beverly Hills 90210* – and the corkboard full of photographs had been replaced by plain cream walls, but it was still Abbie's room.

'Looks nice,' said Detective Sergeant Andy Painter. 'Must have been hard to, you know, take all the stuff down.'

'It was,' agreed Mrs Matthews. 'Very.'

She suddenly seemed distracted by the view out of the window. The street was a quiet cul-de-sac on the edge of Westhoughton and, above the roofs, Painter could see the stone tower on Rivington Pike and the West Pennine moors stretching beyond. He wondered how often Abbie's mother stood here frozen like this.

'Oh, but I didn't throw anything away,' said Mrs Matthews, snapping out of her reverie. 'I kept all her things. I thought, well, you never know when the police might need something.'

'Very wise,' said Painter. 'As a matter of fact, it would be helpful to look at any photos you have of Abbie. It would be good to get a nice one, just in case we have to put something out to the media.'

'Of course!' Mrs Matthews beamed at him and opened the wardrobe to retrieve a large plastic storage box, full of photo albums and bulging folders from Truprint or Snappy Snaps and hundreds of loose photographs.

The girl in most of them was blonde and blue-eyed with a happy grin, her too-short life traced in a blizzard of prints that showed her racing from toddler to teenager.

'Here's Abbie's final year photo from St Mark's,' said Mrs Matthews, holding a cardboard frame embossed with gold. Painter thought the dark green school blazer, neat tie and sober skirt were belied by the somewhat worldly smirk on the girl's face.

'That's perfect,' said Painter. 'But I wonder if I could take this one as well? I'll get them copied and return them both of course.'

It was an image of the girl sitting on the shoulders of a shirtless teenage boy, surrounded by hundreds of other young people at a music concert. She was dressed in cut-off jeans and a flimsy white T-shirt, her hands in the air and her eyes closed, a silk scarf tied around one wrist and her face upturned to the late evening sun of a day long ago.

The lovesick boy watched the beautiful girl stumble into the bushes behind Rivington Barn. She was totally drunk, but the brain dead idiots gathered around the van didn't seem to care. They were whooping and hollering and passing around joints and bongs and bottles, music blaring from the speakers to a crowd of starstruck admirers and hangers-on.

He had been following the girl for most of the day, hoping for a chance to speak to her, to explain his powerful yet jumbled feelings. After the concert – called Rivi Rock '96, and featuring several big Britpop and American alt-rock bands – she had joined the crowd streaming into the woods, determined to keep the revelry going all night. They had arrived here, eventually, at the Barn, and found one of the bands – a US west coast grunge outfit named Alcatraz Dirtbag – at the centre of a fire-lit party in the car park.

That was almost two hours ago, and the first flush of dawn was now beginning to lighten the sky behind the Pike. After the girl had been gone for around 15 minutes, the boy began to fear that she had passed out in the bushes. He moved quietly through the throng to investigate, nobody paying much attention to the slight, unremarkable figure with an earnest expression and a bowl haircut that was saved from being memorably bad by a cowlick in the middle of his fringe.

Away from the car park, the light from the fire and the headlights soon faded to black. The boy could see virtually nothing, although there were sounds all around him – groans, giggles and the occasional shout – to prove he was not alone. He walked on, the path climbing gradually and his night vision improving as his eyes got used to the darkness.

Then he saw her. She was with one of the long-haired American freaks from the band, reaching up to kiss him and then dropping to her knees, before eventually she broke away and pulled him down on top of her. The lovesick boy watched and listened until it was over.

Later, when the Yanks were finally driven away, he found the courage to approach the girl and offer her a lift home. Yes, he was fine to drive. He hadn't had a drink all night. Just, you know, a couple of tokes.

Later still, after he had told the girl what he thought of prick-teasing sluts like her, he punched her in the face until she lost consciousness and then strangled her to death with her silk scarf.

'Morning, DS Painter,' said Graham Satchell, one of the technicians at the Forensic Alliance lab in Risley. 'I had a feeling we might be seeing you today.'

'Morning Graham,' replied Painter. He had brought coffees and muffins from the drive-thru Costa on the ring road, no expense spared to keep the lab rats happy. 'I guess you heard then?'

'Oh bloody hell, we've heard alright. Haven't we, Sukes?' Satchell called over to Suki Jolly, the white-coated and bespectacled pin-up who featured in the dreams of many male – and female – police officers from Crewe to Carnforth.

'Yep, got a call from your pal Marcus first thing, said the long-awaited parcel had arrived from the States,' she said, picking up a coffee. 'These for us? Thanks, Andy.'

'Marcus is sweating bullets. Reckons he's taken over 300 quid that says you're gonna be left looking like a chump,' said Satchell.

'Three to one on apparently,' replied Painter, biting into one of the muffins. 'Trust me, he's going to be in the money tonight.'

'Tonight?' asked Jolly, raising her perfectly sculpted eyebrows. 'No chance, we've got samples coming in from a triple up in Oldham. Wife and two kiddies.'

Painter's shoulders slumped. 'Shit, I heard about that,' he said. 'How long then?'

Satchell guffawed and Jolly gave a feline smile of delight. 'Don't worry, mate,' said Satchell. 'We'll get a rush on yours. I've got a tenner on with Marcus meself.'

'Oh ye of little faith… ah, not you as well, Suki?'

'Fraid so, twenty quid,' said Jolly. 'Anyway, come on, don't keep us in suspenders any longer, hand it over.'

Painter had joined Greater Manchester Police's Cold Case Unit five years earlier, after a stellar start to his career in Trafford CID. He made his name on a string of tit-for-tat gang stabbings which threatened to blow up into a PR disaster for the city, organising the dawn raids that brought the burgeoning turf war to a relatively peaceful conclusion, before sealing his status as one-to-watch by bringing down a gang smuggling heroin from Istanbul via Rotterdam and into an industrial unit on the southern bank of the Ship Canal.

There were other options open to him when the time came for a promotion, but he was most attracted by the challenge (and the glory) of closing a case that had defied other detectives for years. The Abbie Matthews murder was one of the first he had been assigned to and he felt an immediate connection with the case, perhaps because if she had lived they would have both been around the same age.

On August Bank Holiday weekend in 1996, 17-year-old Abbie had attended the Rivi Rock music festival – another connection, many of the bands playing that day had also been Painter's teenage favourites – in a field on the shores of Rivington Reservoir near Horwich. The land was owned by the water board and had once formed part of Lord Leverhulme's estate, including swathes of landscaped gardens on the hillside leading up to Rivington Pike – a stone tower that had originally been lit to warn against the Spanish Armada.

Abbie was last seen by her friends several hours after the concert had finished, near an old manor house complex called Rivington Hall Barn that was a wedding venue and tea room by day and a popular hang-out for after-club ravers by night. The police estimated that at least 2,000 people had been roaming around the area at the time and yet – largely because most of them were completely wasted – nobody could recall with any clarity when they had last seen Abbie.

At some point, however, she must have got into a vehicle and been driven north along the winding hillside roads up the chain of Victorian reservoirs that still supplied drinking water to Liverpool, 25 miles away across the Lancashire Plain, before being brutally murdered and her body hidden inside a stone overflow pipe.

Abbie's parents reported her missing to the police the following day and a somewhat cursory search operation was launched (teenagers going astray after a rock concert not being entirely unheard of) before her mortal remains were discovered by a man walking his dog. The murder of pretty Abbie Matthews became headline news but, despite national press coverage and several appearances on the BBC's *Crimewatch* programme, it remained unsolved.

There was an abundance of forensic evidence. Abbie had had sexual intercourse in the hours before her death and semen samples were recovered from both her vagina and her underwear. However, the DNA database threw up no matches and a huge DNA sampling exercise among men from the Horwich and Chorley areas – as well as thousands of concert-goers who came forward – yielded no matches.

Abbie's head injuries were extensive and had been inflicted by a blunt instrument, possibly a fist – in which case the murderer would have had significant bruising around his knuckles for weeks afterwards – but the ultimate cause of death was asphyxiation with a silk scarf, a material which at that time defied fingerprinting.

Her blood alcohol level showed that Abbie was at least five times over the legal driving limit when she died and her stomach contents included white wine, beer and vodka, as well as a partially digested meal of cheeseburger and chips. Toxicology results found she had also consumed small amounts of the drugs ecstasy and cannabis before her death.

The detective team at the time had a working theory that Abbie's murderer was not the same person with whom she had had sex, based on the lack of defensive injuries consistent with a rape. However, this detail was never released to the press and the newspapers tended to refer to the crime as a rape and murder.

After he picked up the case, Painter found himself intrigued by this aspect of the case. He spent a lot of time with Abbie's mother, who still lived alone with her grief in the house they shared in Westhoughton, and re-interviewed all of her friends that he could trace. She had an on-off boyfriend at the time, a local lothario called Daz Watts, but the relationship was very much in the 'off' phase when she was killed. Daz also had a cast-iron alibi as he was locked up on remand in HM Prison Hindley at the time.

Her friends also remembered Abbie sitting on the shoulders of a handsome blond kid, a stranger from London, or somewhere 'down south' at any rate, who was called Gary. Or possibly Barry. After a deal of hard work, Gary Newlands had been traced to Andover in Hampshire and interviewed at some length. After the concert he had returned to Manchester with his mates and had a few drinks before crashing out in their hotel, a fact apparently confirmed by several witnesses. Nevertheless, Painter had tracked Newlands down once more and made him go through his story again.

Then, finally, a breakthrough. Several witnesses had mentioned that one of the bands from the concert had been up at Rivington Barn at around the same time as Abbie and her friends. One local girl, whom Painter tracked down in Chorley, had even had a son as a result of a brief liaison in the woods with the drummer from the band, identified with some bitterness as Alcatraz Dirtbag.

Painter vaguely remembered them from his youth, a sub-Pearl Jam outfit that upon further investigation were revealed to be a four-piece from Santa Rosa in Sonoma County, north of San Francisco, consisting of lead singer Peanut (real name Edward Klein), guitarist Stretch (real name Francis Doyle), bassist Terry Bretton and drummer Leo St Michael.

Stretch had passed away from a prescription drug overdose in 1999, but while Terry Bretton appeared to have dropped out of the music scene altogether (there was a T Bretton listed in the Sonoma County phone book at a vineyard outside Wikiup) Peanut and St Michael were still making a living from touring and playing as Alcatraz Dirtbag.

As St Michael was the father of the child in Chorley, Painter thought it was unlikely that he was the same man who had sex with Abbie Matthews, leaving him with only Bretton and Klein to pursue – but also the certain knowledge that GMP would not pay for him to fly to California on such flimsy evidence. Then, a chance discovery on eBay had electrified his investigation and ultimately led to him becoming the talk of several police forces across the North West.

Peanut, although now well into his forties, was still renowned for his long, flowing black mane and a Dirtbag fan in Colorado was selling one of his hairbrushes on eBay. The fan claimed to have stolen it from Peanut's dressing room after a gig at the Bluebird Theater in Denver and posted photos showing a black brush with a grubby handle inlaid with mother of pearl and bristles tangled with hair. Painter had ended up in an online bidding war and the damn thing cost him $215, plus shipping fees, paid for out of his own pocket.

However, while the hairbrush was never going to adorn the walls of even the most desperate of Hard Rock Cafes, he knew it would be a treasure trove of viable DNA evidence – a fact confirmed by Graham Satchell one night in the pub, before the technician spread news of his scheme to every living soul in the job he could think of.

Now, after waiting for almost two weeks, the day of reckoning had arrived. Painter produced the brush, wrapped in a plastic evidence bag, from his briefcase and handed it to Suki Jolly.

'Careful with that,' he said. 'That's my life's work you've got there.'

Two weeks later, the hairbrush sat in the middle of a polished wooden table in a conference room on the top floor of the new GMP headquarters building in Newton Heath. A battery of top brass and force lawyers were looking at it as though it might possibly contain a new strain of the Ebola virus while they discussed their next move. Painter sat at the back of the room, gazing out of the window over the anonymous industrial park and thinking how much he missed the old HQ in Old Trafford, just off busy Chester Road and around the corner from the United ground.

'Do you recall the band, Alistair?' one of the lawyers was asking the ACC.

'Can't say that I do,' he replied. 'Not really my scene, grunge.'

So far, they had established that none of them remembered Alcatraz Dirtbag but very little else.

'And it's definitely his DNA then, the singer's?' asked the ACC.

'Yes sir,' said Painter, turning his attention back to the suits. 'A solid match to both semen and hair found on the body.'

'Good Christ,' said the ACC. 'Doesn't mean he killed her though? I mean, these rock stars can barely keep their dicks in their pants at the best of times. Look at what's his name… Harry Styles.'

'So,' said another lawyer after an uncomfortable silence. 'Next move?'

'Sensitive,' said the ACC. 'Not a good time to be rocking the boat with our American friends.'

'How so?' asked the lawyer.

'Never is,' replied the ACC obliquely. 'Still, we can't let this one lie. If Andy were to go over there to speak to this Peanut chappie purely as a witness, surely that couldn't cause too much of a problem.'

The lawyers exchanged a flurry of worried glances but said nothing.

'Good, so that's settled then,' said the ACC, suddenly as bright as a spring morning. 'Well, Andy, it looks as though you've bagged yourself a jaunt to San Francisco. Smashing city, have you been before?'

'No, sir.'

'Well, enjoy it but don't go spending too much time in lap dancing clubs. Or more importantly, any taxpayers' money.'

The lawyers giggled dutifully.

'No, sir.'

'Excellent work, Andy, really first rate. Talk to Sheila on your way out, she'll sort all your travel details. Now, I'm afraid we've got a few other, ah, issues to discuss.'

'Of course, I'll be on my way then,' said Painter. He stood up and collected the hairbrush from the table and said his goodbyes.

Once outside the HQ, he took out his phone and called Mrs Matthews in Westhoughton to keep her up to speed with the latest developments. As he spoke, he took the photo of Abbie at the concert from his jacket pocket and studied it again. There was the girl, with her eyes closed and her face turned to the sun, and there in the background was the lovesick boy, watching her.

Painter raised his head and looked at his reflection in the mirrored glass, seeing his resemblance to the youth in the photograph; the same earnest expression and the same cowlick in the middle of his fringe. Much had happened since that night on Rivington Pike but the lovesick boy knew he could never forget.

THE COLD CALLING

Lynne M Blackwell

Jackie is lost in a drowned village, swimming over twisted spires, ornate columns and cobbled streets. Within the watery ruins she tastes a strange mix of pond weed and stale tobacco, recognising the brand. Through a collection of tree stumps, blackened, as if destroyed by fire, she stumbles across another opening. From this door, she enters a dark wood, inhaling the smell of pine and cigarettes, again.

She hides behind giant oaks and sycamores, scratching skin on thick warty trunks that are bifurcated, splayed wide. She can sense a man's presence, close by, thrashing a torn branch at the ground, swiping weeds, beating a path – heading her way. Out of the corner of her eye, she sees a flash of pink. There's nothing Jackie can do but wait for events to unfold. She takes in every detail, watching the frail girl as she limps through the forest, crunching pine cones underfoot, squelching mud and mulch – making too much noise.

An engine is running. A huge weight is pressing down. Great wafts of damp air pass her by, flashes of sky, the coldest of nights. Something jagged is rubbing against her sore back – a zip with wide teeth, clenched tight. There's a single splash, ripples of moonlight on black water – then nothing more. The image fades. Doors slam. The shutters come down.

The girl put her tracksuit clean on, months ago. Now the wool is bobbled from sleeping in it and the colour has turned a dirty pink. She turns up the frayed hems, puts her arms in the air and runs barefoot through a gauntlet of vermin.

It seems strange that she knows her way around, but she's had clues during captivity: mother sheep's disapproving baas, birds shrieking rather than singing, raging gales and whiffs of manure.

She leaves the cobblestone yard, clearing slurry, stubbing toes on uneven ground, catching nettle stings and the snatch of brambles. She reaches a wooden stile, staggering over the slimy step to get to another empty field.

Although the land stretches out for miles, the atmosphere is oppressive, making her feel woozy and penned in. She wipes sweat from her brow, but it's already dripped into her eyes, messing up her vision; blending sky with fields, turning a traditional watercolour into an abstract.

She struggles to remain upright, side-stepping towards a meadow, back against the dry stone wall. Then, leaning into the long grass, reaching for the finishing line, she collapses in a heap.

She starts to stroke her back, tracing circular indentations. He used to put a blanket over the grubby mattress, as if that would soften the blows. With every movement she'd feel either stone floor or rusty springs, but she got used to pain. It overshadowed petty nuisances. She dealt with the head lice like a bad case of dandruff, scratching her scalp, picking out scabs – drawing blood without realising. Even the rancid fusty smells that at first made her gip didn't register in the end.

The wind has picked up, blowing across the meadow, parting blades in thick clumps. She feels massive, a clumsy oaf that's no more concealed within a patch of grass than a pink elephant. His voice is carried along in the breeze, whispering her name. She looks for him, scanning walls and fields, hearing the twang of barbed wire and a heavy thud, left of the bridleway.

It's 1pm and the curtains are already pulled, shutting out neighbours who have taken to staring in. Jackie Phillips has been pacing the floor for hours, plagued by a psychic's instinct, fearing the worst. She stops to consider the girl's mother anxiously waiting for news – every second slowly ticking by: five months, three weeks and six days.

Her fingers shake over the dials, prodding at the three nines. It's a female voice again, calm as the last one, another irritating bitch. Jackie is standing for no nonsense. She's had enough of everyone fobbing her off.

'I need to speak to someone in Sheffield,' she gulps, 'DC Ben Hammond – he'll have to do.' She puffs up the cushions, ruffling feathers, punching gold embroidery, catching a dangly tassel.

'You're wasting time,' she huffs. 'A child is in danger.'

Frustratingly, this sense of urgency doesn't seem to be reflected on the other end of the line. Jackie's voice rises to a desperate yell.

'You've got to find the second girl before its too late.'

Initially, DC Ben Hammond questioned Jackie's authenticity. Rather conveniently the image of a kidnapper kept freezing, but she knew things that had been kept from the press – things that only an insider would know. He examined the information available to the public, scrutinising everything that had been posted online, scrolling the missing persons website, finding nothing more than the girl's name and description. There were no references to footwear, and yet the psychic was able to describe the lost trainer, matching the one his colleague had found half a mile from the last known sighting. 'One of a pair,' she said, 'white, transparent heels, orange label, no laces and a muddy sole.'

The police traced Bethany's mobile, which had gone dead a few miles down the bypass, within walking distance of her home. It seemed a foregone conclusion that this kid had been snatched. They didn't need supernatural intervention to confirm that. Her mother knew this too, but school friends were less convinced. They explained that Bethany had planned to find her dad. In their words, 'He'd done a midnight flit and she wanted compo for sending her mum doolally.'

Ben found him living in a two-up two-down in the Scottish borders, where he'd been shacked up with the estranged wife of a Mr Brown for a year. He said that his ex had refused all offers of money, insisting that she didn't want anything to do with him. The lover took her eyes off daytime TV to back him up, rolling the sleeve of her onesie as if preparing for a cat-fight. Ben raised his eyebrows at her, taking every word with a pinch of salt.

It didn't take long to search the dingy property. He didn't see the point sending for a JCB to dig up the back yard. Neither did he feel the need to start lifting floorboards or rifling through the eves. He couldn't get the psychic's voice out of his mind. Her concerns tapped into his subconscious, like a persistent rattling at the door, until he started to picture the things that she saw. As if he was watching a film, each shot clicked into view: the girl, a damp cellar – the man with greasy hair and nails bitten down to the wick.

A strip of brightness shines under a gap at the bottom of the door, illuminating the stairwell like a light sabre slashing through the air. Bethany can see his shadow cutting across the light. She listens as he slowly turns the key, coercing the stiff bolts, cursing them for refusing to budge.

She tries to judge his mood from the way he's looking down on her: standing proud on the top step, beneath fluorescent tubes that flicker and buzz – arms crossed, smirking. She steps back, touching grit and flaky paint, inches from the outside.

He's getting close, thrusting his weight against her, breathing instructions down her neck.

'Be a good girl while I'm gone.'

What was once in focus becomes a blur.

Ben is standing by Jackie's bay window, framed by a velvet pelmet, floral drapes and fussy tie-backs. She's muttering to herself beside the elaborate fake marble fireplace, encapsulated in a nicotine haze – a yellowy ectoplasm, straight out of a Victorian séance. Other than that she doesn't appear to be a stereotypical psychic. In his opinion, her feathery high heeled pink slippers are more Danny La Rue than white witch. He would have expected to find several dream catchers

72

or at the very least a crystal ball. It's what he'd imagine Liberace's house would have looked like if the pianist had lived in a ten-year-old semi.

Ben asks if there could be other victims and she begins to put on a show: scratching feverishly, talking about rats scurrying over cobblestones. He backs away, as if madness is contagious. Then, all of a sudden, she starts staggering around, feeling her way past obstacles which are not there – walking in the dark.

Ben moves towards her extended arm, cupping his hands beneath a long line of ash, waiting to catch it before it falls. To his horror, she drops the whole cigarette – not onto her sheepskin rug, but into his palm. He throws it out of the window, inadvertently inviting a disgusting mix of animal waste and pre-treated sewage into the room. And all the while, she's picking out non-existent splinters from the soles of her feet. One minute she's seeing stagnant ponds, then fresh deep water the next – too many contradictions for his liking. He makes his way to the door, but she's hollering after him.

'It's no good. The shutters are down.'

He leaves before she wastes any more of his time.

Bethany stops to cradle a stitch, keeping vigilant, looking for signs of civilisation, rubbing her tummy, talking to the foetus – giving it a name.

In the distance, wispy clouds thinly veil the mountain tops, creeping into the deep crevices like billowy smoke, concealing all exits. She wonders if it had all been too easy. What if he left the door open to test her loyalty? Her breathing is rapid, and out of control. She's fearing the consequences, but unable to move.

She looks around for the other girl: pink tracksuit, long dark hair. He put her into isolation, months ago when he thought the two girls were up to something. They had made a pact to escape when, and if, the opportunity arose – together or alone. They reckoned it wouldn't take long to find help, but there's nothing out here, only fields and barbed wire.

She starts to scratch at the many open wounds, forgetting how to breathe – more scared of freedom than captivity. If she gets back to the farmhouse before he does, he'll not notice she's been gone.

Jackie parks up in a lay-by, gasping for air. She tries to envisage the girl's movements, willing her to make for the road. She's been here before. She remembers low beams, vinegary chips, hand-pulled ale, and a beer garden with breathtaking views. Inside the pub, there's a collection of photographs hanging off lumpy whitewashed walls. These images of children with awkward grins and stiff postures were taken on the streets of Derwent, before it was flooded to make way for a reservoir. Jackie has seen the village under a vast stretch of water: stripped down to its foundations, beneath what is now known as Ladybower.

There's a hose pipe ban in place. It's not rained for months, but Jackie is shivering. The air conditioning isn't on, but it's suddenly gone cold. Goosebumps prickle as she visualises the girl, sprawled over pine cones, mud and mulch. Infuriatingly, she knows this is somewhere near here, but the exact location eludes her.

Jackie heads off into the forest, treading carefully as if walking on someone's grave. She comes to a standstill by the edge of the dry reservoir, mesmerised by the sight of rippling water, sniffling and foaming over the girl's feet.

Bethany watches as a van backs up practically through the farmhouse door. He's getting out with a bullmastiff in tow – looking for her.

She turns, ripping brambles out of the way, yelping, snapping twigs, splintering the soles of her bare feet. She dodges a scattering of feathers and a mauled rabbit with maggot-ridden abdomen and empty eye sockets that seem to be staring back. In the distance there's a road, but the closer she gets, the more it moves further away.

Jackie takes a left fork under a canopy of overhanging trees. The wispy foliage, like emerald feather boas, makes her think of girls in dark dives, waiting for clients and pimps. This thought makes her queasy. The nausea is made worse as she swerves around pot holes, trying to block out the sound of blood-curdling screams. An image springs to mind – the back of a man's head. Then nothing more, until she's startled by the sight of a car directly in front, and traffic lights that are red.

Beyond the towering pine trees, a never-ending stream of cars and lorries wind their way through the snake pass. There's a trail of exhaust fumes, mists of windscreen wash, gargles of spit – and a bridge. She has to take the police there.

Bethany wakes up shivering and yet she can feel sweat seeping from every pore, aggravating the spots on her face, back and chest. She's wrapped in a nylon cocoon, the sleeping bag from the cellar. He must have put her here: on this cold corrugated floor, close to a draught – the back of a van – the one she saw at the farmhouse. It's probably early morning, before the dawn chorus, because it's eerily quiet. She can't hear the man or the dog, but she can smell skunk. If her hands hadn't been bound, she might be able to reach the zip or the string that's tied above her head. She presses her tummy gently, waiting for a reaction, feeling sure the baby ought to be kicking by now.

A bang makes her jump. It sounded like a glove compartment slamming shut. He's on his mobile, lowering the tone into an indistinguishable whisper. Her empty stomach somehow churns. She's forgotten the last time he gave her anything to eat, or drink, and yet her bladder is full.

The back doors are flung open and a cold breeze rips under the sleeping bag in a succession of icy waves. She wets herself, the urine coming out in a flood, warm and stinking like an old lady who's not been drinking properly.

He's beside her, rattling a match box. He was always threatening to set her alight.

She curls up inside her nylon shroud, feeling nothing except an urge to cry out for Mum.

Jackie can smell the man's cigarette and something more distinctive – roll-ups – weed. She closes her eyes tightly, watching him heave out a bundle from the back of a van. He lets go, giving it a push, waiting for it to roll into a watery grave. It makes a single splash. She sees ripples of moonlight, then nothing more. It's gone, without trace, beneath a jet-black sheen – a lid on the matter – simple as that.

She's visualising a human form, crouched inside a sleeping bag. There's a stench of decomposing flesh – midges and flies. She jolts up, staring into darkness, seeing the back of the man's head, a great mop of greasy hair – the bastard that killed the first girl.

At the same time, children are stepping over what looks like a fallen wall, unaware that this was once a church. Without a spire, stained glass windows, a font or pew, no one recognises its significance. Something has excited their dog's sensitive nostrils. Far ahead, he has discovered a package of some sort in the old fishpond on the edge of a water-depleted reservoir. As his inquisitive nose sniffs and snorts, a section of red quilted material bloats out. The children gather round, noticing strands of hair sticking through a knot in the cord – a blessing in disguise, a forewarning not to touch.

Their father pulls the dog away, clips on its lead and warns the family to stand well back.

At the police station, officers pace the floor, polystyrene cups in hands, exchanging information, which is coming in by the second. It's the news Ben has been dreading. The psychic was right all along.

She's with him and DC Briggs now. They're escorting her to Ladybower on the Boss's orders. He wants the case wrapped up by whatever means. She knew there was a body in the reservoir weeks before the water levels receded, so there's a chance she might lead them to the murderer. Anything's worth a try but Ben is careful not to sound like the converted because Briggs is the biggest sceptic around. Ben tells Jackie that he intends to park by the road-block, without mentioning that this happens to be next to the bridge she keeps going on about. He looks in his rear view mirror, expecting some acknowledgment from her, but it looks like she's in another trance.

Jackie doesn't need to close her eyes to see the murder scene. It's embedded in her memory, a snapshot in time, faded like the photos in the pub by Ladybower. She wants to nail the man who did this, but it's infuriating because she only ever sees the back of his head. She waits for the image to turn full circle. Egging him on, until she sees his face for the first time. For a split second she's looking at his demonic eyes, caught in the glare of headlights.

She taps Ben on the shoulders, insisting he stops the car. He parks half-on, half-off a verge close to a bridleway and an old packhorse bridge. Jackie clambers out, steadying herself against a wall, fretting in case they're too late to save the girl.

Bethany was dragged from the van and kicked down the hill in the sleeping bag. Great wafts of grass passed her by, flashes of blue sky and will o' the wisp clouds. Her direction kept changing until she came to a halt against something sharp, maybe a pile of rocks.

She's not sure of the time. It's hot – an intense heat that usually comes from the midday sun. A bird is flapping its wings. In the distance, there are many cars and lorries. Someone's coughing nearby – a chesty, smoker's cough.

Jackie tells the officers to run on ahead, drawing their attention towards a heap of limestone packers where she's sure they'll find a tatty sleeping bag. She clutches her chest at the point where it's rattling, staring intently, looking for movement – praying the girl is still alive. Ben stops to kneel down, reaching out to touch something. He seems hesitant, afraid of what he might find.

Bethany can hear the reassuring sound of sirens.
A noxious odour accompanies a slight hiss. She can feel something rubbery and smooth, pressing down onto her face.

She's in a dark confined space like the back of a van. Someone in a uniform is leaning over, readjusting the mask, explaining that she's having oxygen: 'Don't worry. You're going to be all right.'

Bethany's voice is croaky, but she manages to ask if anyone has seen her friend.

The paramedic seems puzzled.

'He's killed her, hasn't he?'

She strokes her shrunken tummy, feeling the emptiness of a baby that's gone. Her arms go limp, flopping through the cot sides. The metal feels ice-cold, but she's too tired to flinch.

When Jackie gets home she's determined to do all she can to find the suspect. She shoves a lozenge in her dry mouth and takes herself back to Ladybower – turning blind corners and sharp deviations, passing memorials to dead bikers. Her mind's eye is drawn towards a bunch of shrivelled roses tied to a bridge, hanging over the twisted neck of sun-bleached wrapping. There's interference on a radio. Someone's switching channels onto the local news. A terminal is in sight. He's at the airport – weighing up the options. An engine starts. Everything is in slow motion, a blur: road, runway, razor wire – fencing. The van crashes and yet it's deadly silent. She bites into her sweet, releasing a strong menthol vapour, gulping liquorice shards that leave a sharp sensation in her throat. Drifting out of consciousness the man realises that the liquid he can taste is his own blood.

Jackie gets settled on the cream sofa: kicking off slippers, rounding up cushions, and smiling, her work done.

THE MILLIONAIRE'S WIFE

Karon Alderman

'Hurry up with that cup of tea, Vera. It's the time he normally calls...'
John has the laptop open on the table and he's wearing his blazer.
He's still such a smart man and very organised; he's been on courses
and all sorts, up at the local library; silver courses, they call them.
'I'm a silver surfer,' he said when he first bought the laptop. That's
how the world is now, everything done on phones and computers.
John's explained that to her again and again, all about the net and
the web and everything global. She wonders if they'll ever sort out
a computer that does the housework, putting out the washing and
cleaning up the spiders' webs from the window sills.

She puts the empty washing basket down on the kitchen floor
and pushes the back door closed. The sun is shining, but there's a
breeze; just perfect weather for the laundry, you couldn't ask for
better. She likes it when she can get it out on the line. She always says
it smells so much fresher when it's been out on the line. The doorbell
is ringing. She turns to him in surprise.

'But there's someone at the door,' she says. 'They're ringing the
doorbell,' she adds.

'Well, that's what it's for, woman...' he gets up from the table,
moves into the hall, pushing the door half closed behind him.

'Who is it?' she calls but he doesn't answer. She tries to go into
the hall and he is shaking his head, filling the space, moving her back
into the kitchen.

'No! Don't answer it!'

She stops, gives him a puzzled look. He is breathing heavily,
but pushes the kitchen door closed. The bell rings again, still clear
through the closed door. It's not a big house.

'Mr Babalula will be ringing any moment,' he adds. 'I can't be
distracted. It's important to have a clear head when you're dealing

with finances. I can't have you wittering on to someone on the doorstep when I'm making important financial transactions.'

'They're still there,' she says as it rings again. She hesitates, unwilling to push past him. 'But John... who can it be? It might be important!'

He gives her one of his looks. 'Don't be daft, woman. It'll just be door to door sales or Jehovah's Witnesses! The world's full of sharks and crazies.' His voice is firm. 'We'll just pretend we're not here... You get on and make that tea. Go on – we don't have to be dictated to, or told that the world's ending or some nonsense about the second coming just because they're inconsiderate enough to lean on the bell!'

She turns to the sink and starts to fill the kettle. The sound of the bell is muffled by the rush of the water from the tap but it is still there. Whoever it is does not just walk away. They listen to the doorbell. It rings, stops, rings, stops. There is a pause. Then it rings again.

'Someone's not giving up,' she says, cheerily, looking sideways at John. He is still standing by the door, very upright and smart, like he's guarding it. She puts the kettle on the work surface and flicks the on switch.

'They'll give up and go in the end,' he says, but he still doesn't sit down by the phone, like he normally does, waiting for the important call. Funny how you can hear someone all the way from Nigeria as clear as if they were standing right beside you. It's like magic really. John often explains technology to her, usually while she's trying to cook, but she knows she doesn't understand.

They wait, both standing in the kitchen, the noise of the kettle building. She stares at the door to the hall. Needs a coat of paint, she thinks. Her finger touches a dent, feels the unevenness of the woodwork. John used to be so proud of his gloss work. Every year he'd touch up and then a full strip and repaint every five years... but he hasn't done anything for ages. She tries to count back the years, pinning dates to events, the year he fitted the new kitchen units was the year after they went to Cornwall, so that must be… she can't remember the years. Ten years maybe and he'd not done a full repaint since, had he? For a moment she wonders if he's losing his edge. But the money! Two million pounds! Who'd have thought they'd ever have two million in the bank? Millionaires, that's what they are.

She gazes at the chipped paint and the scuffed lino, every muscle straining to hear the silence after the bell stops. He says it's time consuming making millions and the paintwork will just have to wait. It's a shame, she thinks. It isn't as much fun being a millionaire as you'd think. She doesn't actually *feel* like a millionaire. But John is so hard to explain to. When she tried to tell him that she thought it was time they spruced up the kitchen a bit he got angry. He says she doesn't understand things and she knows that's true, she's not so clever as him and there are so many things now that seem so complicated. She sometimes thinks you need to have a degree to switch on the washing machine these days. But he gets so cross when she doesn't understand things.

'Go away, go *away*,' he is muttering, rubbing his hands against his trousers.

'Who can it be?' she repeats. 'D'you suppose it's important?' she says, hesitantly, putting her hand to her mouth: 'Maybe it's Suzie!'

'No! Of course it isn't Suzie, you st…' he stops before he says it, but she knows what he is thinking. 'Just ignore it!' He is nearly shouting, standing there, his head tilted to one side, listening to the bell, pretending to not be in, which is silly, she thinks, just silly, if he's going to go around shouting like that. Not only the person at the door, but the whole street will know they're in if he keeps on shouting like that.

She turns away, focuses on the steady roar of the kettle. He's not himself, she thinks. He wouldn't even let Suzie in the other day. She'd cried that night, at the thought of Suzie driving all that way from London and he'd not even let her in the house. Not let her make her a cup of tea, even. Not let her… oh, her head got so jumbled sometimes. But it couldn't be right, could it, to turn away your own daughter? She keeps her back turned, feeling the tears come to her eyes as she tries to remember when she last saw the children, not so little now; and then to not let her in… She fusses with the teapot, turning it on the trivet to just the right angle, finding the mugs and the sugar; she has to pass him to get the milk out of the fridge. She doesn't look at him. He'll calm down in a minute. His little moments, she calls them. Even the best of men get impatient, she knows that.

'Why can't we let Suzie know about the money?' she asks, feeling a quick stab of guilt about the little note she'd put in Suzie's birthday card, full of hints of holidays and college fees for the children. 'Why can't I give some of the money to Suzie, so she can take the children on holiday? John?'

He stands by the cooker, very stiff and straight, like some old army man, she thinks, standing there all smart in his blazer. Not that he's ever been military, but always smart… that's one of the things she'd always liked about him, how he liked things just so; a real stickler for things. Now, his hands ball up into fists and his voice is loud in the sudden silence.

'Don't be bloody ridiculous! Suzie! She thinks we're senile, thinks we need her poking her nose into everything – thinks my years of experience count for nothing! She doesn't even understand finance – for God's sake, she's an art teacher! What does an art teacher know about anything!'

She steps back. He's been so angry lately, so quick to fly off the handle. She doesn't understand. She thought the money would make him happier. That he'd feel more secure, more contented. That's why she'd signed it in the first place, to make him happy. Glowing he'd been, when he'd tried to explain it all. Of course there'd been a risk. He'd told her that. You couldn't expect to make lots of money without a little bit of a risk. Mr Babalula had explained it all, about moving money from where it was not needed to where it was needed. It was a service really and you made money from that. That was the way of things now, the service economy, John had called it. And the risk was only a little one; she'd made sure of that.

'We couldn't lose the house, could we?' she'd asked him and he'd promised her it was nothing like that.

'A little bit naughty where the tax man's concerned,' he'd said, rubbing his hands. 'You don't want to know too much about it.' And he'd touched his nose and laughed.

'Oh, the tax man,' she'd said, smiling. 'That's alright then.'

And it had been. He'd shown her the account details, you could do it all on the computer now; well, John could. She wouldn't know where to start; a million pounds, in their account.

But now the door bell rings again and then someone hammers on the door.

'John, John, dear...' she doesn't want to upset him, but – 'they're banging on the door now – I think it must be something important... Jehovah's Witnesses are normally very polite, so I really don't think... can I just go and see who...?'

'No!' his voice is so loud it makes her jump. 'They might be looking through the letterbox!' he says, ignoring her as she shakes her head.

'It's got one of those draught protectors... don't you remember, we fitted one to stop the...'

'Stay right there!' he cuts across her words. He glances quickly round the little kitchen and pulls open the kitchen drawer. He grabs the big carving knife. 'Just wait!' he says in a loud whisper. 'Get on and make the tea... I'll deal with this.'

She claps her hands to her mouth and watches through the half open door as he creeps along the hall, like he's in a silly TV programme. She wishes he'd not taken that big knife. This is a safe area with nice neighbours. You can't go around waving knives at Jehovah's Witnesses, she thinks, even if they are a bit too persistent with the doorbell.

She can hear a voice calling through the letter box but not the actual words, through the noise of the kettle. He's not himself, she thinks, he's just not himself. She pours hot water onto the teabags, two, nice and strong. John gets in a right tizzy if it's weak; dish water tea, he calls it. Maybe he'll feel better when he's drunk his tea.

She wonders if she should make him an appointment with the doctor. She is looking at the phone, wondering if he will let her make an appointment, when the phone starts to ring and she hesitates. John always deals with Mr Babalula– long complicated calls that wear him out, yet seem to rejuvenate him too. She doesn't want to pick up… she's only spoken to him the once and it wasn't at all easy. He had such a strong accent, she didn't want to be rude, but it was terribly hard to understand him. She waits, two rings, three rings. But John'll be so cross if he misses the call and he's already not very happy… she picks up the receiver.

'Mum! Mum, are you alright, Mum?' Just the sound of Suzie's voice makes her choke up, so she can hardly speak.

'Suzie!' she manages to croak, 'I'm so sorry about the other day, I don't know why your dad…' but Suzie isn't listening, she is saying something: 'Your letter… Dad… laundering…' Vera struggles to catch up with Suzie's quick words and then suddenly John is beside her. He snatches the phone from her and something clatters to the floor.

'It's alright, dear,' she says, rubbing her hand. 'It's not Mr Babalula at all, it's our Suzie. It's just something to do with the washing, nothing important… I'll sort it, John, I'll sort it out, you sit down, drink your tea.' But he holds the phone away from her, staring at her and breathing heavily. His face is a strange mottled red. She is crying now; she can't work out what Suzie's done to make John so very angry, as angry as he was when Suzie failed maths and said she'd never wanted to be a doctor anyway. He slams the phone back on its stand.

'Shut the door,' he says, pushing the kitchen door closed. She rubs her eyes, gulps back a sob.

'Let me ring her back, I'm worried about her…' She falters – she doesn't want to remind him how he wouldn't let Suzie in, after she drove all that way, just in case it upsets him again. She pushes the mug of tea towards him, hoping it will settle him, but he ignores it. 'Maybe she needs some help, maybe some money for the children – everything's so expensive these days. Perhaps we could give her some of the money, John?' Her voice is quiet, tentative. 'What's the point of being a millionaire if we can't enjoy it?'

He leans against the door to the hall. The doorbell rings again and she can hear a voice, calling.

'Oh really!' she says. 'Let me see if I can get rid of them… and then we can drink our tea and all calm down and…'

'It's the police!' John is sweating. 'They know we're here!'

'The police?' She is astounded. It is so unlikely. 'Of course they know we're here. We live here.' Her mind is spinning. Suzie is alright, she was just on the phone, only a few minutes ago… She struggles to imagine why the police would call. 'Has there been an accident? Why don't we just open the door and see…'

'No!' his eyes dart madly around the kitchen, from the phone to the laptop to the back door. 'It's trouble. We're in trouble… It's Suzie's fault, all her fault, poking her nose in…' He is rocking slightly, spit gathering at the corner of his mouth.

'Is it about the tax, John? The police? Is it because we didn't pay the tax?' Her mind can't hold all the strands, can't work out what's going on.

He bends, stiffly, picks something up from the floor. It is the meat knife. He holds it awkwardly.

'It doesn't matter,' she says. 'Pop it in the washing up bowl. Let me go and talk to them…' she says. She moves as if to go to the door.

'No!' he shouts, and he pushes her hard against the kitchen units. As his arm lifts she is still surprised.

'Just shut up!' he shouts. 'It's not our money, you stupid woman! You've never understood finance! Ours comes later, when the money's safely through, we'll get it, Mr Babalula promised.'

The knife glances off her shoulder bone, bounces on her arm and sinks into her side like it's going into butter. She screams just the once.

'Oh!' she says and as she slides to the floor, thoughts glide slowly through her mind: he's not himself... that cupboard door's a positive disgrace... he never drank his tea... and Suzie is not the only person in the family who can't do maths.

The phone rings. Maybe it is Mr Babalula... or Suzie ringing back? She cannot reach it. John stands, looking down at her, breathing heavily. He smears his hands against his clean trousers. He doesn't speak. He turns and staggers out of the back door. She can hear the glass on the front door break and footsteps rushing along the hall. The phone keeps on ringing, on and on. She can see through the open back door, the washing, blowing on the line.

Clean, white sheets, blowing on the line.

The laundry's done.

Nothing to worry about now.

MEMENTO MORI

Pam Plumb

The material should have absorbed the sun's rays. Instead, it intensified them, blinding Annabel, forcing her to turn away. An imprint of the tableau was fired onto her retina: her daughter Tia playing at tea parties with Kieran Owens.

Tia had laid her yellow security blanket out on the sand pit, her pink plastic tea set wonky on the lumpy sand. Annabel heard her instructing Kieran on how to hold his cup, how to stick his little finger out like a princess. He giggled and fidgeted despite his princess training.

'Come on, Tia, let's go,' said Annabel. Kieran looked up, scrunched his face into a smile and waved. Annabel returned the wave and called to Tia again. She'd known Kieran from birth, still remembered seeing him as a newborn when his mum, Mandy, was in hospital, the shock of his Down's warping her smile.

'Can I play at Kieran's house?' Tia had stuffed her tea set into its bag. Her security blanket was over her arm, dangling in the dirt.

'Maybe later. I'll have to wash your blanket tonight, Tia.'

Tia shook her head and frowned. 'No. Another day.'

Annabel laughed. 'OK, tomorrow then. Say bye to Kieran.'

It was a short walk home; the village was small enough to feel friendly but big enough not to be in everyone's pockets. Most people knew each other to some degree but lately there had been a few new people moving in.

'Why don't you play in the garden while I make tea.' Annabel opened the front door and picked up the post. She'd hoped there would be a letter from her solicitor saying he'd served the divorce petition, but it was just the gas bill. She wondered how much longer it would take before she and Tia were free from her ex. Not that Tia actually knew him; he hadn't been in her life since she was a baby.

Annabel glanced out of the window. Already Tia had unpacked her tea set and was laying it out on the blanket, the bright yellow fabric like a beacon on the grass. I'll wash it when she's in bed, thought Annabel.

Detective Inspector Liam Foster replaced the phone more gently than necessary. He was trying to gather his thoughts as he digested the news, trying to work out what to do first, trying not to remember what happened last time. He hoped it was nothing. Hoped it would resolve before he'd left the station. Sometimes it worked out like that.

Foster decided he would speak to the mother while his officers started a preliminary search. He hoped the child would be found playing in a friend's garden or in the park at the end of the village. He called to Detective Constable Collins to join him. Foster knew she was good with families, good with women.

As Foster and Collins pulled up outside the girl's house, Foster scanned the street. Nothing stood out. An ordinary row of old weaver's cottages. His parents had lived in a similar street in the next village. He'd made a bit of money selling up after they'd passed away.

Many of the neighbours were outside, grouped in gossiping clusters, grasping tight hold of their own children. Like a shoal of mackerel, they turned to watch him and Collins walk to the front door, the late afternoon sun shining off their faces. Why don't people ever go missing earlier in the day? Foster wondered.

In the living room, the girl's mother was showing the Family Liaison Officer photos of her daughter on the laptop. 'I took this one last month, but she's had her hair cut since then, it doesn't really look like her now.'

Foster stepped into the room and cleared his throat. The Liaison Officer jumped to her feet. He waved her to sit back down and turned to the mother. 'I'm Detective Inspector Liam Foster. Can I ask you a few questions?'

It always surprised him how people reacted when their children went missing. Some could only cry, expecting the worst from the start. Others, usually the parents of teenagers, started out angry, railing at the audacity of their offspring. Foster could see this mother had been crying, but the task of finding a photo had focussed her attention. She turned her clear blue eyes towards him.

Foster took a seat and leaned forward. 'Have you got any family that can support you?'

The woman shook her head.

'No husband? Partner?'

'I'm getting divorced. I've no idea where he is. My solicitor's dealing with all that.'

Foster nodded. 'When did you fist realise Tia was missing?'

Her blue eyes filled with tears and it was some moments before she was able to tell Foster what she'd already told the others.

A low animalistic hum emanated from the crowd that had gathered to search. As people moved about, jostling to demonstrate their good citizenship, a ripple of expectation shivered through them. It reminded Foster of the moments before a fox hunt. Foster stood on the steps of the library, elevated enough to see that around 400 people had turned out. He also had 150 officers, drawn from across the county. The dog handlers would be another hour yet. Nearly at midsummer, at least there were almost three hours of light left.

'Can I have your attention please?' A portable PA system had been set up so his voice was loud and echoey.

'Thank you for offering your help. We are looking for Tia Vickers. She's four years old with short blonde hair and green eyes. She's wearing a pink flowery dress and carrying her security blanket. This is a distinctive yellow blanket made of cotton. Tia might be hiding in a bush, a fox hole or anywhere that might give her shelter. Please take care that you search methodically in your teams. My officers will guide you.'

Foster scanned the crowd. He felt that familiar disgust as he saw the mix of emotions on the searchers' faces; fear, pride, determination. But mostly excitement at being part of this girl's misery, of perhaps being the hero who finds her alive, or the one who will re-tell the tale of finding her broken body in a tangled mess of weeds. What sickened him most was that he knew he shared their feelings.

To override the shame, Foster thought about the perpetrator. Is he or she here? Pretending to be a part of the community? Blending in to help keep their secret? It wouldn't be the first time. Everyone's name had been taken, checks would be done on them, but it all takes time. And time, he thought, is something I don't have.

It had been hard for Foster to go against the villagers' enthusiasm and stop the search. But he couldn't be responsible for a broken leg or worse. They would resume early in the morning. There probably wasn't much more he could do tonight apart from make a statement to the press. His least favourite part of the job. Already the gossip and finger-pointing had started on Twitter and Facebook. The press probably knew more than he did. Several local reporters and a few from the nationals were here already. He knew there would be more tomorrow.

It was easy to see why Simon Wells had become the spokesperson for the village; he was articulate, not handsome but pleasant-looking, and had recently moved into the Old Police Station, which people seemed to think gave him extra importance. DI Foster watched Wells as he listened to an officer give instructions for what would happen in the morning, making notes in a reporter style notebook. There was a childish drawing of a cat on the back page.

Foster walked over to Wells and tapped him on the shoulder. 'Can I have a minute?'

Wells smiled broadly. 'Of course.' With his blue eyes and light tan he looked a little like Paul Newman.

'How well do you know the family?'

Wells shrugged his shoulders in a continental gesture. 'Barely. I first met them at the school fête last summer. The girl was helping her mother on the cake stall.'

'Do your children go to the same school?'

Wells smiled again. 'I don't have children.'

Foster shifted his weight. 'Why were you at the fête then?'

'I'd only just moved to the village. I thought it would be a good place to meet people. Everyone was there.'

Foster nodded, appreciating the social intricacies of village life. 'Did you meet Tia's father?'

Again the smile and a shake of the head from Wells. His charm was beginning to annoy Foster.

'Does anyone know where he's living now?'

Wells cocked his head in thought. Then he shrugged his shoulders again. 'I heard he'd not been back to the village since he put his wife in hospital. Your lot haven't traced him yet then?'

Foster patted Wells on the shoulder. 'We're working on it.'

Wells widened his smile. It made him look younger.

The morning was wet and Foster's hope dipped. The dogs would find it harder to pick up Tia's scent. Evidence like shoe marks or fibres may have been washed away. Foster hadn't mentioned any of that to Tia's mother though. When he'd dropped by the house on his way to meet the team, Annabel had been hopeful. She'd remembered a part of the woods where the village teens hung out. Thought maybe Tia had followed them and got lost. Foster said he'd check it out, but held his promises there. The last time he'd promised to deliver a child home there'd been more than one parcel.

So far there was very little to go on. A short list of suspects. Until the kid's father was located then he was pretty near the top. The mother was up there too, of course, although Foster thought she was genuinely innocent. A known paedophile from the next village had been picked up yesterday but had a tight alibi. There was nothing to get a toe hold on, thought Foster.

When Foster arrived at the village library, Wells was already there, talking to one of the officers. There were far fewer villagers out this morning, partly because it was early but it was also Monday and people were at work. Still, Foster estimated a good hundred had turned out. He noticed almost all were wearing T-shirts with Tia's picture on the front and the Crimestoppers number on the back. It amazed Foster that communities could be so organised so quickly. He often wondered what happened to those T-shirts afterwards; badges of honour if Tia was found safe and well, memento mori if not.

Foster was making the usual speech about gratitude and safety before the start of the day's search when he sensed movement at the back of the group. People were moving aside, making a pathway into the crowd, letting a boy walk towards the steps of the library. Murmurs from the crowd gathered volume so that by the time Foster could see what the boy was holding he had to shout to DC Collins to get a bag. The boy was crying, his tears and snot dripping onto the evidence. People began pulling phones out of their pockets and pointing them at the boy, ready to take a photo to tweet or post. Foster had to bellow to be heard.

'Put your phones away. Do not take photos. He's just a kid.'

Foster ran down the steps and put his arm around the boy's shoulders, both comforting and shielding him from the crowd. He led him up the steps and into the library. DC Collins followed them with the evidence bag containing Tia's yellow security blanket.

The interview room was too small and too warm. Besides Foster and Collins there was also Kieran's mother and the duty social worker. The desk had been removed to help keep it as informal as possible but Kieran was still wary of the strangers. Offers of cold drinks and even an ice cream for the boy had been refused. Foster glanced at Collins beside him. Her face was soft, half smiling as though things were going to be all right. Foster couldn't do that, couldn't turn his real feelings inward and make a show of hope. Over the years Foster had met many different suspects, some disabled, most not. One thing he'd learned was that being disabled didn't make you innocent.

Kieran said he'd found Tia's blanket down a lane but couldn't say where exactly. Foster thought it was strange since the boy had grown up in the village. Maybe his disability affected him more than Foster expected, but still it was strange.

'OK, Kieran. Let's try again.' The social worker stiffened, listening intently. Foster glanced at the boy's mother, who was absorbed with wiping her eyes. 'Why were you in the lane?'

'Looking for Tia. Mummy said she had gone away.'

'Did you know Tia's blanket would be there?'

Kieran shook his head.

Collins leaned forward and spoke softly. 'Can you say "yes" or "no"? We need to hear you.'

Kieran sniffed and looked at his mother. She ruffled his hair and smiled. 'It's OK. Just tell the truth.'

'No.'

'Was there anything else of Tia's?' said Foster

'No.'

'A shoe? Maybe a hair clip?'

'No.'

Collins asked the next question. 'When did you last see Tia?'

The boy gulped back tears before answering. 'Saturday. At the park.'

Foster checked his notes. 'Don't you remember playing in the park on Sunday?'

Mandy Owens leaned forward, her bare forearms sticking to the desk. 'He doesn't know the days of the week. He plays with Tia every day.'

'Weren't you with him?'

Mandy shook her head. 'He's twelve. He's old enough to play out on his own.'

'Don't you think it's a bit odd for him to play with a girl eight years younger than him?'

'Kieran has a mental age of five or six. That's why they play so well together. They're best friends.'

Foster cleared his throat before asking the next question.

'Kieran, do you and Tia ever go anywhere else to play?'

Kieran looked at his mum, as if he needed help understanding the question. Mandy squeezed his hand and tried to smile. 'He means where else do you play with Tia?'

Kieran turned back to Foster and Collins and smiled for the first time since the interview started. 'We play at my house.'

'Never at Tia's house?'

The boy shook his head. Foster noticed he had the softest of dark downy hair on his top lip. Despite his mental age, thought Foster, Kieran was entering puberty.

'What's your favourite game that you and Tia play?'

'Princess tea party. She's teaching me to be a princess.' Kieran's smile widened at the memory.

'Do you ever get angry with Tia?'

Kieran shook his head. 'She's beautiful. She's a princess.'

Foster shifted in his chair. He didn't want to even think about it but he knew he had to.

'Do you ever touch Tia?'

'How dare you!' Mandy put her arms round Kieran and pulled him tight. 'He's just a boy. How can you even ask that kind of question?'

'We don't always know our children as well as we think we do. Please, Mrs Owens, let him answer.'

'I know my son inside and out. He would never do anything like that.'

Foster could see her struggling to keep a lid on her anger. Out of the corner of his eye he could see the social worker bristling. They all needed a rest. He leaned across the desk and made eye contact with Kieran.

'Have you and Tia ever played other games?'

'That's enough, Inspector.' The social worker glared at Foster.

But Foster kept his eyes on Kieran. If the boy knew what he meant he wasn't showing it. The only emotion Foster could detect was fear.

Foster nodded and leaned back in his chair. 'Interview suspended at 12:25.'

The search area had been extended while Foster was interviewing Kieran Owens. All of the lanes in and around the village were being searched by scene of crime officers and other personnel. The sun had come out after last night's rain. Foster was hopeful there would still be some fibres from the blanket in some mud or trapped on a hedge to indicate where Kieran had found it.

There had also been an anonymous call around 10 o'clock this morning which was pulling Foster and the team in another direction. A male caller with a thick Suffolk accent. Foster had listened to the recording of the call before interviewing Kieran. The only information the caller had given was to look in the woods on the other side of the river because there was a series of small caves that 'the girl might have taken shelter in'. He thought that was a strange phrase and sounded like a hoax call. But of course he had no choice but to search. It was, at least, a lead of sorts.

After Kieran's interview Foster needed some fresh air. Despite his paunch he really was an outdoors person. As he walked to the car with Collins, the light breeze was welcome after the claustrophobic heat of the station. Pushing through a cluster of press to reach the house they found Wells on the sofa talking to Tia's mother, his hand resting on her knee. Foster asked the Family Liaison Officer to make some tea.

It took a moment for Wells to notice Foster and Collins standing in the doorway. He pulled his hand away from Annabel's knee and stood to shake hands as if he was at a dinner party. Foster couldn't bring himself to match Wells' wide smile. Collins remained in the doorway while Foster took a seat opposite Annabel.

'This is Simon. He just popped in to see how I'm getting on,' said Annabel.

Foster shot a look at Wells. He was gazing at Annabel, smiling his irritating smile. They looked like two teenagers in love and a thought crossed his mind.

'I thought you said you didn't know Tia or her mother.'

Foster watched Wells' face for a reaction. There was only that smile. 'I don't. I mean I didn't. We'd only seen each other in passing, but since all this…' Wells grabbed hold of Annabel's knee again and gave it a squeeze, prompting her to finish the sentence.

'Simon's been really kind, helping with the search and everything. He organised the T-shirts too.'

The two of them were wearing the new T-shirts. Foster looked at the photo on the front. Tia's face was wrinkled in the folds over Wells' stomach. She was wearing the flowery dress she'd disappeared in. Foster wondered why she didn't have her yellow blanket.

Judging by Annabel's dry eyes, Foster guessed that Wells hadn't told her about Kieran and the security blanket. At least he had some sense, he thought.

'Annabel,' said Foster, 'I need to speak to you.' He glanced again at Wells. 'Alone.'

'Of course. Just wanted to pop by and give my support, you know.' Wells patted Annabel on the shoulder as he left the room, brushing past Collins on his way out.

Collins sat down next to Foster and took out her notebook. Foster saw Annabel stiffen as the Liaison Officer sat next to her, spilling the drinks on the coffee table.

'Have you found her?' Foster could see her eyes dampen.

'No, I'm sorry. But there have been some developments.' Foster leaned forward. 'A boy found Tia's security blanket. At least we think it's hers.'

'Oh my god. Who? Where?'

Foster watched her closely as he said the name. She slapped her hand over her mouth and shook her head.

'Do you think Kieran Owens would hurt Tia?'

'He wouldn't do anything to Tia. He's her best friend.'

'Do you know how old Kieran is?'

Annabel let out a strained laugh. 'His mum, Mandy, is one of my closest friends. We've known each other since school. Kieran's age doesn't matter. He adores Tia.' She looked at Collins and the Liaison

Officer, as if they could corroborate her thoughts. They smiled but didn't speak.

'When was the last time you or Tia saw Kieran?' said Foster.

'I've told you this already.'

'Are you sure it was Sunday?' said Collins, scribbling in her notebook.

Annabel nodded.

Foster cleared his throat. 'Did Kieran ever come to this house? Either alone or with his mother?'

'Yes, of course. The kids would play in the garden together. He loves Tia's playhouse. He hasn't got one, you see.' Annabel tried to smile but the confusion still showed on her face.

'When did you last see your husband?'

Annabel's face darkened. 'Not since he fractured my skull.' Foster had read the reports; she was lucky to have survived by all accounts. At first she had agreed to press charges then changed her mind, claimed it was an accident. At least she'd had the sense to get a restraining order. Since then he hadn't been picked up for anything else, as far as Foster could tell.

'Could he be staying with his parents? His mates?'

Annabel pushed her fingers through her hair. 'I don't know. He could be anywhere. All I know is he's not here.'

'OK. Did he ever hurt Tia?'

Annabel shook her head. 'He doesn't really know her. It was me he wanted to hurt.'

Back in the office Foster swivelled in his chair to face Collins. 'What do you think?'

'The sooner we find the father the better.' He smiled at her directness.

'Has there been any news from the cave search?'

'No, sir, they're still looking. It's a complicated cave system. We've asked for specialist help from Derbyshire.'

Foster nodded. 'Anything from the search of the lanes? Fibres? Clothing?'

Collins shook her head.

'What do you think about the boy?'

Collins shrugged. 'Not sure, sir. Seems unlikely though. He's just a kid.'

Foster turned and looked out the window. He wasn't so sure it was that simple. There had been lots of inconsistencies in the interview. Foster remembered his last case and the mistakes he'd made when he'd labelled a suspect as unlikely.

Foster stretched. He wasn't looking forward to reporting back to the Chief with so little detail. He knew he needed more. Turning back to Collins he said, 'Get across to the Incident Room at the village library and see if you can piece together Tia's last moments from the villagers' statements. There must be someone who saw something. I'll meet you there in a bit.'

Collins reached for the door. 'What are *you* going to do, sir?'

Foster frowned. 'Work out a niggle.'

It was an odd place for someone to live, thought Foster as he pulled up outside. He supposed everyone who moved into a house, unless it was brand new, was like a cuckoo but somehow, occupying a building that had once functioned as something else was strange. Aside from the vicarage, the Old Police Station was the biggest house in the village. Foster reckoned there must have been a cellar at one time, for keeping the prisoners.

Foster knocked on the door. He guessed Wells was in; a blue Volvo was parked on the drive. He seemed to be waiting a long time and was about to go round the back when Wells opened the door.

'Hi, Inspector, what can I do for you?' Foster noticed Wells had changed his T-shirt.

'Can I come in?'

There was a heartbeat's hesitation.

'Sure. I was just having a breather, you know, from the search. Didn't get much sleep last night.' Foster followed him into the entrance hall. There were no traces of the building's history.

'I'll take you through to the kitchen, the lounge is in a shocking mess at the moment.'

It took Wells a few steps to realise Foster had stopped at the half open door of the living room.

'Really, Inspector. My cleaner hasn't arrived yet. There's coffee on in the kitchen.'

Foster pushed open the door with his forefinger. It creaked under its own weight. A faint waft of stale air slipped out through the widening gap. He took a step in, feeling Wells grasp his elbow. 'Please. The kitchen.'

Foster shook him off and walked into the room. Wells was right, it was a shambles. An upright piano, covered in old newspapers and discarded mail greeted Foster. Further into the room, he could see two old Chesterfields, one either side of the fireplace, the leather cracked on their arms. Between them was a glass-topped coffee table. Foster could see a crack in it. Strewn on the floor were drawings. Cats, birds, butterflies, princesses. All drawn with crayon.

'I told you it was shameful.' Wells tried to laugh, but was silenced by Foster's glare.

'These are children's pictures. You don't have children, do you, Mr Wells?'

Wells started to collect the drawings, scrunching them up in handfuls.

'Don't touch anything. Just tell me why these are here.'

For the first time Foster could see Wells lose confidence. His wide smile faltered, only managing his continental shrug of the shoulders. 'I've had visitors. My niece. Not had chance to tidy up, you know, since the local girl went missing.'

Foster walked round the coffee table. 'How did the glass get broken?'

Regaining a little composure, Wells gave a chuckle. 'The removal men broke it. Still waiting for compensation. You know what it's like.'

Foster bent over the arm of one of the sofas. In a crack of leather, he saw a strand of cotton. It was only thin and wispy, but he was pretty sure it was the same colour as Tia's yellow blanket. He straightened up and looked at Wells.

'Does this place have a cellar?'

Wells started walking backwards, shaking his head. 'No, no cellar. I think they bricked it up, you know, flooding and what not.'

Foster took a step towards him. 'Don't make this any worse. Show me the cellar.'

'Please. I can't. There isn't one.' Foster stepped closer and grabbed Wells by the arm, spinning him to face the wall, pinning him against the plaster.

Handcuffs on, Foster yanked him back to face him.

'Cellar. Now.'

Wells began to sob. Foster gave him a shove out of the living room and down the hall. Wells stopped outside a small door, an old-fashioned latch keeping it closed. Foster pulled it open.

Cold, damp air rushed into the hall, carrying a smell of rot. Foster scrabbled for the light switch.

He looked past Wells down the stone steps. Nothing. He turned Wells around and unlocked a handcuff. Wells squealed with relief, 'Thank God. I've done nothing wrong.'

'Shut up.' Foster wrenched Wells' hand, making him stumble back with renewed sobs, locking him to the hall radiator.

Foster stepped through the cellar door, his shoes tapping loudly on the concrete.

'Police. Is there anyone there?'

He heard a sob, but couldn't tell if it was Wells or not. As he got further down the stairs, the rotten smell got stronger. Foster had smelled it before and it turned his stomach. Human waste. And death.

Foster reached the bottom step. At first he couldn't see anything out of the ordinary. Packing boxes were stacked in one corner. A washing machine was against another wall. Then he turned to face the furthest wall and gasped. Slumped on the floor lay the twisted mess of a girl. Her hair shorn. Her pink flowery dress was ripped and blood-stained. A kitchen knife lay by her side.

What shocked Foster most was the smiling face of the person sitting on the floor, watching him take all this in.

After a moment he spoke. 'Why?'

'To punish her.'

'Tia?'

'No, Annabel.'

'Wasn't a fractured skull and losing her husband bad enough?'

'That didn't stop her being a stuck-up bitch.'

'That's not a crime.'

'She always thought she was better than me. Pretty and clever. A good job. Money. So bloody perfect.'

'She didn't deserve this. Tia didn't deserve this.'

'She was going to send Tia to some private school.'

'So?'

'She was going to take her away from Kieran!'

Foster took a step closer, trying not to breathe in the stench. 'Now *you've* taken her away. How does *that* help?'

Mandy's sneer faltered and she dropped her head.

'Why kill her?'

Mandy looked up. 'We didn't mean to. She wouldn't shut up. Wittering on. Wanting her precious mummy, wanting Kieran, wanting her bloody blanket.'

Foster took another step. Out of the corner of his eye he could see Tia, damaged and still. 'She was just a little girl.'

'*She* wasn't. *She* laughed at me, laughed at Kieran. She won't laugh now.'

Foster knew he should radio in, get back-up. But he wanted answers first.

'Wells. How did he get involved?'

'*Him*?' she scoffed. 'He's a bloody pervert.' She spat on the cellar floor.

'What happened?'

She rubbed her face with the back of her hand, leaving a smear of blood. 'I thought he liked me. Thought I was going up in the world, going out with a posh bloke. Took me a while to work out he was only interested in kids.'

'You saying this was his idea? That you had nothing to do with it?' Foster was struggling to keep his anger under control.

'He said we'd keep her just for a while. Overnight or something. I didn't know what he was going to do. What he did. He made her do things.' She nodded in Tia's direction. 'Much worse than this.'

Foster shook his head, nonplussed at her reasoning. Finally he radioed Collins and waited on the steps, his eyes fixed on Mandy.

It wasn't long before the team arrived. While Collins cuffed Mandy, Foster climbed the cellar steps. Walking past Wells he headed for the front door, into the sunshine and took a deep breath. He remembered talking to the press was not his least favourite part of the job after all.

A DEAD MAN IN STRATFORD

Belinda Weir

It is not yet 11 o'clock when Charlotte, Midge and Mo get back to Stratford tube station. The air is warm and heavy, the bridge to the Westfield centre still thronged with people and the Orbit tower glows red in the dark of the Olympic park.

'Quick drink?' says Mo.

'How about a long, slow one?' suggests Midge, looking at Mo in what she imagines is a suggestive and seductive manner.

Charlotte winces and is on the brink of saying:

'Actually I think I'll just head back – early start tomorrow,' when Midge catches hold of her arm and starts walking her away from the underground entrance and the lights of the shopping centre towards the relative dark of the street. It's easier to go along with her, thinks Charlotte, and I'll only have one.

'Where shall we go then, ladies?' asks Mo, sweeping his hat off his head and waving them forward.

This is one of the few things Charlotte has found to dislike about him, this slightly put-on charm and old-fashioned gallantry. Mo grew up on the Wingfield Estate and went to Kidbrooke Secondary; he was brought up by an older sister who insisted on manners and fought hard to keep him away from the rougher kids on the estate. Mo plays down his origins but maintains a kind of old-fashioned formality towards the women, which contrives to seem at once both attentive and condescending to Charlotte.

'Ladies? Aren't you the smooth one!' giggles Midge.

Mo has made it clear he fancies Charlotte and this annoys her because she could quite like him if it were not for Midge, so she is working hard at putting herself off him. Charlotte, mid-twenties, a market researcher for an online travel website, is blonde and brown-eyed, and bears more than a passing resemblance to a young Brigitte Bardot, especially now in her low-cut tie-front midriff-exposing white shirt and navy pedal-pushers. Midge is a junior copy-editor with a small publishing house in Soho and uses a lot of Irish swear words.

Charlotte and Midge live in a terraced house near Maryland station; Midge has the ground floor bedroom, which faces on to the street, in a part of London which has somehow escaped the frenzy of rapidly rising house prices and remains determinedly down-at-heel and often unsafe. On weekend nights cans and bottles sometimes sail over the privet hedge and crash on the concrete paving in front of her window. Midge shares a bathroom with Mandip, a primary school teacher who goes home to Dudley at the weekend and pretends not to know that her flatmates use her room for friends to crash on Saturday nights. Charlotte's room is at the top of the house, her own shower and lavatory compensation for the three flights of stairs and worth paying the extra for, while she battles intermittent bulimia.

The women and Mo have been at a fancy dress party this evening – the launch of a book on nouvelle vague French cinema, on which both Midge and Mo have worked. Charlotte has been, as so often, Midge's plus-one; Mo, who works on the production team, has enjoyed dressing up as Jean Gabin in a Kepi hat and with an eyeliner-pencil moustache, though no one has guessed who he is meant to be, largely because Jean Gabin does not originate, as Mo's family does, from Somalia, by way of south London. The evening has been fun, in a small way. Charlotte dances with Simon, the very tall intern in IT, who is dressed as Jacques Tati and impressed that she knows who he is meant to be, because most people have guessed Inspector Maigret.

'Because of the pipe,' he says, waving it around, M. Hulot-fashion.

'The shorts and socks are a bit of a giveaway,' Charlotte says.

They exchange numbers and then Charlotte talks for a while with a very young Jean Seberg lookalike who works in the legal department and explains that she doesn't actually read books, but knows that some people still do. Charlotte feels old after that exchange.

She goes in search of food and of Midge and finds some retro chicken and mushroom vol au vents, scoffs them hurriedly and then approaches the latter, who is curled up on the reception room sofa, still chattering away to Mo.

'Shall we?'

The invitation is to Midge but Mo decides it includes him and they set off towards Holborn tube. Midge sleeps on the journey, her head on Charlotte's shoulder, and wakes with a shiny drool of saliva like a slug trail down her chin when they reach Stratford. The nap has energised her and she is so obviously keen to prolong the night and the chance to be with Mo that Charlotte, guilty at letting Midge get quite so pissed, allows herself to be led along the night-time streets of Stratford in search of a bar.

'I feel a bit sick,' Midge whispers, as they walk. 'I feel really weird actually – I think someone put something in my drink.'

Alcohol, probably, thinks Charlotte. And then, I am such a bitch. Midge is only wanting to enjoy herself, and she is small and round and lonely and sweet and funny when you get to know her, and Mo is a bit pretentious, but probably not a bad person.

'Where are we going?' she calls to Mo, some way ahead of them.

They have by now left the lights of the shopping centre and are walking towards Maryland which is not known for its exciting nightspots although Charlotte remembers, with a sinking dip in her stomach, that it does contain the pub in which Iron Maiden made their debut, and which she has never ventured into because it has always seemed full of greasy men in biker jackets. Sure enough, 'Cart and Horses,' calls back Mo.

Bugger, thinks Charlotte. She notices with a jolt that Midge is no longer hanging onto her arm.

Before she has time to worry, there is a squeal from somewhere to her right.

'Down here! I've found somewhere!'

It couldn't be worse than the Iron Maiden pub, thinks Charlotte, knowing and not caring that she is being a snob. She traces the squeal down an alleyway which opens out after a few paces into a small lighted square, almost surrounded by blocks of flats. From what Charlotte can see they look circa 1930s, with steel-framed windows and low brick balconies, and the effect is not unlike being on an ocean liner. The illusion is maintained by the tables and chairs scattered in the centre as if on deck, and ringed around by a rope, strung between low wooden pillars. Tall lights illuminate the circle of tables and chairs, casting the rest of the square into shadow. Above, in the flats, a few windows shine yellow or blue but most are in darkness.

Midge can just be seen in a doorway to the left, where a neon sign blinks pinkly. *Theatre Bar*, it announces.

'It's open,' Midge calls to Charlotte, and disappears inside. Charlotte follows.

The room she enters is low-ceilinged, with wooden floorboards and a row of square tables arranged carefully along the outer wall, next to shuttered windows. Along the opposite wall gleams a long mahogany bar, with the usual pumps, and behind, bottles and glasses ranged along the mirrored gantry. There are people sitting in the chairs – a middle-aged couple at the table furthest away in the corner, a group of four men playing cards, and a young couple with a large old-fashioned Silver Cross pram which the girl pokes with her foot to make it rock while she texts.

The young man stands up as Charlotte tries to get past the pram.

'Sorry, I'll get it,' he says. He releases the brake and steers the pram to the other side of the table towards his partner. Neither of them glances at the blanketed lump; the girl plays with her phone and the man sits down again as soon as Charlotte passes, and picks up his pint.

Midge is talking at the barman, explaining the fancy dress.

'Jeanne Moreau, I'm meant to be, can you not tell? Only I lost my beret.' The barman says nothing, just looks expectantly at Midge and then at Charlotte as she approaches.

'What's it to be, ladies?' he asks. A puckered scar above his mouth, possibly the trace of a repaired harelip, gives his face an air of menace to Charlotte, as if he were sneering at them, though she knows that's unfair and more likely a reflection of her own unease at being in this place, which seems somehow unfriendly. The couple are looking at her and Midge, unsmiling; the poker players have barely paused in their game.

'Vodka and diet coke, please. Two.'

'And a pint of Carlsberg as well.' Mo has arrived.

'I'll get these, girls,' he says. 'You go and sit down.'

Charlotte objects to this instruction but can think of nothing coherent to explain why it is insulting, if well-intentioned. So she says nothing. She pulls on Midge's arm and Midge trots obediently behind her, to the door and out into the square.

Mo appears a few minutes later, holding two glasses with the third wedged between them, and a couple of packets of crisps clenched in his teeth.

'There you go, thought you might be hungry,' he says, as he drops the packets on the table. Charlotte sits back in her chair, which wobbles a bit on the paving stones, and sips her drink.

'Thanks,' she says, raising her glass towards Mo.

'Cheers,' he says. 'But I tell you what, this is a weird place, isn't it? The guy at the bar looks like something out of a Hammer Horror – did you see his face?'

'I felt sorry for him, poor man,' says Midge.

'And where is everybody?' asks Mo, as if Midge hadn't spoken. 'I mean, it's dead, this place. And no signal.'

He waves his phone in the air, and Charlotte fishes hers out of her shoulder bag. 'No Service' flashes across the screen.

'Never mind, let's just enjoy our drink, shall we?' she says, shoving it back in her pocket. 'How're you feeling, Midget?'

She leans over and puts her arm round Midge, who has slumped tiredly in her seat. It's like she is the dormouse, thinks Charlotte.

So I must be Alice, or the Mad Hatter. No, that one's definitely Mo with his silly hat. Perhaps I am the March Hare. She stretches back in her chair and stares up at the summer night sky, where a plane is blinking and a few dark grey wisps of beardy cloud drift lazily. London is never completely dark, she thinks, and her eyes are already making out features in the flats above the bar. A bike, propped against the wall; satellite dishes and a clothes airer, and what could be people, shadows behind the curtains, though it is really too dark to make out.

She brings herself with difficulty back to the conversation. Midge has metaphorically popped out of her teapot to ask a question.

'Why Theatre Bar?' she asks. 'Where's the fecking theatre, then?'

Charlotte looks around. All the world may be a stage but this is an unlikely venue, although the blocks of flats rising around them are faintly reminiscent of the tiered seats in an amphitheatre and the square is spotlit.

'Theatre in the round maybe?' she says. 'Like the Royal Exchange. They could have shows on here, or bands or whatever.'

'And who'd come to see that?' says Midge. 'Ye'd have to be a right eejit to come all the way out to Stratford to sit in amongst a bunch of poky old flats to watch a play, would you not?'

Mo is picking his teeth with the corner of a crisp packet, bored. Theatre is not his thing.

'Maybe the barman's an old act-orr,' he says, giving the word several syllables. 'Maybe he got that scar in a fencing fight.'

The door to the bar opens and the barman appears to collect their glasses.

'Can I get you ladies and gent another drink?' he asks.

Midge starts in.

'We were just wondering...' she says and Charlotte interrupts, scared that Midge will ask the man about his scar.

'We were wondering where the place got its name,' she says.

The barman looks at her and stands still, holding the glasses.

'There used to be a theatre here,' he says. "Although, more of a bear-pit you might call it. A very long time ago, of course. Now, can I get you anything else?'

Mo wants another pint and follows the barman back through the door. Charlotte shivers. A bear-pit. He means bear-baiting, she supposes, and she imagines the square filled with baying spectators, pushing and jostling to get a look at the frightened bears clawing chunks out of each other; the shouting and the betting, the blood on the fur and the stone and the shrieks and roars of the injured and dying animals.

Charlotte sits upright as a scream hits the night air, from somewhere behind the flats but it is followed by laughter and she relaxes slightly, but leans over to shake Midge awake.

'Midgey, I think we should go home. I'm really tired. Shall we just go and tell Mo we'll not stay for another, are you alright with that?'

Whether or not Midge agrees with the suggestion Charlotte cannot say because with a crash and a burst of light, the door to the bar swings open and Mo comes tearing out, his shiny shoes slipping on the stones as he runs towards them.

Behind him, the young man who moved the pram is following, not running, but with arms outspread and dancing a little from side to side as he comes forward.

'Quick, we've got to leave. These people are mental,' Mo shouts breathlessly. Then he stops, momentarily confused. In the empty night there are suddenly noises, doors opening and slamming, people running along the balconies and down the stairs, heels clacking on the stones, excited chattering and coughing. Charlotte doesn't really want to turn round to see, but she is aware that there are people beginning to crowd into the square, separating out from the shadows to become men, women and even some children, steadily coming from all sides to surround them like the tides in Morecambe Bay.

The young man is getting nearer, walking slowly and purposefully, now rolling his sleeves up and smiling as he looks from

Mo to Charlotte to Midge and then to the people, now standing round the three.

'He woke the fucking baby up, didn't he? Clumsy cunt. Can't have the baby woken up, took me hours to get him down. Got to teach the fucker a lesson, ain't I?'

There is a murmur, some nods, a woman shouts:

'That's right, Mikey, you show him!'

'Mate, I honestly didn't mean to... it was an accident, sorry,' says Mo. He is appealing to reason. He stands protectively in front of Charlotte and Midge, holds his hands out, shoulders lifted, a small smile on his taut face.

'You think it's funny, do ya?'

Mikey is very close to them now. He pushes Mo in the chest and keeps moving forward so that Mo is forced to lean backwards to avoid getting spit in his face. Mo hisses to Charlotte out of the corner of his mouth, all the while holding eye contact with Mikey:

'Get out, Charlotte, run! Go and get help.'

Charlotte turns clumsily and falls over her chair, which clatters to the ground. She sees Midge pushing under the arm of an onlooker and go running off and round him but Charlotte herself is too slow, too late. She stands up slowly, rubbing her hands, which were grazed as she fell, moves back a step and then another, but is prevented from going any further by two hands tightly gripping her arms which she sees, as she looks behind her, are attached to the middle aged woman who had been sitting in the corner of the bar with her husband. The woman has dyed-copper hair, white at the temples, and her lipstick has bled into the lines around her mouth. She calls to the youth as she tightens her grip on Charlotte.

'Let him have it, Mikey,' she shrieks.

Charlotte looks around her. To her right is one of the card players from the bar, a little man in a greasy blue suit, now waving a notebook in the air and shouting:

'I'll give yer ten to one on the darkie.'

To her left Charlotte can see the husband of the woman who holds her; he is red-faced and sweating, breathing heavily and shifting from one foot to the other as he focuses on Mikey and Mo. Mo, minus his hat and indeed his shirt, looking scared and cold as the man from the bar, the young man who moved the pram, jogs up and down in front of him and flexes his fingers.

There is actually going to be a fight. A dense mass of people now crowds the small square, from which the tables and chairs have been cleared. People are jostling for a better view of the men, roaring insults at Mo and encouragement at Mikey, waving notes at the poker player, who moves among them, writing in his notebook and stopping occasionally to wipe his brow with a tissue.

With a sudden thud of her heart Charlotte realises with certainty that this is the theatre from which the bar takes its name; they are the show, and Charlotte is now very frightened for Mo. Her eyes search the crowd for help – a friendly face, someone who might come to Mo's assistance and stop this terrible spectacle, but even as she squirms, the woman's fingers dig in to her upper arms and a voice hisses into her ear:

'Alright, dearie, just stay where you are and nobody'll get hurt.'

This is so patently untrue that Charlotte almost laughs. She twists again, tries to turn round and the woman's thumbnail, false and pearly, catches in her hair.

'Ouch,' Charlotte cries and jerks her head forward, so that the nail comes off and tangles in the curls.

'You little cow,' shouts the woman, and sticks her thumb, babyishly, in her mouth; it is all the space Charlotte needs and she pushes backwards as hard as she can so that the woman stumbles and lets go of her and Charlotte is propelled forwards. The people in front of her make way and Charlotte finds herself now in the centre of the crowd, next to Mo. Tears are staining his face, and a bubble of snot forms in his nostril as he breathes out but he is still trying, poor Mo, to be gallant.

'Get behind me, Charlotte,' he says and she does. She can smell his sweat and fear and realises that not only is he going to get hurt, badly hurt, but she probably will as well, because why, after this, would these people let her walk away?

Charlotte's legs start to shake and she wants to cry. She closes her eyes briefly and begins to bargain with herself: if I get out of this I will never complain again about the tube journey, I will phone Mum more often, I'll stop drinking. She opens her eyes just as Mikey takes a swing and lands a punch on the side of Mo's head. He staggers, blinks and totters, nearly falls, shakes his head and then whirls round and suddenly launches himself at Mikey, screaming 'Bastard! Bastard!' and jabbing with his fists, poking at Mikey's eyes with his fingers and kicking, aiming for the other man's groin. It is unexpected and shocking, and the surprise works in Mo's favour. A sharp kick connects with Mikey's undefended knee and he goes down with a crack onto the stones.

Any relief Charlotte feels is short-lived. There are willing hands helping Mikey to his feet, and others pushing Mo forward again.

'Go on, son!' yells the man next to Charlotte, and it is not clear to her who he is cheering for. Mo stands for a minute bravely, in a boxing stance that is, like much of Mo's actions, hopelessly old-fashioned. He is shivering and holds his hands in front of his face, as Mikey launches at him. The youth grabs Mo's head, one arm bent at the elbow, squeezing Mo's neck and tilting his head, the better to aim blows at his face. Mo's feet slip on the stones, he throws wild flailing punches but Mikey arches backwards, keeping his body out of reach while he purposefully and rhythmically turns Mo's face into a mess of blood and swelling. Charlotte doesn't want to watch but can't look away. There is really no contest. Mikey is practised and Mo is hurting, he is bleeding, he is crying out in pain and shock and he is, finally, out cold and lying on the stone of the square.

The noise and hubbub around her quietens, as people move away from the spectacle. There is a cluster of people around the bookie, the barman puts a bar towel round Mikey's shoulders; the young woman kisses him on his cheek and Mikey rubs his knuckles and shakes himself down like a wet dog.

Charlotte goes over to Mo and strokes his head. There is a large lump and something spongy beneath it and she recoils and then looks at her fingers which are now bloody and wet.

'It's OK, Mo, I'll get help.'

But from where? Charlotte is unsure whether to try to move Mo, and decides that he is in no immediate danger from the people who still linger in the square but she is loath to leave him. She looks around without much hope – and there at last is Midge, coming towards her, talking away to the policeman by her side. A proper policeman, with a badge and high-vis jacket and everything. Charlotte is so relieved she almost wets herself.

'Midge! Over here!' she calls. Midge sees her and comes running up, pushing through people who stand aside and let her pass.

'Oh my god, Charlotte, is Mo alright?' Midge cries. 'I didn't know what to do, I ran all over, knocked on doors and everything, and none of these feckers would lift a finger to help. Thank Christ I found Sergeant Dixon over there, he'll sort them out. He's going to call up a police van and an ambulance... and where's Mo?'

Midge finally sees Mo, lying unmoving on the ground behind Charlotte. She goes over and slumps down at his side, bends over and then sits back on her heels and starts to cry.

'He's dead, Charlotte. He's dead, he's dead!' She lifts Mo's head and lays it on her knee, stroking and sobbing.

The policeman ignores the women for the moment. He has walked over to Mikey and slaps him, hard across the face. Charlotte is sure this is not correct procedure but she admires him for it. Around them the people who have not left the square are also watching.

Sergeant Dixon hits Mikey again, shoves him in the shoulder and the young man almost falls over.

'What was that all about then, Mikey?' says the policeman.

'I beat him, didn't I?' Mikey is defiant, but cringes away from the slaps the policeman is landing on his head.

'I had money on this, Mikey,' says the policeman. 'Fifteen minutes I reckoned he'd last. And you had him down in three. So. What – were – you – playing – at – Eh?" Each word is accompanied by a prod from the policeman's index finger, the final grunt resonating with a punch in the young man's face which sends him reeling backwards, into the arms of the barman, who dragged him into the bar.

The door slams shut. The policeman turns and walks, slower now, towards Charlotte.

'I suggest you get your friend home,' he says, nodding over at Midge, who still sits on her haunches, rocking back and forward and cradling Mo's head and shoulders.

Charlotte goes over and prises Midge's fingers out of Mo's wiry hair. She pulls the girl up, gets her standing and then, each supporting the other, they turn and stagger towards the alleyway. In the distance a siren is wailing, drawing nearer to the square and the theatre bar. It will be much too late for Mo.

A SMALL REBELLION

Alex Reece Abbott

In the early spring, when blossoms were still buds and the days were still short, Chloe Henderson's first small rebellion took place.

With more of a shove than a nudge, Lawrence had issued a string of suggestions, all equally uninspiring. Learn a language. Or what about knitting. Something to keep your mind off it, he'd insisted.

Redesigning the garden was her choice – gardening wasn't even on his list of projects. But plants were healing and it would keep her occupied, get her outdoors. Anyhow, it was supposed to be her recovery, not his.

One dimming afternoon, after an hour of fossicking, she left her favourite bookshop with her calico bag laden with advice on garden design. She stepped out into the chaos of the high street, buoyed with doing good. One in five shops in town had already closed and she loved Gaunt's for being a survivor; the calm hush, the glowing coal fire and the serendipitous pleasure of browsing always lifted her. If she could, she'd bottle the steadiness, the continuity and serenity that flowed from Elizabeth Gaunt's packed shelves.

A rattling cough barked from the doorstep of the empty shop next door and a news story flashed through Chloe's mind. *Killing with Kindness*: giving beggars money humiliated them, it didn't improve their quality of life or help them off the streets. It only funded their drug habits.

But the bundled girl didn't look like an addict. Lonely, yes. Friendless – probably. With her almost new kid-skin gloves, her well-cut trench coat buttoned to the collar and a black beanie, pulled down to her dark, straight eyebrows, she seemed more like she'd broken away.

Chloe braced herself for the old gimme-gimme but it was as if the girl had given up and huddling in the doorway had become more appealing than asking strangers for money. From her foetal position, she refused to beg.

Her face was without expression. She made no move. As much enthusiasm for begging as I've got for going to therapy, thought Chloe, admiring the girl's defiance. She rummaged in her pocket for a pound coin and fished out her car keys instead.

'I'd kill for an *espresso*,' the girl murmured.

The words came out before Chloe realised what she was saying. 'Come on, the coffee's better round at my place – and that way, you can have all you want.'

My place. Lawrence would hate that, much as he claimed to love how impulsive she used to be. Mostly she let him believe that she was still her old spontaneous self, when really what he welcomed as an impulse decision was a case of abandoning herself to an option.

But this felt different. The girl reminded her of someone she'd known, before York, before Lawrence, before the recession, before the baby. What harm could one cup of coffee do – especially if the girl was gone before he came home?

Ten years together had taught her there was no point juggling with him. *Feel flattered* her envious friends at university had said when he'd courted her with constant attention – and for a while, she'd buried her reservations.

Then he'd ambushed her with a very public proposal in front of the Eiffel Tower. After roping in a passing Chinese tourist as photographer, grinning Lawrence had shaken the stranger's hand and told him that he always got what he wanted. It was only supposed to be a weekend break and he'd rounded her up like a Dales gun-dog for his engagement.

Dead romantic, said her friends when the couple arrived back in York.

After the wedding, he'd become more protective of their privacy. His home was his sanctuary; visitors ruffled him. Her old friends who'd cared ebbed away.

The confectionery factory was already gearing up for Easter, pumping sweet, malty chocolate into the damp air. Chloe breathed in and refused to dwell on Lawrence. She'd done her therapy homework; she'd spoiled herself with gardening books – and now she'd treat herself to a little adventure.

'C'mon.' She rattled her car keys and the girl stretched and moved stiffly to her feet.

The roads were greased with mizzling rain and already choking with early rush-hour traffic. The street lights flickered into life as she steered the girl down by the swollen river, jostling with tourists and tipsy race-goers lurching back to their hotels.

The sepia Ouse stank with debris from the Dales and swamped the paths with cocoa-coloured sludge. She piloted them through the hissing brown geese who patrolled the banks. The girl stood like a sentinel as she unlocked the car.

Chloe started the engine and when she checked the wing mirror, noticed that she looked brighter than she had for months.

'You're not dropping me off at the station.' The girl clicked her knuckles. 'Not trains, the cop-shop. And I'm not going back to that hostel full of drunks and smack-heads.'

She tapped her forehead. 'Mental.'

Chloe beamed like a fairy godmother. 'Coffee, that's all.'

The medieval city walls circled them and the drizzle had transformed the Minster into a lurking tower. She wiped the condensation from the windscreen and peered into the blurry world. 'And warm food and a shower – if you want.'

She had a rising sense that something significant was going to happen, that her life was about to change. Not exactly a warning of danger but some deep-down knowing that she'd always remember that place, that moment they set off together.

'I forgot to ask...' she started.

The girl took Chloe's sunglasses from the dashboard and slipped them on, even though the weak sun was struggling against the clouds. She slid down in her seat again, collar pulled up like a gumshoe in a novel. 'No names.'

Chloe was dying to find out how long she'd been on the streets – and where she'd come from. She snuck a sidelong look and realised that the girl was probably about her age.

A surge of compassion unfurled inside her, tempting her with the possibility of a new friendship with someone she didn't know. Someone who couldn't judge her or her choices. Or how she'd been coping since The Baby.

As the car warmed, the girl scratched at her arms and Chloe's imagination shifted into overdrive. One hundred and one itches burst into life, flaring across her skin. She could have picked up anything living on the streets.

They parked in the driveway and the girl chewed her lip as she studied the large detached house, the honeyed gritstone, the gleaming Thirties stained glass. Chloe shepherded her through the front door but the girl paused at the hall dresser to admire a vase of peacock feathers.

Chloe smiled. 'I love the way their colours shimmer but Lawrence says they're bad luck.'

The girl shook her head. 'Eye of the devil? No, peacocks guard the gates of paradise. They're protection, the symbol of our potential, renewal and immortality. If you're Greek, the tail commemorates Argus and Hera's faithful watchman with one hundred eyes.'

She tilted a feather to the halogen spotlights, sparking flashes of gold and emerald green and ultramarine. 'I used to paint them… among other things.' She replaced it carefully in the vase.

Sunny-Olga was skulking in the kitchen and texting. She wore a face like a haughty sphinx, although Chloe was sure that she heard and saw everything.

Lawrence had noticed her ad somewhere and thought an au pair would be useful with The Baby coming. Then, not long after The Baby's funeral, Lawrence had announced that Sunny would be staying longer. Any exception to his *No Visitors* rule surprised Chloe but there was no point arguing. She was still unclear whether he'd been anticipating another birth or if he'd decided that she wasn't coping.

Fresh from Lodz, petulant Olga had advised that she wished to be known as Sunny – which Chloe regarded as outright misrepresentation. Still, it had become a case of the unhelpful blonde devil she knew.

Somehow Lawrence tolerated Olga. Chloe wondered sometimes if she had something on him, but she didn't dwell on it since Olga ironed all his shirts and did the things that were beyond Chloe's interest. He said that she was delighted to have a nice place to live while she continued learning English. Chloe had never detected any signs of gratitude, although she'd noticed that Olga's mysterious classes often stretched late into the night without any improvement in her fluency. Lawrence even accepted Olga's annoying, expensive habit of keeping the central heating turned right up year round, which Chloe suspected was a ploy to swan about the house half-dressed.

'This is a f-friend,' said Chloe to Sunny-Olga. 'Coffee?'

'Double *espresso*. Please.' The girl looked Sunny-Olga in the eye and Sunny-Olga glared at her.

After a heavy sigh, Sunny agreed to light the fire and bring drinks and snacks. In the front room, the girl shed layers of cashmere like skins, until she was down to a single sweater. When she pulled off her gloves, Chloe saw no wedding rings, although a chunky antique silver fob-watch chain glinted on one wrist; a tattoo circled the other: a bright Celtic bracelet.

'Food and drink first, then could you organise the wet-room for... our guest?' said Chloe.

Sunny gave a curt nod and huffed off into the kitchen.

'Please, close the curtains,' said the girl.

'No one will see you here.' Chloe drew the curtains tight. 'And trust me, Sunny only sees herself.'

The girl prowled the room, inspecting the artwork, the rugs, the hand-thrown ceramics – all carefully chosen by Chloe. She was sure that the girl was wondering when she'd have a home again and it crossed her mind that she could stay more than one night, even help out with the garden make-over. Except that when it came to spotting deceit, Lawrence was like a vulture hunting carrion.

Chloe eyed her up. 'You're my size. Sunny can wash and dry your things and I've got some clothes upstairs to recycle.'

Before Chloe could intervene, the girl flopped into Lawrence's armchair and shot her a wary look. 'That's kind. I couldn't take much with me.'

Sunny barged in and dumped a tray of sandwiches and cupcakes on the table.

Chloe smiled as her guest helped herself.

'Is all,' said Sunny, slamming the door behind her.

Chloe winced and wondered what it would take to persuade Lawrence to get rid of Sunny-Olga.

The misty rain sealed them in the house and Chloe was pleased that they were out of the weather. The girl seemed lulled by the crackle of the fire. Stretched out in the soft glow, her features were beautiful and well proportioned – yet apart from an occasional flicker of recognition or disagreement, she held her face in neutral.

Finally, after polishing off the contents of the tray, the girl rewarded her by confiding. Chloe made herself focus. '… suffocate. He has friends everywhere, a web of men looking for me. Taxi drivers, people who know people… out and about, people who see things. And his best friend's the head of social services here…'

Chloe felt rewarded that the girl was coming out of her shell but the way she spoke made her sadder than she'd felt for a long time. She struggled to listen to her low, flat drone. 'Everything will be alright,' she said. It was the best – or least worst – platitude that she could find.

The girl carried on until Chloe felt that unless she concentrated, she'd drown in this unexpected flood of blame and accusations.

She began to jig one leg. '… He broke my jaw last time so I couldn't talk. Once I'm away from here, I can rebuild my life.'

Chloe breathed in the silence. Her stack of untouched garden design books beckoned out of the corner of her eye. Then she saw the girl. 'Rebuild your life,' she said. 'I can only imagine.'

The girl dropped her voice. "Sorry, I haven't spoken to anyone in weeks. Sold my phone so he couldn't track me.'

Chloe blinked slowly, sinking with how much they had in common. Lawrence was good at hating too and he was another one with a big enough stubborn streak to follow it up.

The girl stretched her slender hands, then went to the piano in the corner of the room.

She perched and went straight into some fast boogie-woogie, one foot stomping, head swaying, sinews rippling under her smooth olive skin as she played.

Chloe closed her eyes and wished that she could sing like her, deep and passionate.

Then, the girl stopped as abruptly as she'd started. She plonked herself down in Lawrence's armchair again and toasted Chloe with the last of the coffee. 'Absent friends.'

She'd painted a clear picture and Chloe believed her. Far stranger things had happened under the cover of love and honour.

'Tried the police?' she suggested.

The girl's laugh was brittle and Chloe wished that she could erase her words. 'He's got good reasons not to involve them. He has his own ways of doing things.' She examined the small wedding photo that Chloe kept in a silver art deco frame on the bookshelf. 'He's not right for you,' she said, as if it were a fact.

Chloe flinched. 'What do you want?'

The girl let out a ragged sigh. 'Get to the next main train station down the line, further out of the reach of my husband and his even lovelier friends. A last night to rest and prepare.' She held out her empty cup. 'And another coffee?'

It was more than she'd bargained for that afternoon but Chloe calculated that she could get the girl settled in the spare room before Lawrence came home from rehearsal – usually late. She'd give Sunny the morning off, buy her silence, then they'd leave without anyone knowing. In for a penny.

The girl's plans, the possibility of so much freedom and choice was intoxicating. She checked her phone diary, her gut twisting. 'Lawrence has rehearsals all tomorrow so I can take you wherever you want. And you can stay tonight. Just to get you back on your feet.'

The girl nodded and yawned. They were beginning to relax into each other's company and Chloe sensed that she'd grown on the girl enough to be able winkle out her name, when Sunny burst in.

She pointed at the door. 'Wet-room.'

The night came down like a drawn blind and Lawrence turned up early. Slouching in the doorway of the front room, he preened, taking in the cups and plates.

Not yet forty, a pot-belly lurked on his belt and his grey-flecked beard couldn't disguise the second chin creeping around his jaw. His heavy eyelids made him look perpetually sleepy and round wire-frame glasses added something smug to his expression. With the remains of his hair gelled into dark glistening spikes, he reminded her of a malevolent Foss otter. 'I wasn't aware that we were expecting anyone,' he said slowly. 'What's the story?'

Chloe laughed and tried to make the girl's visit seem small and ordinary. 'She's a very good pianist,' she added, as if that made everything OK.

He stroked his beard. 'I thought that we'd agreed – no house-pests.'

Following him into the kitchen, she made another spot decision – not to tell him about the escape plan. 'She's got no one close to her and no money.'

Lawrence sucked his teeth and poured a large whisky. 'Madness, bringing a total stranger into our home,' he said, as if nothing could dispute it. 'What are you going to do with her?'

'She only needs food and a hot drink. She'll be gone before you know it,' she said, enjoying his irritation. 'Be nice.'

After her shower, the girl joined them. Chloe noticed a shift of expression flicker in Lawrence's eyes when they were introduced. The girl gave him a glare and a curt nod, then went to the front room.

He poured another whisky.

'For a moment, I thought you knew her...'

'I'm a musician, I meet people all the time. You know that.'

Yes, she thought. I know. But wherever the girl had been – and whatever had happened to her – she was thawing. She looked more relaxed, shining with something almost like innocence.

He drained his glass and banged it down on the counter. 'Get shot of her.'

Chloe frowned. 'I like her.'

'You've got no idea where she's been.'

'I want to help her,' said Chloe, without budging.

He washed his hands in the kitchen sink. 'You don't even know her. She's not a fucking project - and I want doesn't get. Get rid.'

'But it's alright for you to have Olga,' she said through gritted teeth. She turned on her heel and went to get some money.

The husband was sure to be tracking or blocking any bank accounts – at least she could save the girl the embarrassment of asking and dull the guilt of ditching her.

Sunny bailed her up on the landing. 'Paid leave. For to go on English Intensive.' A ragtime tune floated to them, then Lawrence's staccato machine gun laugh. Sunny raised an eyebrow and studied Chloe's face. Chloe did her best to be the sphinx. 'Only four days. Like long weekend,' pushed Sunny, still blocking the stairs. A flirty giggle carried up the stairs, followed by the sound of something ceramic smashing. Sunny curled her lips in distaste. 'Musicians.'

Chloe tried to concentrate. 'What?'

Sunny sighed. 'English Intensive. OK.'

'Do what you like,' she said.

Sunny flicked her hair and stalked off to her room.

'You usually do,' muttered Chloe as she gathered up clothes. She grabbed her emergency roll of banknotes from her sock drawer and hurried back downstairs.

The silent front room still glowed from her carefully positioned lamps but the tray had gone and the fireguard enclosed the embers on the grate. The piano lid was closed. Shards of the vase lay in the hallway and she thought how stupid she'd been, how condescending to think – for even a moment – that this attractive young creature had needed rescuing. She left the neatly folded clothes in an armchair and gathered up the peacock feathers from the tiles, wondering if the girl had seen right through her hostess performance, seen her need for a friend.

From the kitchen, she scanned the shadowed back garden before checking the front room again. The shy moon crept out from the clouds, casting the driveway in a dull silver-blue light and exposing the empty parking space.

Sunny was in her bedroom, supposedly studying. Chloe knocked on her door and eventually she answered, blocking the doorway with her semi-naked body. Chloe could glimpse the computer screen flickering in the background and thought she could hear a man's voice.

'He has gone… out,' said Sunny, over-pronouncing her H's.

'I can see that.' Chloe took a deep breath. 'Do you know *where*?'

Sunny shrugged.

'And the… lady?' pressed Chloe.

'Ah, stranger is gone also? Huh. Must study.' Sunny pursed her glossy crimson lips, then closed the door.

Chloe went to her bedroom and took the bottle from her bedside dresser drawer. She sat on the edge of the bed, counting the sleeping tablets, then put the bottle away again. For the first time since losing The Baby, she didn't want to be dulled and numbed. If she could feel without interference, that would surely protect her somehow.

It had felt good, doing something for someone, to take her mind off things even for a couple of hours – not that she could've kept the girl against her will. Disappointment pressed down on her. Unable to sleep, she paced, looking into the darkness and wondering who would rescue her.

The inky dawn was breaking when the halogen headlights scythed her bedroom walls. His four-by-four shuddered to a stop in the drive and she watched from her window as he searched the seats. Sweat beaded on her forehead and she cursed Sunny-Olga and her damned heating obsession.

She went downstairs when she heard the back door slam.

'You're late. Or early,' she needled. 'I didn't even know you were going out.'

He pulled off his gloves and held up his hands. 'Guilty as charged. Last minute rehearsal. Went well, so we kept going.' He poured a tumbler full of whisky, took a long swig and groaned. 'I'm cream-crackered.'

Chloe watched him. 'You'll be pleased to know that the girl's gone.'

He drained his glass.

'Did you hear me? She just up and went.'

'I heard.' He ran a hand through his dishevelled hair. 'I gave her a lift to the station on my way to rehearsal. She was keen to get off.'

The words hit her like a kick. 'But she's got no phone, no money – what's she going to do?'

He yawned. 'Not a clue. Still, waifs and strays always turn up somewhere.'

She eyeballed him in disbelief. 'Why didn't you tell me? Or call me so that I could say goodbye?'

'Why are you making a mountain out of a molehill? I didn't know she mattered.' He rived his forearm red-raw. 'I need a shower.'

Still yawning, he lumbered off, leaving a trail of mud on the terracotta tiles and her worrying and uncomforted. She stared out the window, swamped with cold rage at his need to control everything, at how he'd stolen the girl, at the way he spoiled everything.

When Chloe came downstairs that afternoon, the house had already been primped, as if no one had used the front room for days. She could have imagined the whole thing.

A week later, Sunny-Sphinx suddenly left for Poland, taking her moods with her. She'd been vague about leaving but Lawrence said that she'd unexpectedly come into some money. She was taking over the family guest house in Lodz and carrying on her English studies online.

While Lawrence was in the car, waiting to take her to the airport, the Sphinx used the hall mirror to touch up her perfect cerise lipstick. She looked at Chloe with something like concern.

"Good luck. Look after self," she said, before slamming out the front door.

From the lounge bay window, Chloe watched them drive off. Lawrence was smiling and beaming Sunny-Olga had one arm wrapped around the back of his seat. She hoped that Lawrence would want to visit Lodz.

Chloe began to enjoy the strange relief of having the house to herself again. She hadn't worked since the cot-death and she didn't need to, not now that she'd inherited from her parents. It left her with plenty of time on her hands, too much time some days.

She flicked through her gardening books and jotted down ideas and remembered when she'd met the girl. If Lawrence asked what her problem was, she said that she missed Sunny.

She explained her garden plans but he didn't like gardening any more than he liked surprises. At the end of every summer, he attacked the hornbeam hedges with a noisy, fuming chainsaw to keep them under control – but only because he hated the idea of getting people in to do the job.

His narrowing eyes and strangled tone told her that he was trying to be patient. 'You're not thinking of bringing someone in for this.' It was supposed to be a question but it came out as a statement of fact. He crossed his arms. 'They only take advantage and you're soft as a brush – you'd kill them with kindness.'

She shook her head. 'I wasn't…'

'People can seem perfectly normal, then turn on you for no reason. One in four people are mentally ill. I saw it on the news.' He wrapped a heavy arm around her shoulders. 'No need to bother with anyone else, Mrs H. Happy enough, aren't you?'

Happy as most people, she thought, then she wondered how could you ever *really* know how happy someone was. When he approved her new garden design with only one amendment, it gave her hope that things might improve.

Every so often, intense as a vision, the girl drifted back into her mind and then she felt an ache, as if she'd lost an old friend. He'd only say that she was wasting her time, so she didn't tell Lawrence that she'd been scanning faces in the streets and doorways, looking for the girl.

Whenever she went into town, she passed the bookshop. One day she dropped in and – trying to sound casual – asked Elizabeth Gaunt about the girl. Ms Gaunt stood as solid and enduring as the shelves of old books that surrounded her. Leaning on her high oak counter, she clasped her hands and spoke in a low, quiet voice. 'There was this woman about your age and build, but she wasn't exactly homeless. Said she was on her way somewhere. Haven't seen her… probably since you came in for your gardening books at the end of winter.'

She took off her glasses. 'I brought her a strong coffee a couple of times but I'm embarrassed to say that she was almost on my doorstep and I can't even tell you her name. Did you know her well?'

Chloe nodded. 'She was a friend of mine.'

Elizabeth Gaunt cocked an eyebrow. 'So many people pass through. And the train station's only five minutes. She could be anywhere by now.'

Chloe checked the train station for the haunting shadow of a girl, but all she found were shabby, emaciated men picking over butts in the gutters. She wondered whether they'd always been there or if she was simply seeing them for the first time.

She worked on her garden make-over, trying to get it perfect and planted a rosemary bush for the girl in a sheltered corner. It smelled clean on her skin, like sun and hope. She tamped down the surrounding soil and wondered if the girl would have been better off without her help. All the while, Chloe had a nagging sense that she was overlooking something more important.

They'd just arrived home from their wedding anniversary dinner at the desperately cheerful Sicilian. Chloe found it contrived, like some kind of theatre for the diners. She imagined the staff at the end of the night, feet on tables, drinking lager and talking about the weather in perfect broad Yorkshire accents. But Lawrence loved it and kept booking the place. He said it reminded him of *The Sopranos*.

He sprawled on the front room sofa with a glass of red wine and tried to get her to join him, but once Chloe realised she'd mislaid her mobile phone, she couldn't settle.

'Stop mithering,' he snapped. 'I'll get you another one, something better.'

But she didn't want to be upgraded, she wanted *her* phone, the one she'd had for two years, with the leather case that she'd chosen, the one she knew. The one that held her history, numbers, photos, texts, her diary – her life, before it all went pear-shaped.

He switched on *Match Update*, put his feet on the coffee table and poured himself another glass of wine. She called herself on the landline and traced her ringtone out to the four-by-four in the drive.

It was spontaneous, to slide back the passenger seat and check the cavity beneath it.

Her phone screen flashed and as she grabbed it, her fingers brushed cool metal.

She slipped the phone into her pocket and picked up the fob-chain. It weighed heavy in her hand and she dropped it as if she'd been scalded. A vice tightened around her ribs and her breath was too short. She understood exactly what the girl had meant about suffocating.

Even though she knew the simple, straightforward explanation, she was already dismissing it. A woman's – now tarnished – fob-chain was in her husband's car. It was a line of thought that she refused to pursue.

She cursed her stupid pre-occupation with herself and the new friend she'd lost, which had stolen her focus from what should have mattered: where had that girl gone?

Towards the end of summer, she was nursing an espresso when the buxom breakfast newsreader announced that a dog-walker had found a woman's body tucked under the shrubby undergrowth, down on the floodplains beside the Ouse. The woman had a distinctive Celtic tattoo on one wrist. It made her think about listening to ragtime that night and the way the girl had played with a kind of freedom that she had never experienced.

Chloe switched off the kitchen television. She found Lawrence sitting in his dim study, door ajar, his body jerking to some new track. When she pushed open the door, it creaked like a Hammer Horror prop. He wheeled around without removing his headphones.

Through his window, she could see the garden. It still looked perfect, not quite ready to go over. She shivered and wrapped her arms around herself. 'The girl... they've found her down by the river.'

He nodded and turned back to his screen. 'Yeah, saw the news. She was lovely, poor thing.'

She stared at his hunched shoulders and had the feeling that she was allowing herself to see him for the first time. Their home, the place where everything matched, had been tainted and ruined. The newsreader could tell her nothing that she didn't already know: there was always a price if Lawrence didn't get what he wanted. Her second act of rebellion was forming in her mind.

'Off out?' he said, without turning.

'Just the bookshop.'

'Tracking down something special?' he asked.

Her throat tightened. 'Nothing much.'

He gave her a thumbs-up. In the stifling hallway, the eyes of the peacock feathers seemed to watch her and she thought about what the girl had said about them. She glanced in the hall mirror and her face was drawn and blank, as if she'd completely lost hope.

She stepped out into a bitter cloak of chocolate, hanging dark and heavy in the morning air. Swallowing hard, she tried not to gag. Murder had a tongue – she would talk to the police. It was the least she could do for her friend.

TULPA

MJ Wesolowski

When Carly Walters hears the familiar *ping* noise that indicates
she has received a message, she jumps. Carly Walters never usually
jumps at that noise. That *ping* noise is a welcome noise, a life-
affirming chime that indicates to her that someone has taken the
time to sit down (or stand, as is probably more usual these days) and
type out a message, a message to *her*. Carly loves that noise. That
simple *ping carries* her, at least for a few, fleeting moments, to a place
where she is not just wanted, but *needed*.

Ping.

Message received.

When Carly was a little girl, the house used to smell of furniture
polish and fresh air. When Carly was a little girl, those smells were
infused with fresh flowers; bright blooms that shone from various
vases on top of the piano, the mantelpiece, even the bookshelves.

No flowers sit on any of these places now and the windows are
shut tight. She can't remember the last time she even used half the
rooms upstairs. Carly is no longer a little girl.

Mum doesn't like it when she opens the windows in the living
room, Mum says there's a draught. Carly sometimes tries to remind
Mum about the flowers.

'You remember when I was a little girl and we used to go up the lane?'

'Oh yes,' Mum says in that high-pitched creak of a voice she uses
when she has no idea what you are saying to her.

Which is often.

'On the way to the woods? I always picked the dandelions
because I thought they were pretty, didn't I?'

'Oh yes.'

Mum sits in her chair, staring past Carly into the middle distance,
blanket wrapped around her legs. Her eyes are rheumy and pale, her
mouth sunken to an upside down smile. Carly doesn't carry on.

'There's a draught, darling', Mum says, pointing at the closed window with her finger, bent into a hooked claw. Thick, yellow fingernails.

Carly sighs.

Inside the house has that off-sweet cooked-meat odour that you smell inside a hospital or a home for the infirm. The air inside is thick and warm.

Mum's eyes are closed; her face slumps even further and Carly stands up. The laptop is in the kitchen; Mum doesn't like it, even with the sound off. 'Is it like a telly, darlin'?' she says over and over again. Carly's tried to explain.

From the kitchen, mum can't hear the *ping* but Carly can. That little chime has sent an ember of excitement deep into her stomach and she can feel it glowing. Carly keeps the curtains closed, that laptop is her own little window to the outside, a glowing place that is always warm and where people always want to talk. Outside is the grey passage of day. Carly sometimes wonders what she'd do without it.

Carly can't see the rest of the kitchen. The blind is closed and the glow from the laptop creates a pale pod of light at the tall table. She knows it's bad for her eyes, but if she turns the kitchen light on, she'll see the dishes in the sink and on the sides; the blurred window of the microwave splattered, as if something died in there. She'll see the row of pot plants that are nothing but little brown stalks, the mould that holds the room in a great, black claw. She'll see what was once Mum's domain, where she would flit from cupboard to worktop, a stern white tick. It smells of the bin in here.

Carly sits down at the screen; the tiles are cold and crumbs flit between her toes. A fly buzzes half-heartedly behind the blind, trapped in a plastic prison. The blinds used to be bright green but that was years ago.

The little speech-bubble icon at the top of the page has a red notification floating over it. That sight ignites her little ember of joy even further. Notifications are all well and good, but most of the time they're a let down. *'So-and-so posted in the group', 'So-and-so liked your comment.'*

Carly's joined a group, *Mildon Mums*. Today she's learned that yoghurt packaging may cause cancer , the 120 comments below it somehow turning into a debate about biting. One of Mildon Mums is Carly's 'friend' (on here anyway) and she is sure that 'biting back' is the only real way to prevent your child doing it. *'IV bitten my kids nd it does em good LOL.'*

The biting woman's name is 'Sam Lass' and in her pic, she's glaring into the camera from folds of sunburned flesh. A toddler stares from her lap. Carly often wonders what that toddler's doing while Sam's posting here all day. She wonders if she should ask, but she doesn't. They're 'friends' but not that good 'friends'.

Carly doesn't comment often, but she 'likes' other people's comments so she'll get the notifications. It's a bit like being back at school; if there was a barney or owt, two of the lads knocking lumps off each other, she'd hang about at the edges with Rachel, watching. Rachel was a proper friend.

Carly's got a *message* though. That's what that *ping* noise was. Notifications are a blunt little *bloop*.

A personal message shows that someone cares.

Sometimes.

Carly clicks on her messages tab and takes a little breath. It isn't one of her 'friends', the majority of whom are men whose 'likes' are a miasma of amateur pornography sites. Most of their names are indecipherable: Russian, Ukrainian, Arabic, Nigerian. Their profile pictures are of cars or weed. They sometimes message her but she never replies. *'U want good cock????'* they say. *'Meet me' 'Sending me money???' 'I like marry??? U???'*

Some of the Mildon Mums are her 'friends' too. Sam Lass is one of them. Sam Lass has over 1,000 friends. Some of these friends include Carly in messages about children: *'Do u know ne one whos good wiv kids to babysit so we can go out for a change LOL.'* Sometimes they send photographs. Carly leaves those conversations. She doesn't know what to say.

'I get so lonely when the kids are asleep,' they say. *'that's why I live on here LOL.'*

Carly knows all about these people. Nothing about their kids.

Mum is snoring in the living room. The television mumbles.

From: Rachel Pike.

The name hits home with a terrible severity, each syllable crashing into Carly's mind, through her chest and deep into her stomach. There's no profile picture. She gives an involuntary gasp. It's like a hole has opened up inside her and freezing air is rushing in.

There's a draught, darling.

Rachel Pike.

With shaking hands, Carly grips the mouse and opens the message; the room seems to hum, to vibrate around her, consciousness pulsing in and out; the ragged beat of some bloated heart.

The message is only a few words and Carly reads them over and over again, her breath coming in little pallid gasps and her hands dancing a mad jig over the table.

'They've found Linda, Carly.'

It says.

'If you get this now, put on the news.'

Carly doesn't know if she can stand; her legs seem to have gone numb.

The black mould claw that holds the kitchen closes in; Carly can smell the bin, the dishes, the bags of green liquid in the fridge. The fly is going crazy behind the blind, thudding against the glass.

They've found Linda, Carly.

Detective Chief Inspector Kaja Kyllonen catches herself in the mirror and jumps. In films and on TV, the parents of dead children leave the bedroom of their lost untouched, silent mausoleums where dead-eyed toys stare out through a veil of dust. Mr and Mrs White have done no such thing. Their daughter's room is now the 'spare', with new wallpaper and a chest of drawers. A lamp bends in mourning on a bedside table beside a bowl of pot pourri that smells of nothing. It is silent up in here, no murmurs drift around the door of the living room. Constable McKnight is down there on small-talk duty. It's a rite of passage: weather, flowers, pets, between the relentless tick of a brass carriage clock.

'It's under the bed', Mr White said. He's 60 but his face looks thirty years older. That's what grief does to a man.

Kaja looks at her own reflection for a few more moments, caught in the tall mirror fastened to the wall. She knows they call her the Ice Queen behind her back. It's all in the face, a grim, flat line of mouth and her pale eyes. *Wolf-eyes*. She doesn't care. If she cared she'd like it or not; she gets the job done, ice or no ice.

Under the bed in the heavy silence. No one has slept here since. Kaja's willing to put money on that. Death has a funny way of tainting people. She's glad Mr and Mrs White have each other. One day they won't. The man will go first, they usually do; consumed and withered with grief. It's the not knowing that gets people, once it's shrunk and withered them it dispatches them with a cool blade.

She's glad they've got one answer for the Whites today. A body.

'It's under the bed'.

Kaja pulls out a wooden box. It's larger than a teenager's stash box. Linda White never made it to teenage-hood.

'We gave away the books, the toys,' they told her downstairs. 'Charity, you know? It's what she would have wanted.'

Kaja admires the Whites for attempting the exorcism of their daughter. Thirty years is a long time. Especially with no body.

'She kept her special things in there. The things that mattered to her.'

Kaja kept her face still. The Ice Queen.

She turns away from the mirror and sits on the bed. Lifts up the metal catch. What is she expecting? A new revelation, an answer? It's not like no one's looked in here before.

They didn't have a body before.

Linda White wasn't even ten years old when she disappeared. Kaja Kyllonen was barely out of nappies. Mildon's outrage filled the red tops: 'Give her Back!', the leafy streets of the town's more affluent suburbs in stark black and white, a younger Mr and Mrs White, arms around each other. 'Just tell us that she's safe.' As the years went on, white van and satanic cult speculation passed over Linda White, psychics and forensics came and went, determination faded from their faces as the story dripped out of existence.

Then they found her. Thirty years on. A week ago. An early morning dog-walker in Jessop Wood. Stupid thing went jumping into one of those marsh ponds, came out stinking, green duckweed trailing from its coat like witch's hair, three black fingers in its mouth.

What does a nine-year-old keep? What was special to Linda White?

Kaja leafs through worn postcards from friends, back in the days when France was a world away. Blue Berol pen, kisses, cinema tickets, shells, smooth beach-glass and bits of pottery still stained with soil. Nothing else. They told her it was pointless but she needed to come and see for herself. Now they have a body.

Kaja runs her fingers around the inside of the box but knows there's no secret compartments, no sudden clues. It would have been a sex offender, a violent, clever fucker with a penchant for little girls. They're still working on the body at the lab, what's left of it. Most of Linda White's been eaten by life, lain still in the dark waters in Jessop Wood. There'll be nothing left. Nothing but closure.

What's that?

Kaja stops. Her fingers have met something sharp. She lifts the last of Linda White from the box and places it beside her on the bed. There's a birthday card from Mum and Dad – lots of love; she's kept that one, a cat on the front. Reminded her she was loved. The Ice Queen's heart gives a jolt. Beneath it there's something at the bottom of the box.

Something sharp.

At first it looks like nothing, a knot in the wood, an accidental mark. Kaja can feel something rising in her chest, a revelatory breath of frozen air that rises in her when a crack appears in a case. Is this what's happened? Has she really found something that everyone else missed? This cold wind would usually be a galvanic, driving force but not now, not this one.

She stares hard at the mark on the wood, stares until she is sure it has been done on purpose, that it's not some freak occurrence, some chance.

DCI Kyllonen feels her limbs stiffen and a surge of memories thrum through her. Chanting, singing, little girls' voices.

Chalk strokes on a pavement in the dying summer sun.

His mark.

Now there's work to do.

Carly Walker doesn't care what time it is. The radio mumbles somewhere from one of the windows open on the computer. She can't remember if she gave Mum her tea or not but she'll be fine. She'll be *fine*. They've found Linda, they've *found her*.

It's dark outside.

Carly's fingertips are cold, freezing; she's gone upstairs and got her duvet, hunched it up around her so she can stay here at the kitchen table. Sam Lass is debating with the others about when you should give your kids fizzy drinks. Sam Lass gives her kids Coke in their bottles. '*Theyve only got baby teeth so wat duz it mattr? LOL.*' Carly's duvet stinks like mould.

Bloop, bloop, bloop. The discussion keeps going and Carly looks every time, but that little red bubble above her messages stays quiet. Sometimes she stops and looks at what she sent back.

Rachel Pike. *Friend request: Pending.*

Where r u? Carly has written. It says her message has been *seen*. Nothing has come back.

Mum is calling from the living room; she's making those noises she makes when she's hungry. High and long like a old cat. There's a smell of shit too; Carly needs to change her, to put her to bed. She will, she *will*, but she needs to do this first.

She's requested to join the group *Mildon, past and present* but her request is fucking *pending*. It's 1.36am. Admin will be in bed. She's posted in *You know you grew up in Mildon when...* and *Mildon*

Massiv, which just seems to be teenagers posting pictures of their dogs and their cars.

Bloop.

One of her posts has been *liked.* Carly goes straight to her Friends page.

Rachel Pike. *Friend request: Pending.*

Rage boils.

She goes back to *Mildon Massiv.* No new dogs. Her post is still there.

Carly likes the post herself, just to get it bumped. She adds a comment too, *anyone remember him? Cum on I know U do!!!!! :) :) :)*

Mum's noises are coming again over and over, *wooo, wooo, woo.*

Carly shuts the kitchen door.

She's going to have to wait it out. Carly pulls her duvet around her again. She hunches forward at the kitchen table; it reminds her of being a little girl, sitting here.

Night ticks on.

'He lives here,' she said; little Rachel Pike in her red dress.

'Who?'

'Come on.' And they run, wellies splish-splashing in the mud, the brown path that smelled of rain.

The trees around them are tall and they had faces like in the stories, big black eyes.

Carly was never scared when Rachel was there, because Rachel was brave; she never had a raincoat, she never had her wellies on.

Rachel Pike never stayed on the path either. Rachel Pike danced through the trees. Rachel Pike wasn't scared.

'Does your mum mind you being out in the rain?' Carly says. 'I'm dead when I get home.' Her jeans and jumper soaked, hair hanging like a dead thing from the back of her head.

They stood in a little copse that stank of dead leaves. Carly's wellies were silvery with squashed slugs. Rain rattled around them. Carly and Rachel have been here before.

'Here it is,' Rachel Pike said.

Up ahead between the trees are red bricks; moss growing in great clod like moulds, a rusted iron door.

'He lives here.'

Linda's scared. Carly can see Linda's scared. She keeps looking back, through that gap in the trees where the path is.

'I want to go home.'

Carly slaps her.

The noise and Linda's red face sends a warmth through Carly's fingers, to her hands, her arms, through her chest and all the way down.

'My dad says…'

'Fuck your dad.' That word warms her too, nearly as much as the slap.

Linda's in the year below; she wants to be bad. She wants to be like Carly.

'Fuck your dad.'

Carly's not sure what it means but that's what Mum said last time they were down the lane. 'Fuck your dad.' She slapped Carly's face with one of her long, pink hands and she dropped the flowers. The dandelions and yellow poppies.

'Even that shit's too good for him.'

And Carly had cried.

'Don't you dare fucking cry,' Carly says and Linda stands up straight, her lips taut.

'If you cry, I'll leave you here.'

She knows what it's like down here on your own with the mud and the trees, the noises and the rustlings, the dark.

Linda's looking past her to the mossy wall, the iron door.

'If you cry, he'll hear you.'

There's a file on Kaja's desk, as brown as her morning cup of shit coffee from the machine. She opens it, still half asleep and there it is again. The symbol.

His symbol.

The sight of it is almost funny – neat, rounded edges, created with a computer. Someone else remembers him.

The rest of them are coming in and out; she can smell rain on their coats, cigarettes and coffee on their breath, unwashed hair. Cars growl from downstairs; her desk is next to the window, the pane spotted with rain. Grey Mildon outside.

The file's not very thick: a few pages, forum posts, and entries in online encyclopaedias. They all say the same thing. They all mention Mildon, they all show the symbol.

Kaja remembers.

'What's that?' and Melissa had drawn in a little breath.

Chalk it was, white chalk, outside a front gate. The rain only seemed to thicken it, a soft white sludge. It wasn't words.

'What's that?'

His mark.

Dad had cleaned it off with the broom out of the shed, muttering in Finnish. Mum had told Kaja not to play with chalks. She was nine years old – *as if.* But Melissa told her not to tell; if you told, he would come for you.

Kaja calls at the Whites' house on her own. Their street is silent save for the fat songbirds that squawk from the hedges. The Whites' rhododendron is getting too big, its fat pink heads sniffing along the window sills. Pea pods hang fat and untouched. Like swollen fingers. Kaja looks away.

They sit together in the front room where a brass carriage clock ticks down time. The Whites know what happened to their daughter at last. Two white-haired ghosts. 'It's good to have closure,' they say 'after all this time'. Kaja knows they wish she would just go away.

'We've already told them,' Mr White says, gesturing at the window. 'Back then and now. How could she have enemies? She was nine years old?'

Kaja brings out the file from her bag and shows them his mark.

If you tell, he'll come for you next.

Mrs White's lips get thin. She remembers the story, the rhyme.

'We'd like you to leave.'

Kaja doesn't blame them.

It's 8 o'clock in the morning when Carly gets a reply. Mum's stopped crying and the house is quiet. The fridge rattles in the kitchen as if something's trying to get out.

Someone's replied to Carly's post.

'He's real alright.'

She sighs. There's heavy relief in her stomach; it blooms like roses. Of course he's real.

'If you don't pack it in, my girl..." Mum's voice, like the caw of a crow. They're in Jessop Wood again. Carly's crying; her hand is covered with freakish white bubbles. The nettles leer back at her in defiance, their spines savouring her flesh. 'If you don't pack it in, I'll leave you here all night. He'll find you then for sure...'

Carly reaches out for Blue Bear but Mum's got him by the ear.

'Stop fucking crying, girl.'

She can't she can't she would if she could, she promises, please.

Blue Bear disappears back into the nettles.

'What did I tell you, Carly? What did I say? Now look what you've done.'

When Carly crawls back out onto the path, her eyes almost swollen shut, Blue Bear in her hand, Mum is gone.

The path through the wood curls into the mist. No one else is here, not on a day like this. Carly can hear things rustling and branches creaking. She holds Blue Bear tight, grits her teeth against the pain in her hands, her legs, her face.

'Bitch,' she thinks, the words black and cruel in her stomach. 'Fucking bitch.'

'Why are you crying?'

Carly turns round. Wood pigeons clatter from the branches.

Nothing. No one on the path. The trees creak and gasp in the wind. She can smell soil, leaves, the iron reek of old rain.

'Over here.'

Carly looks back, winces at the snapped stalks of the nettles. There's someone else in there.

'Watch it,' Carly says. She can feel swollen bubbles on her lips. 'Those things hurt.'

It's another little girl.

'Are you scared?'

'No.'

'What's your name?'

Carly tells her.

'What's yours?'

There's no DNA on Linda White. Her body is a wizened, blackened thing that curls at an obscene angle on the gurney. Linda White will never rest in peace. Kaja can't stop staring at the single black tooth where there had once been a little girl's face.

Dr Flood's words still hang in the air like the reek of bleach.

'80-90% sure that cause of death was blunt head trauma.'

Pathologist words, dressing death up in little veils. Flood keeps his face blank.

'Limbs bound. Evidence suggest the burning took place pre-mortem.'

Pre mortem

Jesus Christ, she was only a girl. A child.

Bound and burned and beaten.

Kaja can't look any more. She drives back to the office with the radio on loud. The mist chokes Mildon, grey mourning. Jessop Wood up on the hill, a brown streak of sodden mould. She remembers the rhyme.

He'll tie you up and burn your hair,
How many girls he eats down there
One... two... three... four...

There's another file on her desk. The techies have been up all night searching for *him*. Half of them have heard his name; they talked of him in the playgrounds when they were kids, the parks, they whisper his name when they wake from gasping dreams.

He'll never leave here. Made in Mildon.

Memories writhe like white worms. The smack of a skipping rope on the playground, ten pairs of feet in white socks. Each syllable pushed out like a punch. Jump and breathe and jump and breathe.

She went walking late at night,
In the woods and out of sight,
Then she got a great big fright,
And her name was…

Rachel Pike.
Friend request sent
Message seen.
Nothing. Still.

Carly snarls, spits at the screen and wipes it with her sleeve. It's morning and its quiet. There's a smell in the house but she won't look in the fridge. She won't move from here; she's safe in the kitchen. The laptop is her window.

Ping.
Message from: Sam Lass:
'*Yeh I av told em about im coz it stops em bein norty LOL.*'

All that pink flesh, her mouth can't even smile. Carly imagines Sam Lass is a bit like Mum.

'*Stop fuckin' crying, girl, cos he'll hear you and this is where he lives, just here.*'

'*What do you remember?*'
Ping.
'*I remember im from when I woz a kid. My bro used 2 tell me about him.*'

Carly's mouth is dry. She wants to go to the sink but it's dark. The house is silent. She types.

'*What did he tell you?*'

She waits and it seems like days. The house stays silent, the smell wafts, flies buzz.

Ping.

'*He lived in th wood. Jessop Wood. In a house. Did u ever go up dere?*'

Carly wants to laugh.

'Yeah,' she types. '*I've been there loads.*'

She waits for a few seconds. Waits until Sam Lass had read her message.

'*Still do.*'

Ping.

It's immediate.

'*Wow LOL.*'

'*Yeah. Not so scary these days.*'

'*smh :p*'

'*He's not real though is he?*'

There's a longer pause. One of the flies Carly thought was dead has somehow resurrected itself and has begun thudding against the window again, crashing about behind the blind.

Message seen 6:45am.

The silence is huge, it presses down hard.

Ping.

'*I fort he woz reel.*'

'*Still do?*'

Ping.

'*Yeh LOL.*'

Relief. It's like hot chocolate, warm and sweet pooling in her stomach. Carly remembers that book at school: *Charlie and the Chocolate Factory*; that chocolate river; the fat kid, Augustus Gloop, dipping his hand in there. That's what it must have tasted like, that's how it felt in his stomach, warm, and comforting and sweet, like a hug.

Ping.

'*My mam told me about Rachel Pike. The mark on da pavemnt the nyt before. Dey never found her right?*'

'Right.'

'Dey still dnt no wat happnd to her. Even wiv dere computers an that. Long tym ago now. Propr scary LOL.'

'You want to come see for yourself?'

Another pause. This could be it.

Message seen.

The fly stops buzzing, gives up. That stink.

'OK LOL. U wanna meet?'

'Yeah. Bring your kids.'

Ping.

'LOL yeh. Datll shut em up 4 a bit LOL.'

Carly smiles. There's a thud from the living room; feet on the carpet. Carly's smile broadens. Of course. It makes sense now. Rachel Pike's friend request, of course it's still pending.

'Carly...'

Rachel Pike in her little red dress. Her feet are wet with mud and the house stinks of mud, of rain, of Jessop Wood, of *him*. Carly gets up from the table, her legs ache. It's dark and there's a shadow watching her.

'Carly...'

Carly wants to cry; she can feel the tears heaving at her. Rachel Pike at last. It doesn't matter that they've found Linda White, there's two of them now, just like there was two of them back then.

Rachel Pike stands in the living room in her little red dress. She's got his stick in her hand. The black wood and the black nails like something from a castle.

'I'm coming!' Carly staggers against the kitchen wall. Her voice feels gravelly, harsh, as if she hasn't spoken for days. 'I'm coming...'

Rachel will help her. Rachel will show them that he's real.

Just like they showed Linda.

Kaja doesn't feel victorious when they catch her. If anything, she feels sad. It wasn't hard. They waited in the wood, behind the trees.

The dogs never stopped growling. They watched her car pull up and waited for her to get out. She pissed herself when five officers jumped her. One of the dogs had her round the wrist. Fucking animal.

It's a victory for the techies really. It's the web where people hide these days: dog fights, paedophiles, even drug deals. People will tell anyone anything online. People are stupid.

Kaja can't help thinking that maybe they're not, that some people are just desperate.

Back at the station, they tell her how they broke into the house and it was like something from a horror film. Piles of rubbish and a skeleton in an armchair, fucking blanket still wrapped round its legs. One of them big old detached places up on Scurmore Road. No neighbours to complain.

There's champagne in the office. Someone brings out a bottle of Jack. Linda White can rest at last.

'You ever heard of a tulpa?' Dr Flood asks her when there's a quiet moment.

Kaja sips coffee. The rest of them are hoping Carly Walker gets life. Bitch.

'It's a Buddhist thing. Brought to the West at the end of the Twenties.'

Kaja wants to ask what Buddhism's got to do with all this mess. She doesn't. Dr Flood doesn't talk much.

'It's the idea of creating something from nothing. Creating a *thing,* an *entity,* by just *thinking of it.*'

Kaja gets cold. Icy. She thinks of chalk marks on the pavement. Dad with a brush.

'In the Seventies they called it an egregore, a thought-form.' Dr Flood scratches his head.

'It's like if a group of people believe in something hard enough, it becomes real. Becomes *independent.*'

The techies have joined the party. They stand awkwardly on the periphery clutching cans. Kaja wonders which one of them is Sam Lass. Maybe they took it in turns?

'These days they call it a *meme.*'

Flood puts down his cup.

'I'm getting home before it becomes a circus, Kaja.'

They both look out the window. Through the mist, vans are arriving. News anchors brush Mildon mist from their lapels and adjust their expressions.

'See you, doctor.'

Kaja watches as Flood's car negotiates the drabs of media and disappears into the darkness.

Soon Mildon's tulpa will be on the lips of every news update in the country. Social media will swell with his name, his symbol, his mark. That rhyme that she skipped to in white socks when she was a girl.

Mildon's monster.

They'll not remember Carly Walker.

Just like they didn't remember Rachel Pike

They'll remember him.

BADLANDS

A TALE OF FIVE PARTS

BLJ Langham

Part 1: Darkness on the Edge of Town

'It's almost time, kid,' he says in his usual drawl. 'I got to know you want this, ain't worth doing otherwise.'

I nod, 'I know what's at stake.'

He flashes that winning smile, reaches over and squeezes my shoulder. Even though those eyes are hidden behind aviators, I know they're crinkled with warmth.

'We're in this together, son.'

I fish a crumpled pack of Marlboro's from my pocket and light up. It's a maddeningly hot day in mid-July. The car windows are wound all the way down but there's no breeze, so there's no relief and we just sit there, sweat seeping from every pore; my plain white tee and jeans are soaked and any exposed skin immediately sticks to the seats. We need a good storm and it looks like one's on the way. Black clouds boil over the hills to the east, lightning dancing across the billowing mass.

We'd swung by this gas station a dozen times over the past three weeks, sometimes in the morning, sometimes the afternoon, trying to determine its peak hours. Usually at around midday it would be quiet, and today is perfect.

Every Friday and Monday is deposit day. At closing time on these days they take their earnings from the week or the weekend and drop them off at the bank.

This particular gas station sits on a little road on the edge of town, close enough to the highway that drivers can stop off without too much of a detour. All this means big money, all of which is sitting in a little safe in the manager's office out back. There's two cars parked at separate pumps, their owners, a redhead and a middle-aged business-looking man, are filling up their tanks, the cashier watching from inside.

I throw the smoking butt from the window and it hits the ground, a thin blue trail snaking into the air.

The Boss reaches into the back seat, takes his Smith & Wesson, holds it between his legs, checks the cylinder, snaps it back into place and nods at me. I reach for the sawn-off Winchester I've stored under my seat; even on a day like this the metal barrel is cool to the touch.

He opens the door and steps out with the gun held behind his back and is careful to angle himself so it is hidden at all times. I follow but the sawn-off is hard to hide so I'm moving awkwardly.

He gives one final look up and down the road; there's nothing coming either way, so we cross the forecourt. As we reach the door, the businessman is heading out. I freeze but The Boss steps up and with his gun hand behind his back holds the door open for the man. He flashes the driver a smile and when he's passed gestures with a flick of his head that I should go first.

I take a deep breath and enter the shop. The air-conditioning is on full blast and the wave of cold air washes over me, then I hear the door close behind me and the soft turn of a lock. I look back at him and he gestures up the aisle. The cash register is directly to our left by the window.

I make my way up the aisle in front of me towards the back wall; at the end is the keypad-locked door to the manager's office. I look back to see The Boss standing head held high, his weight on his back foot, hands behind his back.

I turn left and make my way along the aisle, sneaking looks towards the cash desk; a heated argument has broken out over how much money is owed.

I'm running out of shelves so I turn my back towards the desk, pretending to be checking out the drinks fridge. I bring the sawn-off up into a better grip in my hands and slowly start edging backwards.

The cashier thinks Red owes more than she's willing to pay but neither is paying any attention to the guy taking tentative steps back from the Coke fridge.

I look towards the front door.

He's still there, watching silently. He gives me the slightest of nods. It's now or never. I grip the shotgun in my hands, take another deep breath, and turn on my heel, raising my arms and the gun.

'Show me your hands, this is a robb…'

The words stick in my throat as I look out the window.

The black and white patrol car sits out in the forecourt, its owner frozen, about to slam the door shut; his aviators are perched atop his forehead, his mouth hanging wide open and he's looking straight at me.

Part 2: Tenth Avenue Freeze Out

We stare at each other for a few moments, not quite believing what we're seeing.

I shift my aim to the window and squeeze the trigger.

The glass frosts, the other side obscured, then explodes. All noise stops when the shot rings out – all I can hear is the ringing in my ears.

The officer has already dropped to the ground, my buck smashing his windows and peppering the side of his cruiser.

I've got seconds before he composes himself enough to return fire so I leap to relative cover under the windowsill. It's about three feet high and solid brick on the other side. I feel every shard of glass as they hit my skin. Red dropped to her knees as soon as she saw the gun and as I try to press my body as close as possible to the wall I see the cashier disappear out of sight down the aisle towards the drinks fridge.

I look to The Boss. He's still stood by the door, hands behind his back.

'Lock this shit down, kid.'

I point my gun towards the end of the aisle and I call out:

'I'm going to need you to come back out here.'

I hear him laugh.

'Get fucked!'

'I don't want anyone to get hurt, but my buddy here, he doesn't care either way.'

The edges of The Boss's mouth curl into a smile. I don't know how the cop hasn't seen him but he hasn't opened fire.

There's no noise for a few seconds then the sound of him getting to his feet. In a sudden blur he lunges from one aisle to another, I squeeze the trigger, and the glass door of the fridge shatters, its contents cascading to the floor.

By the door The Boss casually raises his gun arm, aiming down the aisle towards the manager's office. I know he'll do it if he has to and this shit storm only gets worse.

Keeping low I run a few steps before diving through the air and land at The Boss's feet, pointing my Winchester in the same direction as his New Century.

The cashier is struggling with the keypad, and it's the only reason he's still alive. If he'd got that door open he'd already be dead.

'Fucking freeze!'

He doesn't so I pump the reload lever, aim the sawn-off into the ceiling above his head and let off a round just as the lock clicks open. He freezes as the ceiling fitting disintegrates and he's showered in dust.

'Don't fucking move.'

I glance back at Red, she's staring straight ahead with the same manic look in her eye, and then I look up at The Boss.

'You got her?'

He smiles and nods.

I crawl across the floor to the door as the sound of sirens wail in the distance.

'Looks like their response time is quicker than we thought,' I call back to The Boss.

'Didn't think they'd be on the doorstep,' he yells back.

I smile in spite of myself and continue crawling towards the cashier who's staring at me, wide-eyed with fear. As I reach the door I prod him with the tip of the barrel, encouraging him inside.

The office is tiny. There's no other door and only one window that a cat wouldn't fit through. There's a desk, a filing cabinet, and the safe tucked in the corner. The cashier is on his knees in the middle of the room, he can't be older than twenty. His name badge reads, 'Service with a Smile: Joe', but he isn't smiling. The shotgun in his face probably isn't helping.

'I need you to open the safe.'

Quietly he says, 'I can't,' as a tear runs down his cheek.

'Excuse me?'

'I can't. I don't have the combination.'

Didn't see that coming.

Shots fired, no money, and sirens drawing closer. We were going to end up on one of those dumbest criminal shows and The Boss didn't need that kind of bad press.

'What's in the till?'

'Forty bucks.'

Fuck.

I grab Joe by the scruff of his neck and drag him back out into the store. We keep low as we make our way to the front of the store. The Boss is leaning against the wall below the window, gun trained on the Red. She's staring straight ahead, utterly silent and ghostly white; I'm afraid she's gone into shock. I throw Joe to the floor next to her before collapsing against the wall next to The Boss.

'We've got a problem.'

I bang the back of my head against the wall.

'There's no money.' He just looks at me, but his eyes are still covered so I can't read his expression. 'Joe can't get in the safe.'

'Well shit, son, that just ain't gonna fly.'

The sound of screeching tires fills the air and the sirens suddenly stop. I turn to The Boss.

'How many do you think are out there?'

He shrugs, and then nods to the fallen sunglasses stand next to the cash desk. I'm confused, then see my own face staring back from a cracked mirror. I reach out my leg, hook it under my ankle, and pull it towards me.

I take the cracked mirror and hold it above my head, angling it so I can see outside.

It's starting to get dark, those black clouds creeping over the sun. There are three cars outside, scattered across the forecourt and the road. There are officers stopping traffic, and others crouching behind their cars, firearms pointing in our direction.

Feedback whines across the forecourt and a voice booms:

'THE BUILDING IS SURROUNDED. PUT DOWN YOUR WEAPON AND YOU WILL NOT BE HARMED.'

The echoes bounce around as I lean my head against the wall with my eyes closed. The only other sound is an occasional sob from Joe. I turn to find Red staring straight at me, her mouth wide in a Cheshire cat grin.

'This is so fucking cool!'

My mouth is hanging open in shock but The Boss bursts out laughing.

'I've dreamt about being in situations like this all my life!'

The Boss turns to me with a wide smile.

'I like this one.'

I hold the mirror up, using it to survey the scene outside; a few more patrol cars have shown up, lights flashing. The voice booms outs again.

'IF YOU GIVE YOURSELF UP, YOUR CO-OPERATION WILL BE TAKEN INTO ACCOUNT. YOU ARE ONLY MAKING MATTERS WORSE FOR YOURSELF.'

'Patronizing fuck.'

The Boss turns to me.

'We ain't going out like this, kid. We gotta take control. Make 'em play by our rules.'

I shake my head in exasperation.

'How? We're in way over our heads.'

'Show 'em that we ain't afraid to fuck up their day. Make 'em respect us. Make 'em fear us! Think, son,' he barks at me. 'We've fired shots, they're within their rights to blow us away. But what have we got up our sleeve? What protection can we give ourselves?'

My head's swimming and I can't think straight. I look away at Red's wide smile and bulging eyes and at Joe curled up in a ball in front of the cash desk.

Then it hits me.

'Hostages,' I whisper.

Red gives an excited gasp as Joe lets out a terrified whimper, but The Boss gives me a wide smile.

'I don't think they'll give in to our demands.'

'Who said anything about demands?'

I give him a puzzled look and he flashes me a wink. The mirror still in my palm he takes my hand and forces it slightly to the right. I see the cop infested forecourt and then…

The Chevy.

I nod slowly.

'Use them to get to the car…'

'Then we get the hell out of Dodge.'

I thought Red might hyperventilate at this.

'Amazing!' she blurts.

Joe's mouth opens and closes like a fish for a few moments.

'I can't believe this is happening.'

'Son,' I pump the reload lever, 'you best start.' The Boss's words coming out of my mouth. I hold up the shotgun, 'Everyone to the back of the store.'

Keeping low we snake our way to the back, so we can get behind our hostages without breaking cover. We make our way between the aisles until we're in front of the door. I turn to The Boss.

'You're sure about this?'

He nods at me. 'Only one way out of this a free man.'

'You take Joe and I'll take Red.'

He nods, draws his gun and points it at the cashier, but Joe doesn't even notice, he's staring at me, eyes wide with shock. I wrap my arm around Red's neck, keeping her close to me while keeping my other arm free to point the Winchester. I feel a shiver run through her body as I touch her but she doesn't look unhappy.

I take a deep breath, and then I nod at Joe.

'Get the door.'

Part 3: Born to Run

I take a few tentative steps out the door, but no one fires for fear of hitting Red or Joe. There is no noise except the wind, bringing the oncoming storm ever closer and I feel tiny drops of rain hit my face.

After a few more steps a voice calls out.

'Put down the gun. You've nowhere to go. No one needs to get hurt.'

I flick my eyes to The Boss who gives an arrogant smile. He's not even using Joe for cover, just has his gun pointed on him. Joe's eyes flit between me and the cops; he's looking for an escape route but knows that if he makes one wrong move, he's dead.

'Oh my God,' Red moans. 'All these guns.' And she lets out an excited sigh. I keep moving, never leaving enough of myself exposed for them to get a clean shot.

Joe's eyes flicker towards the cops again, but I point my sawn-off at him, and he's reminded that we'll do whatever it takes to get out of here alive, so he bows his head and falls in step.

As we draw closer to the Chevy I check the roads. There are two cruisers blocking the road to the left, but only one, parked bang in the middle, to the right. The direction the Chevy is already pointed in.

'OK,' I whisper in Red's ear, 'I need you to drive. The keys are in the ignition. As soon as we get in I want you to gun it straight forward and head for the high…'

Joe makes a break for it, running towards the nearest cruiser but The Boss doesn't do anything. I turn and raise the shotgun, pointing it at Joe's retreating back.

'Joe!'

I don't know why. He knew no more about us than the cops but I feel my finger tighten and the shot ring out.

The buck tears into his back. Strings of red plasma explode backwards as he cries out, audible above the ringing; and in slow motion crumples to the floor with a single bounce and is still.

I barely hear them as I stare at Joe's body. A trail of blood seeps out from under him and snakes toward me. The rain really starts coming down and I try to back away, but it's hard with Red in tow.

I reach the Chevy, keeping Red in front and the car behind; I clumsily open the door, lay the driver's seat down and crawl into the back seat, pulling the front seat up behind me. I lay flat as Red climbs into the front seat. The Boss is already in the passenger seat.

'Go,' I whisper, barely audible over the rain hammering off the roof. Red shifts the gear into drive and presses down on the accelerator. As we pull out I risk raising my head a little. An officer runs to Joe, turns him over and leans his head closer to Joe's mouth. Then he turns and points a blood stained finger at a medic.

The impact of the colliding with the bumper of the cruiser knocks me back into the seat. Red navigates the queue of traffic that has piled up. Faces turn as we pass, trying to catch a glimpse of the reckless criminals who have just killed a man. They are quickly obscured as the rain streams sideways, turning everything into a Dali painting.

As we tear down the road The Boss turns to me and lets out a laugh.

'Shit, boy! That got their attention!'

I stare back at him, speechless.

'Now they know which side of the fence you sit on.'

He flashes me a wide smile and I want to knock every one of those perfect teeth right out.

'We just killed a man,' I whisper.

'Nah, boy, you just killed a man.'

I hate him right now but all I can do is kick the back of his seat.

'How did you let him get away from you?'

'I knew you'd have it under control.'

I let out a loud hollow laugh as I sit upright.

'Oh yeah, because it's all in fucking order!'

I lower my head into my hands and start to shake uncontrollably.

I feel a hand take mine and I look up. It's Red. She looking at me in the rear view mirror, her excitement replaced with concern.

'Joe ran,' she says. 'He knew what would happen.'

The Boss looks at her sideways, then at me.

'This girl is way off the reservation.'

I kick the back of his seat.

'Shut. Up.'

Red looks hurt.

'Not you, him,' I say, with a nod to the passenger seat. She turns to look at The Boss, who turns in his seat and looks out the back window.

'When you stop being a pussy, we need to come up with a plan.'

I turn too and see flashing lights on the horizon, illuminating each raindrop like a kaleidoscope.

'Well, we can't keep running,' I say.

'My daddy's farm is about a mile up this road. He's ain't around much though…'

The Boss flashes her his wide grin, then looks back at me.

'Hell, she may be some use after all.'

Part 4: Adam Raised a Cain

The rain's so thick we can hardly see as we take the mud path up to the farm and the car swings in a large arc, dirt flying everywhere as we reach the house. Red is out the car like a shot, lowering the seat so I can clamber out with my Winchester. We leap the stairs to the porch in one, burst through the door, bolting it shut behind us – but I still feel like I've jumped in a lake.

Dripping, I throw my gun on the sofa and run to the only door leading out of the room, which goes through to a large kitchen. Before I slam it shut, I throw all my weight against a bookcase by the door, setting it toppling in front of the entrance. Books hit the floor with an almighty crash.

I dart back over to the sofa and give it a shove. It's heavier than it looks. I turn around. The Boss is leaning against the window that looks out onto the front porch, staring out.

'Don't just stand there! Give me a fucking hand!' He doesn't even turn around.

He doesn't move but Red pushes from the other end and it slides along the floor at an agonizingly slow pace.

'Chickens come home to roost, boy,' The Boss says.

I cross to the other window. I can barely see beyond the porch, but I can clearly see the red and blue beacons flashing through the gloom. Lightning flashes and I see the outline of four cruisers, two figures behind each, weapons raised and just waiting for something to shoot at. Something like me.

I hit the floor just as a deep rumble crashes from the heavens, so deep I feel it in my guts; the window above me explodes and glass rains down upon me. I curl into a ball, covering my head with my hands and I see Red take cover behind the sofa but The Boss just stands there, taunting them. In that moment I want them to turn their fire on him, to see those bullets blow through him and his dead body hit the floor. But it doesn't happen. He just stands there like he hasn't a care in the world.

The bullets finally stop and I force myself to look up at the tattered window. There isn't a pane of glass left intact, the central wooden frames are hanging by splinters, and the tattered curtains flap helplessly in the wind.

The Boss smirks and collapses into one of the armchairs; resting his right ankle on his left knee, he begins picking at his teeth with his fingernails.

I look up at him. 'You're an arrogant son of a bitch, you know that?'

Looking at me over the top of his shades he spreads his hands and dips his head in a bow.

I shake my head and scramble over to the sofa. Red is staring at The Boss and her expression of disbelief tells me she can't quite believe him either.

We sit in silence and the only sound is the rain drumming off the roof. I know it's only a matter of time before they find a way in and the tears make my eyes burn and before I know it my body is convulsing with sobs that I can't control. I think of Joe and how scared he'd been and how none of that mattered anymore because his innards are sprawled across a garage forecourt; how someone is going to have to tell his mother that some kid with a sawn-off killed him for nothing. And then I think of my mother, how the police will tell her that her son is a murderer, the humiliation and guilt that she'll feel for having raised me wrong, and no one will believe me when I tell them it isn't her fault, that she did a good job.

A beautiful smell suddenly washes over me, familiar and sweet. I open my eyes to find my vision obscured by masses of red hair.

She has her arms wrapped around me, one hand stroking my hair. It's been well over a decade since anyone has just held me.

We finally break apart and I wipe away tears with the back of my hand.

'I don't even know your name?'

She smiles softly at me.

'Wendy,' she says.

'Wendy.' I can't help but smile, 'Thanks for letting us use your place.'

Her eyes narrow at this.

'Us?'

The sharp whine of feedback fights through the rain.

'THERE'S NOWHERE LEFT TO RUN. LET THE GIRL GO AND COME OUT WITH YOUR HANDS IN PLAIN SIGHT.'

I grab the sawn-off from the sofa and scramble over to the window, leaving Wendy looking confused. I poke my head above the windowsill and see more patrol cars have arrived.

'Looks like you're royally fucked now, son.'

The Boss is standing just behind me, surveying the scene outside.

'You mean we're royally fucked,' I spit back. 'We're in this together. You said so yourself.'

'That was before you killed a boy.'

'You forced my hand.'

'I didn't force shit.'

'This whole thing was your idea.'

He smirks at me and shakes his head.

'Guess again, kid.'

I stare at him. A lightning flash illuminates the room and there's a smile I've never seen before on his face.

'This isn't the time to start playing games!'

I scramble to my feet and push him hard in the chest and he takes a few steps backwards. He still doesn't say anything and his face cracks into a wide grin.

I've never felt hatred like this before. My arms rise, locked and braced. Slowly I squeeze the trigger.

He just grins at me as the buck peppers the wall behind him. It's a clean shot but somehow I missed.

A peal of thunder booms across the fields, echoing for miles.

I look down at the gun in my hand and then back at The Boss. He grabs the sawn-off and tries to tear it from my grip but I don't let go. He gets it above our heads and brings the butt down onto my nose twice. I feel it break and hot blood begins to flow.

I double over, cupping my face in my hands. I feel his hands grasp my shirt as he throws me into one of the armchairs; I topple over it, my face hitting the floor with a sickening thud.

'You can't kill me, boy,' he snarls.

I hear a crash in the kitchen.

He kneels over me and with one hand lifts my head by the hair, with the other he lands a square punch to my mouth. I feel a few teeth come loose.

'You need me.'

The banging is just on the other side of the door now, but the bookcase is holding true.

He lifts my head and punches me again. I'm choking on one of the teeth, spraying blood everywhere.

'You've always needed me.'

Another punch and my head slams against the floor. My vision goes blurry but I see his hands reaching in for my throat. I feel them close around my wind-pipe. I struggle but he's too strong. The blood is pounding in my ears when I hear another sound that cancels everything else out.

Crying.

I turn my head as far as I can to see Wendy. She's cowering into the sofa, tears flowing down her cheeks. I want to hold her and make her feel safe, the way she did for me, but she's looking at me with terrified eyes.

I feel the grip loosen and I act upon it. I knock The Boss's arms away, his shocked expression makes me laugh out loud. I close my eyes and shout, 'Not any more!'

I must have passed out because when I open them, he's gone. The doors are still barricaded but he isn't in the room. I roll over to see Wendy, head buried in the sofa, sobbing uncontrollably.

'Wendy...' I croak.

She looks up at me. I try to smile, it's agony.

'He's gone?' I ask. I reach my hand towards hers and she reaches forward and grips it, then crawls forward on her hands and knees, completely bewildered.

'It's OK,' she whispers, 'I'll get you some help.'

She pulls my limp body into hers, my face is buried in her hair and I breathe in that sweet smell.

The kitchen door breaks off its hinges and lands on the floor with a crash. Three police officers step through the doorway, one after the other, guns pointed at the both of us and see the mess I'm in. One of them whistles softly.

'Shit. Did she do that to him?'

The officer holsters his weapon and bends forward, grabbing Wendy under the arm and pulling her away. I take one last deep breath and, as the sweetness is replaced by bitter iron, she's gone.

Part 5: Lonesome Day

'So when did you first meet "The Boss"?' She holds up her fingers to signify the quotation marks. I turn to look out the window.

It's early December and the grass is laced with frost. It's close to sunset and the sky is a glorious blood orange. My ribs are still tender and it hurts to strain them for too long, but I don't want to turn back.

She sighs and runs her fingers through her short, red hair. It's neat and perfect, not a strand out of place. It's not a patch on Wendy's.

I know she won't leave until I answer some questions. We've danced this dance for the past two months. My eyes look longingly towards the top drawer of the white bedside table. Everything is white here; I don't turn on the lights for fear of blinding myself. In that drawer is a pile of letters, each signed with a different name, but each from the same person.

Even though I almost got her killed she writes to me at least once a week without fail. She's careful not to write anything about that day but it's definitely her. She always signs off with, 'I love you with all the madness in my soul.' I'm allowed the letters as the doctors think a little bit of normality will help me along the way to recovery. I can't write back though. I'm not allowed pens. She knows I'll find her, as soon as I get out.

'So when did you last see "The Boss"?'

Nine eyewitnesses say that no one left Wendy's father's house from the moment we entered to the moment the officers kicked down the doors and found Wendy and me in a bloody heap on the floor. They also tell me that The Boss was on tour in Europe at the time.

She sighs and rises from her chair.

'Same time tomorrow.'

I don't think about him as much as I used to. I felt nothing but pure hatred for him in the aftermath but these days I mostly feel indifferent. Some mornings though, before my memories catch up with me, I expect to see him leaning against the wall the way he used to. To be greeted with a nod and a warm smile.

He won't be on tour forever.

MAY TRICKS

Martin Robins

In his idle moments Jason liked to recall his favourite lovemaking memory: the time he sneaked his wife into his barracks, having bribed his dormitory pals to conveniently be somewhere else that night, before staying up half the night having sex. In the morning, as a thank you to his co-operative comrades, he sneaked out of the dorm early, taking all her clothes with him. He knew she wouldn't stay in there all day, even if she had nothing to wear. In the end, just after breakfast had been called, she streaked out down the corridor wearing just his camouflage jacket. And all his colleagues were treated to a sight they wouldn't be forgetting in a hurry, whooping and catcalling as her pert bottom disappeared through the double doors at the end of the hall.

The only thing Jason liked better than fucking his wife was stopping other men from fucking her.

Anya had always been popular with the boys. In a textbook case of growing up as an attractive girl in a working class suburb, school became been more about avoiding getting caught smoking in a distant corner of the games field than learning, bunking off with boys just after lunch when the afternoon lessons were taken by a teacher who was too soft to report absences, or too senile to notice. By the time sixth form came around, hazy afternoons spiced with cheap wine and the occasional spliff were more regular than not. She'd had her fair share of boyfriends, and by the time her dismal A-level results dropped onto her parents' doormat, she was near-permanently sleeping on the grubby futon of a gangly youth named Chris, whose main claim to fame was to have a regular supply of weak amphetamine and a couple of cardboard boxes filled with dog-eared happy hardcore twelve-inch singles.

When the inevitable pregnancy came around, Chris was none too impressed and felt a sudden and pressing compulsion to investigate a DJing opportunity in Bristol. Anya had little choice than to move back in with her parents, who despite numerous *told-you-so* lectures, were secretly relieved to have their daughter back under their watchful gaze, pregnancy or no pregnancy. The grandparents naturally took on the role of carers to Kaylie, while her mum attempted to carve out a modest career for herself, eventually landing a job in a high street building society.

The final piece of the puzzle slipped into place when she met Jason in the local sticky-floored nightclub. It was the night of Kaylie's fifth birthday – the first of May. Earlier, the family of four had treated themselves to pizza, pasta and ice cream at Giovanni's, the Seventies-throwback high street Italian restaurant which resolutely refused to go bankrupt. Anya had stayed on in town to meet up with a few friends, have several vodka and Cokes, and hopefully get lucky on the dancefloor. It was love at first grimy gyration; by this time the primary colours of Britpop had run their course, and even the most provincial of DJs had heard of Dizzee Rascal. Anya had always had a natural flair for dancing, and her Saturday night moves were by now legendary – a graceful, sultry, sex-dripping amalgam of styles which shrugged off any challenge the DJ could throw at her. She very rarely had to pay for her own drinks after such a display, and every now and again she, or rather a friendly bouncer who had made it his life's goal to keep a particular eye out for her (perhaps in the vain hope that she might turn her fickle fancies on him), would have to physically fight off the amorous advances of some young pretender whose alcohol consumption had overcome his tact.

But Jason was somehow different to all the rest. Self-confident, but not cocky. Charming, but not oily. Good-looking but modest enough not to think too highly of himself. In a sea of wannabe urban hoods and bearded hipsters, his simple dress and clean-cut manner was just what Anya was looking for. It was certainly what her parents were looking for, as they took to him as if he were their long-lost son, or rather son-in-law, which in a way he was. The very idea of a soldier, an upstanding, brave boy, making an honest woman of their wayward daughter was quite the dream come true. Conversely, just a few months after their first meeting, Anya would have confessed to more than a tinge of boredom in the relationship had anyone she trusted thought to ask. She was going out with her friends less, staying in more, often at her parents' house when Jason was on leave, watching gun-toting hero movies in a state of tepid disillusionment. But her guilt about the stress and worry she had caused her parents over the years, and the joy she saw in their eyes when she was with Jason, was powerful enough for her to put such concerns to the back of her mind. Permanently – or so she hoped. They were married a year to the day after they met.

Adam liked a drink, and could take it too. The consequences of a demanding but ultimately dull day job, and the child-care commitments of a young family, meant that by the time the weekend came around, he felt he deserved to let his hair down. He rarely went out by himself, but if he heard that even the vaguest acquaintance was heading to the pub on a Saturday night, he'd make a point of inviting himself along. His wife was perfectly happy to stay at home and babysit the kids. Pubs and nightclubs weren't her thing, and it did him good to let off some steam as long as she didn't have to be there to see it.

One of the happy side-effects of the increasing popularity of proper ale, thought Adam, quite apart from having something else to drink other than the usual piss-tasting lager, not to mention the kudos of ordering something that nobody in the group has ever heard of, is that it's usually a lot stronger than your usual pint. High 4's, 5's, even 6% ABV's aren't uncommon, which is exactly what one needs to get in the mood for a boogie, especially if there's a bit of catching up to be done. Which there usually is, if one has to see the kids in bed before heading up into town. So, a couple of pints of XB would do the trick to start with. Everyone else is on Staro, the fools. They don't know what they're missing out on. The only bummer is the Carlsberg later if we head to the club. Best get a real hoppy one in next to make up for it.

He must have spotted her within five minutes of hitting the dancefloor. In a sea of floppy tits and overhanging bellies, her lithe, trim figure stood out like a Manet amongst Bacons. Her dance moves were incredible. Hips swaying, arms up, a demure glance to the side – she surely can't have looked at him, but dammit it seemed that way for a second. What a rare sight in a dump like this. Adam fancied himself as a bit of a dancer, and a bit of a looker as well, particularly in his younger days. And because each year was taking its subtle toll on his cheekbones and chin line, he wanted to know whether he could still pull. Full of beery bravado, he made sure he edged closer with every beat, until there was no doubt about it – she was dancing with him. The occasional glance, the 'accidental' bump of the hips – he couldn't believe his luck. It was just like being single again, and, well, there was no harm in it. They weren't kissing or anything, just dancing. What could be more innocent? People dance with each other all the time in ballrooms, in front of their spouses, too. There's nothing wrong in it.

Eventually they broke apart and went back to their respective groups of friends. But when she headed across to the bar, Adam made sure he got there at exactly the same time.

'Hi there. You dance really well. You've got me worn out! Can I buy you a drink to say thanks?' This was Adam's first time to have a proper look at her and she was even prettier than he had first thought.

'Aye, go on then, but I'm driving my friends home tonight so nothing alcoholic. I'll take a Red Bull.' This was brilliant news to Adam. She's into me, and she's not even drunk. Not even slightly tipsy! Fantastic.

There wasn't much time for smalltalk, not that much could be heard above the colossal racket of the disco PA system. He established that she was married (but for some reason wasn't wearing a wedding ring), in her early thirties, one kid. He said he was married too, mid-thirties, two kids. He made a point of making sure his wedding ring was clearly visible as he collected his bottled lager. She lived just outside of town, and took it in turns with two friends to drive each other in to save on taxi fares. She asked why his wife wasn't with him, and he mumbled something about clubbing not being her thing. And that was as far as the conversation went. But they kept meeting up on the dancefloor for another bump-and-grind session, each one more raunchy than the last, or so it seemed to Adam. He'd had a few by this point, but was still in control, or so he imagined. Eventually, the lights went up and the euphoria slowly ebbed away. It was difficult to accept that the night was over. He offered to walk her to her car.

'Go on, then. I don't want to be around these two right now.' Her friends were both insensible – one on drink, the other with a man's tongue halfway down her throat.

As they strolled to her car, they exchanged pleasantries, Adam fighting off the urge to reveal what he was really feeling – that he wanted, desperately, to make love to her. That would be a huge mistake. And the beer must have been wearing off, because he successfully managed to stick to innocent topics of conversation. As they reached her car, he was resigned to his fate.

'Thanks for a great night. You're a fantastic dancer.' He decided that since this was the truth, he could get away with saying it.

'I know. I get that all the time. You could see how the men in there look at me. I kind of get off on it.'

'Well, maybe we'll do it again some time. See you around.' A resigned smile, and he turned to leave. But after only a few steps she shouted after him in a hopeful voice, 'Hey, do you need a lift anywhere?'

He looked back at her. 'Well, I was going to look for a cab. And it's only a half-hour walk if I don't find one. What about your friends?'

'They won't be ready for ages. One's gone for pizza, the other... well I dread to think what she's up to! Come on, it's freezing out here. I'll take you home.'

Appreciative of any opportunity to spend another few minutes in her presence, Adam didn't need much persuading. They set off, with him giving directions. Then she said what he had been half-hoping, half-dreading she would say.

'Fancy a nightcap?'

He looked across at her. A half-smile crept across her lips; apart from that her expression was pure innocence. She went on, 'I could murder a drink. The others can get a cab. It's awful having to stay sober when everyone else is pissed. Will you join me?'

'What about your husband? Surely he'll not be pleased to see me?'

'He's away in some war zone or other. And anyway, it's just a drink, right?'

Temptation played around Adam's brain. He could go home to the spare bed, with only his hangover for company, or he could spend another hour in this amazing woman's presence. He made his mind up.

'OK, just one drink. But I'll have to be getting back soon. I don't want my wife to wake up and find me still out at four in the morning.'

Her half-smile turned into a full one. 'I've got some lovely bourbon you might be interested in.' And they both laughed at that.

She pulled the car into the driveway, switched off the ignition, and ran around to the passenger side, dragging him out of the car and slamming the door shut with considerable force. And noise, thought Adam. She scrabbled around in her handbag for the front door key, and paused for dramatic effect before turning the key in the lock.

'After you, sir,' she teased, standing aside. Adam took a deep breath – the very act of crossing the threshold was straining every moral fibre he possessed – and stepped into the hallway.

It was dark in the hallway, as was the rest of the house, but Adam had the uneasy feeling that the house wasn't as empty as he had been led to believe. As he turned back to Anya to tell her as much, he caught a brief glimpse of a man's face behind the front door, covered in camouflage make-up and contorted into a wide-mouthed, guttural battle-cry, before a dull metal object came hurtling through the blackness towards him. The world exploded in a flash of light and pain, and then there was nothing.

'Jason, you've killed him! Fuck, Jason, you promised you'd never do this again. We've got enough problems with the other two!'

'I haven't killed him, you daft bitch, just given him a scare. Grab his hands, I'll get his legs. We need him on this chair. You've not been drinking, have you? You know I need you sober for May Tricks night.'

'Of course I've not been drinking, I've done exactly as you said, all night. Jason, you bastard, you said you'd just beat him up a bit and let him go. He's bleeding like fuck! Why did you have to hit him with such a fucking big hammer?'

'What do you expect me to use, you stupid woman, one of Kaylie's Bob The Builder toys? Get fucking lifting.'

They dragged Adam's limp body over to a small, wooden chair in the middle of the kitchen's lino floor, and bound him to it with plastic cable ties. Jason slapped him hard around the face until feeble groans emerged.

'Can you hear me, you dirty fuck?'

'Mmmmhhh… yeah…' Adam blinked through a sea of red. Despite the searing pain in his head, he could just about make out a pair of figures standing just a few paces in front of him.

'Right, listen to me, you sheep-shagging skank. If you think you can fuck my wife in my own house then you've got another think coming. A very fucking long think. In fact, you won't be fucking anyone for quite some time. So make the most of this little display, won't you?'

And with that, Jason grabbed the back of his wife's head and roughly pulled her towards him, clamping his lips on hers with one hand whilst tearing off her blouse with the other. Then he turned her around, lifted her skirt, bent her over the narrow kitchen bench and unceremoniously, and rather briefly, had sex with her. When he was spent, he pushed her to the floor and turned back to Adam.

'Did you enjoy that, you dirty pervert? Not as much as I'm going to enjoy this, I can tell you.' And with that he headbutted Adam so hard that the chair fell backwards. The back of Adam's skull cracked hard on the floor, and he passed out.

It was as if the smell had always been there. There never was a time before the sickly stench of faeces and the sharp, vinegary tang of stale urine was buried deep into his pores. Cleanliness was as rare as sunlight, as the pale, emaciated frames of his fellow prisoners wordlessly testified. Adam had lost track of how long he had lived in this underground hell on earth. He had no way of knowing how long his wife and children had been mourning his disappearance. The hardest part of every waking second was to banish from his mind the possibility that they all might have accepted his disappearance – his death, even – and moved on with their lives. Perhaps she had got married again. More than once he had been made physically sick just by thinking that thought.

They were held in a basement hewn from the very earth itself, connected to the house by a narrow, padlocked door. Most days they saw Jason, who visited ostensibly to bring them scraps to eat, but whose primary motive for visiting appeared to be to taunt them mercilessly. Sometimes he masturbated through the bars on the door, leering at the prisoners as he dribbled whitely on the threshold. He rarely bothered to remove the cess bucket, which had over time overflowed to create a foul pit in one corner. The other two inmates rarely spoke, but Adam could piece together that one had been there for longer than the other, and he himself had arrived quite a while, possibly a year, after the second. No names were shared. Occasionally they would catch a glimpse of Anya in the shadows behind Jason, but she never showed her face, never spoke.

How he kept himself sane, Adam didn't know. He'd attempt a routine, a bit of exercise, encouraging the others to do likewise. Simply keeping their spirits up helped his own mood, and the days eventually passed. Adam was dozing against the mud wall when he dreamt he heard his own name being whispered.

'*Adam… Adam…*' He blinked and looked towards the door. Anya was there, looking as beautiful as he remembered. She carried a plate of proper food and three full glasses of water. He scrambled over to see her. Tears rolled down her cheeks.

'Adam, oh Adam, I'm so sorry. He left the key in the door at the top today and I just had to come and see you. If he knows I'm here he'll kill me. I'm so, so sorry. Jason is a lunatic and I can't leave him knowing that you're still down here. Please forgive me.'
And Adam did forgive her. It wasn't her fault that she married a man who turned out to be insane. All he knew is he wanted to escape. To be free. To see his family.

'Anya, Anya. You need to get me out of here. There must be a way. Think. Please think!'

'There is a way. It's nearly May Tricks night again. Every first of May, on our anniversary, he sends me out for another victim. When he brings him down here, I'll knock him out or stab him or something and you can escape. And the others too. I'll bring some fresh clothes and you can come with me in my car. I'll leave him once and for all. We can go anywhere you want to go.'

So the day came. Adam stayed up all night waiting. The noises came from upstairs – the struggles, the shouting, and then the silence. After an age, Adam could hear the upstairs door being unlocked, and the shuffling thuds of a limp body being dragged slowly down the stairs. Evidently this year's catch was a little different.

'Why the fuck you had to pull a lardarse I'll never know. It's demeaning, you know that? To think you could even talk to such a fat fuck gives me the creeps. I'm sweating buckets just getting him down here. For fuck's sake.'

The dungeon door was unlocked and Jason began to drag the morbidly obese frame of the latest victim of May Tricks night inside. As he had just about managed to squeeze the fat man through the narrow opening, Anya rushed into the room, brandishing the very hammer that had been used on Adam exactly a year ago. But Jason sensed something, and at the very last moment looked up and managed to grab the hammer before it hit him. Adam had been waiting for his cue. He grabbed the toilet bucket and slammed it onto Jason's head, covering him in putrid, disease-ridden liquid. Anya recoiled in disgust, but Adam grabbed her wrist and dragged her back through the dungeon door, looking back just in time to see Jason vomiting copiously onto the fat man. He slammed the door shut and twisted the key.

'Fuck you, Jason. Fuck you very much.' And he snapped the key off in the lock.

As Adam closed the door at the top of the stairs behind him, he realised just how little of the angry bellows coming from the cellar could be heard. In fact, nobody could hear Jason at all from outside the house. He might eventually be released, via an anonymous tip-off to the police, but Adam was happy to let him stew in his own juice for a while yet. He turned to Anya.

'I can't believe what just happened.'

Anya turned to him, and even in his foul-smelling, bedraggled state, gave him a tight hug.

'I'm so, so, sorry, Adam. I can't believe I got you involved in all this.'

'Well, we're finally free of that freak. I need a shower and some fresh clothes, then let's get out of this hell-hole.'

Laid on a kingsize bed clad in cotton sheets, Saturday night TV murmuring in the corner, and quaffing the most delicious, ice-cold ale he'd ever tasted, already Adam had begun to regard his year in captivity as a bad dream. And, as if he had just woken up, it was already fading in his memory. Anya had driven them to a five-star hotel with a spectacular view over the city, and his reality was as fresh and unique as if to a newborn baby. His family could wait one more night. He was going to enjoy himself.

Anya looked over from the other side of the bed.

'Is sir comfortable?' she smiled.

'Very. But I think this is the last beer. And I'm still thirsty.'

'Then your servant will get some more for you. Whatever sir's heart desires.'

'Beer first, and then...' His voice tailed off.

'First things first, darling. Back in a minute.' And she blew him a kiss, grabbed the room key, and vanished.

Adam lay back and buried his head in a soft goose down pillow. Despite his excitement, he couldn't resist the fatigue that swept over him. He closed his eyes and slept the peaceful sleep of a free man.

He was suddenly awoken by a click at the door. How long had he slept? What time was it now? And why could he hear a man's voice mixed in with Anya's familiar whisper? The anger suddenly welled up inside him. After all they'd been through together, she dares to bring someone back to their room? Tonight! The unspeakable bitch! His rage was at full pitch now. All the time I've waited for this moment, and now there's some other dirty bastard here! He could hear the door gently snick shut, and tentative footsteps coming deeper into the room. There was a narrow chink of light from the bathroom, by which he could just make out a man's face: young, eager, excited.

Adam grabbed the beer bottle from the bedside table, and in one motion lunged across the bed towards them. He just had time to register the look of surprised terror on the man's face before he brought down the neck of the bottle into his left eye socket. There was a crunch of bone; a gentle spray of another man's blood misted his cheek. The stranger staggered backwards and Adam hit him again, this time holding the bottle with both hands and bringing it down square on his nose. A jet of sticky black liquid shot out of the man's nose and the bottle cracked in half. By this time the man was collapsed on the floor, but Adam kept smashing his face with the jagged remnants of the bottle until his features were an unrecognisable pulp. Eventually, gasping for breath, he threw the murder weapon to one side. His hands and clothes were covered in blood. The silence was heavy with death.

He slowly dragged his gaze away from the carnage in front of him, and, filled with an unknowable dread, looked up at Anya. She looked back down at him. And smiled.

KEYS ON THE MANTELPIECE

Pat Black

The first time I break into your house it's a Friday evening, still quite light, about three weeks after you've moved in. Miserable weather; rain-stippled windows, the house washed in tinny blue except in the corners where you keep the time-switch lights, to fool any burglars.

But I'm not a burglar.

You've gone to your brother's for the weekend, your nephew's birthday party. I'd waited an hour among the parked cars, making sure you'd definitely gone. Then I let myself in.

The house is one of the better rentals you get around here. Tall trees, front and back garden, flowerbeds weeded. Nice crunchy driveway. Good solid flooring inside, not long laid down, the walls fresh in magnolia.

Of course, there's always the fear that you'll reappear. Perhaps you've forgotten something: a present, a bottle of wine, maybe even your purse. You've been forgetful before. I never knew a girl with so many reissued bank cards.

Or maybe you'll see the state of the weather and decide to turn the car around after a quick tussle with your conscience at one of the service stations. You haven't been in the mood for this party since the divorce – you told me so. Your brother is getting a little bit smug in his old age – the wife, the kids, the big house, the fancy car, three holidays a year – and you're not sure you can stomach it. So perhaps your headlights will sweep across the driveway and douse the kitchen.

Perhaps I'll have to run and hide. Or perhaps something else will happen.

That's the buzz, frankly.

I creep upstairs.

Heather pulled into the driveway and engaged the handbrake. She peered at the block of flats, blurry through the rain.

'Nice facade,' she said. 'Very art deco.'

Donovan tightened his grip on his backpack. 'Yeah, I keep expecting to see King Kong peering through the windows.'

Heather chuckled. 'If you've got any blonde neighbours, they might want to check their tenancy agreement.'

Here it was again, that awkward moment, same as last time she'd given him a lift home. The one where her heart began to race, and she recited her mantra: it's only been four months. You're a mature woman, not a child. Get a grip of yourself.

Donovan smiled. Even in the dashboard-lit gloom of early evening, his blue eyes were a startling flare. 'This has been great, thanks a lot,' he said. 'Umm… I was thinking… This time next week… How about we head out for a drink?'

'Oh. Right. I guess we could do that. I mean, I don't think I've got anything on. I'll have a look at my diary.'

'Sure. No worries. Listen, thanks again.'

Donovan waved as he darted between the raindrops to the security door. As she reversed out, Heather's hands quivered on the wheel. Once she pulled out onto the main road, she chuckled. 'Yep. Got a date. How about that?'

It's not so difficult to set these little cameras up. To spot them, you have to know what you're looking for. How often do you look in the corners of your room? Certainly you'd never think to check the top bracket of the venetian blinds.

The batteries last a long time. It helps that they're movement-activated, only blinking into life when you appear, kicking your shoes into the corner, hurling your cardigan onto the bedspread.

If you turn out the lights, I can switch to night vision. I prefer it, in a way. Especially when you're asleep.

I take lots of screen grabs of you when you're naked. Proper little narcissist, aren't we? You stand in front of the mirrors on the built-in wardrobes, grabbing little handfuls, posing, tilting your shoulder, angling your jaw, tugging your hair this way and that, pouting like a blow-up doll. Haven't you put weight on since you gave old Ross the heave-ho? The spare flesh at the cheeks, the back of your neck, the hips. Look at those thighs! To think you once ran marathons. Cuddly is fun, they say, but not for you.

Even the tits have started to go. Gravity has its way, as does time, as does death. You're so proud of them, all the same, aren't you? Thrust in the face of everyone who'll look at the office – and no shortage of spectators, either. But once your bra comes off, things go south, don't they? You pull, you tuck, you suck in. Acts of disguise, masquerade.

You're not what you thought you were. And now you are alone.

Well… Not quite. You've got me.

Drinks turned into dinner, dinner became a date. They asked to shift their seats from dead centre in a Mexican theme restaurant to a booth. The waitress took the request to heart, and barely cracked a smile as she brought them their chimichangas and beer, eyes smothered in thick black eyeshadow. 'Phaedra', said her name badge.

'She's doesn't look like a Phaedra,' Donovan said, picking the lime out of the bottle.

'She looks like a Joy.'

'Or a Serenity.'

What surprised Heather so much was how comfortable it all felt. He was the perfect gentleman about dessert, taking the blame over the chocolate nubbins they ordered when they were both already full up.

'So,' he said, licking the spoon, 'what now?'

'I was thinking we could pop over to Dusty Den's for a quick drink?'

'There's dancing at Den's later, would that be right? Late licence?'

'Dancing. If you want it.' She smiled, and drained her beer. Already, the warmth, the buzz of drink. It had been so long. When was the last time she'd done this with Ross? She'd been in her twenties, perhaps.

'Is binge drinking going to feature in this part of the evening?' Donovan asked.

'Well, who knows? We're both responsible adults. Why do you ask?'

He peered at the menu, mock-serious. 'Cos I really want to know what a vanilla daiquiri bomb is.'

Two hands slapped down on the table; a slab of a person blocked out the light.

'Well now,' a voice boomed out. 'Inter-office bonding, I see?'

Donovan's face froze. 'Oh. Clive. How's it going, mate?'

A balding, pudgy face loomed. 'Oh, fine and dandy. I'm just out with the good lady and my bairn. You both having a good night?'

The colour rose in Heather's cheeks. She took a deep breath. 'Absolutely fine, Clive. Fancy meeting you here?'

'Ah, that's your bad luck. We come here every week.' Clive nodded at the clotted remains of the dessert they'd shared. 'The chocolate nubbins went down a treat, I see?'

Heather smiled. 'We've got big appetites. Hey – why don't you sit down, Clive? Pull up a chair and join us.'

To their astonishment, he did – squeezing into the booth seat beside Heather and picking at the corners of a spare napkin. Clive was no taller than five foot six, but his girth contrived to squeeze Heather into the corner of the booth as he shuffled his buttocks into position.

'It's just great seeing you guys out and about. You've both had a hell of a year.'

Phaedra swept past the booth; Donovan hailed her. 'Bill, please.'

'You off somewhere a bit livelier now?' Clive asked. 'Couple of drinks, yeah?'

'Oh, we're off to Baskin's,' Heather said, as Phaedra came back with the bill. 'Big place. Other side of the city.'

'You have fun now.' Clive raised a finger. 'And stay out of trouble, you hear?'

He waved at them from the window as they passed outside. They waved back, grinning broadly.

'In all your life,' Donovan muttered, still waving, 'have you ever met anyone like Clive?'

'I can't decide if he's wilfully malevolent, ill, or just thick.'

'Jesus. He just left his wife and kid sitting there. While he barged in on us.'

'Did you actually *see* this fabled wife and kid? There are some people who think they're a figment of his imagination.'

'I just want to know – who promoted this guy? In whose mind was he a decent administrator? Did someone do it for a laugh? People skills? Hello?'

Heather shook her head. 'How could you even think to come over and interrupt two people out on a date? Surely you'd spot us, think, 'Oh,' and pretend you hadn't seen it?'

Donovan arched an eyebrow. 'So it *is* a date, then?'

'Well… What I meant, was…'

He kissed her not long afterwards.

Heather dropped the bottle into the blue bin as quietly as she could. The old lady next door gave a small cough from her back step, and smiled when Heather glanced round.

'Mrs Harrigan,' she said, straightening up. 'If I'd known you were there, I'd have made you a cup of tea.'

Dishwater eyes peered over the fence that separated their properties. 'Blue bin's not till Tuesday,' she said.

'Yes, I know, Mrs Harrigan. I'm not taking the bin out.'

'No, you're just filling it.' She grinned with blinding white dentures. 'I heard a little tinkle.'

'You must have very sharp ears.'

'Sharp enough, dear. Though I don't need them to hear your music through my walls.'

Heather folded her arms. 'If you're referring to the night when you banged the walls, it was my television, not my music. At normal volume. At half past nine at night.'

'Whatever. It was loud enough for me to hear, so it was anti-social. But you'll know for next time.'

'I think in future it might be best if you minded your own business, Mrs Harrigan. I'm an extremely busy person.'

Mrs Harrigan chuckled, a sound like something circling a drain. 'Oh, you're busy with those bottles, aren't you? I can see that.'

'You see lots, don't you, love? Perhaps you might want to get out a bit.'

'I *do* see lots. I saw someone hanging around your house the other night. While you were out, gallivanting.'

'I beg your pardon?'

'There was a man hanging around here, in your garden. He looked in through your windows. Round about where you're standing now.'

'And you did what? Called the police? Took notes? What did he look like?'

'Oh, never you mind, lass. I'll just go back to minding my own business.' Mrs Harrigan smiled thinly, limped back into her conservatory and closed the door.

Shame about poor old Ross. It was hilarious to watch you stake out the back garden from your room, without an inkling that I was watching you.

I'd looked in on Ross once or twice; I'd even caught him driving around your street a few times. Something you probably missed, in your state of constant ignorance.

You're lucky you've got me around, you know. Ross could have been one of these bitter exes.

You can't really know what goes on in someone's head, of course, but I don't think Ross meant you any harm. In his poky little flat, he just got lonelier and lonelier. He saw the way things were going, and the ticking of the clock got louder and louder. He recognised his dwindling cleanliness and rapidly decreasing standards. He took a long look in the mirror – the jowly cheeks, the comically hairy arse – and realised his best years had been spent and wasted on you.

He couldn't phone you, of course. Not after everything that happened. He knew it was over. The truth is, he just missed you. Pathetic creature that he is, he thought hanging around your new house would inspire pity.

He hadn't banked on you finding Donovan. Neither did I, to be fair. I'd looked forward to years of keeping you trapped. Next thing I know, you're not at the house any more. Then I see you coming home, flushed, full of the joys, throwing yourself onto the duvet and giggling like a schoolgirl. Then your cutesy little calls.

I'll admit it, I was hoping for a juicy confrontation. Donovan v Ross; intriguing match-up. Your front room had a mic installed, ready for action. But instead of confronting Ross, you called the police.

They're very efficient round your way. That's something to take note of.

Donovan cracked the foil on a third bottle, then applied the corkscrew, tight-lipped with concentration.

'Danger,' Gloria said, draining her glass. 'Golden rule; never open the third bottle.'

'That's only applies when you're alone,' Heather said. Her speech was already slurred. 'Or… before you go driving.'

The cork finally popped. The two women applauded, even though he slopped some of the wine over the lip of the bottle – enough to cause a rill over the tabletop. 'The situation is… almost… under control,' Donovan said, grinning, pouring out another three drinks. 'I'll go grab a dishtowel, in fact.'

The night had been double-booked; Donovan was meant to come around and put up a bookshelf, while Gloria was meant to come around and bathe in the gossip about Heather's new man. Both parties had been polite and offered to cancel, until Heather insisted they should pool their wine and nibbles. Heather had at first been a little put out by how well Donovan and Gloria got on – Gloria, so effortlessly beautiful as always, even with her hair tied back and a pair of joggies on. But the night had lapsed into easy laughter, and a lot of wine.

While he was in the kitchen, Gloria slurped at her drink, smearing lipstick on the end of the glass. 'I have to say… I approve of your new toy.'

'He's lovely,' Heather said, stifling a yawn. 'I can't believe my luck.'

'Looks quite canny in a pair of cords.' Gloria's eyes glinted in the candlelight. 'It's not every bloke who can carry that look off.'

'He looks OK without them too.'

'We shall have to discuss this in more relaxed surroundings, more conducive to gossip.'

'I agree.' Heather peered into the hallway; Donovan was still busy in the kitchen.

'So, what's the score with Ross?' Gloria asked.

Heather squeezed her eyes shut. 'Ross. Poor bastard. I don't know. Seems like he's not adjusted as well as I thought.'

'Playboy lifestyle not to his taste after all? My heart bleeds for him.'

'I couldn't have him hanging around here though. I don't think Ross is violent, but… You can never tell. I think he was cautioned, and warned about coming round here again.'

Gloria nodded. 'Good. Hopefully he just needed a fright, and he'll see sense from now on. But just you remember: any nonsense, any sign that anyone's messing around outside, give me a call.'

'What you going to do? Kung fu?'

'Maybe. I've got some moves. Speaking of which…' Gloria lowered her voice and leaned in conspiratorially. 'What's the story with the little picture frame on your mantelpiece?'

'What picture frame?'

'You know. The one of Luke.'

'Ah. Well, you know… It'd be silly if I didn't have a pic of my baby bro. You know how it goes. You lost your dad last year, it's… It helps, once they're gone.'

'Yeah, but… What was Donovan doing with it?'

'You what?'

'He put it in his toolbag. I saw him. He lifted it, had a look at it, and stuck it in.'

'Why would he do that?'

Gloria blinked, colour rising in her cheeks. 'Oh, I just wondered if there was something wrong with the frame. If maybe it needed mending. You might have asked him to do it when he was putting up the shelf.'

'He's got no reason to put Luke's picture in his bag. Are you sure about this?'

Donovan appeared with a fresh dishtowel. 'Sorry about that. I got prawn cocktail on your other towel. Had to find a clean one.'

That was unexpected. A set-back, of sorts.

You'd gone out with your overnight bag. You can't pass up any opportunity these days, with all the to-ing and fro-ing in your house; old friends, get-togethers. Quite the diary you've got now.

Of course the old wench next door had probably seen me before. She moves like a cat, out there in the dark. Familiar with every individual paving stone, knowing exactly where to tread without making a noise. You could say we are birds of a feather.

She doesn't even clear her throat, or cough. 'Back again, I see.'

I give no indication of alarm. 'What's it to you?'

'Well, you don't live here. Most people who visit use the front door. You used it the last few times you've been around. But I don't understand why you're creeping around here, at this time of night, sneaking in the back door.'

'You should mind your own business, and get back into your own house. Heather will hear about this.'

'Oh, she will,' the old bitch chuckles drily. 'As will the police. I'm sure you've absolutely nothing to worry about.'

How pleasing it is to see those grey eyes flare wide, and hear her breath catch in her throat. As I vault the fence, she staggers back against the conservatory door, clipping her ankle on the ledge and falling backwards. She doesn't know it yet, but she's already uttered her last coherent words. My hands are around her throat, knees crushing her sparrow chest to the tiling, and she's gone in moments, embarrassingly quick. If she had any fire in her, it was quickly snuffed out.

The witch will have to stay on her kitchen floor for now. Hopefully the smell won't kick in for a while. I'll figure something out. The great thing about nosey old bitches is that they're so sly about things. No one misses them when they don't show up.

It wouldn't do, you see, to have someone like that on the outside looking in. Nosey old sorceresses can be the source of so many problems in life.

I congratulate myself on a solid evening's work, pulling into my driveway, and then…

Oh.

'Hey,' Heather said, from the front doorstep. 'I just thought I'd pop round, see what you're up to. Fancy a glass of wine?'

Gloria closed her car door and bleeped the central locking. 'Bit late, isn't it?'

'I didn't think you'd mind.'

'Suit yourself. Come on in.' Gloria unlocked the front door, and disabled the alarm.

Heather followed Gloria into her open-plan kitchen.

'How's it all going anyway?' Gloria asked, filling up the kettle. 'I hope I didn't get Donovan into any trouble with the photo frame thing.'

'No trouble at all. It's all sorted.'

'How come?'

'We straightened it out.'

'Oh yeah? Did he admit to it?'

Heather sat down at the end of the breakfast bar, pulling the chair close to the countertop. 'Well… we straightened it out, because he quite obviously didn't put the picture into his toolbag.'

Gloria snorted. 'I'm here to tell you that he bloody did, love. I saw him.'

'Oh, it *was* in his bag,' Heather said, nodding. 'But he didn't put it there.'

'You'll have to explain.'

'*You* put it there, Gloria.'

Gloria smiled. 'I see. Let me get this right. You confronted him about it. And he gave you some sob story: "Oh, I don't know how it happened, Heather. It must have fallen in by mistake." Something like that?'

'No, nothing like that,' Heather said, her voice even. 'He hadn't touched it.'

'What are you, a fingerprint expert?'

'No, but my cousin Mark is. He works in forensics. You see, when I confronted Donovan… He was horrified. Especially when the picture frame turned up in his bag. But by that time, I already sort of knew how the picture frame got there.'

Gloria said nothing.

Heather went on: 'I made sure Donovan didn't touch it. I took the picture frame back and gave it to my cousin Mark. His analysis showed no sign of Donovan's fingerprints.'

'Maybe he had gloves. I'm only telling you what I saw.'

'Spell it out then. Did you see him with gloves on, or not?'

Gloria clicked off the kettle before it came to the boil. 'I don't think I'll bother with the tea. I think you have to leave.'

'I've a lot more to say though, Gloria. A whole lot more.' Heather opened her handbag. 'You want to tell me about these?'

She fished out some print-outs; black and white images. Heather stood in front of a mirror, stark naked.

'Can you tell me about these?'

Gloria spluttered: 'Tell you about what? Christ almighty, you're into naturism, that's your business.'

'I'm not into naturism, at least not voluntarily. These are from a website – revenge porn, it's called. I was forwarded a link from an anonymous address. Once I'd done some checking, it turned out it was from my boss, Clive. He'd seen these pictures, but, you see…

Even though he might be a bit of a pervert, not to mention socially inept, he's not a bad guy. He had a conscience. It's obvious it's me, isn't it? The birthmark on the neck's a giveaway. Clive couldn't bear it. He wanted to let me know. I found the video cameras. And that led to some very interesting questions.'

'Questions like, "What's this got to do with me?"' Gloria said, mouth twisting at the edges.

'Well, for one thing, you were the only person I gave a set of keys to. You leave them on the mantelpiece. I bet if we go through to your living room, they won't be there, will they? I'll bet they're in your pocket.'

Gloria grinned wryly. 'This is… delusional. Seriously, darlin', get some help.' Then she hurled the kettle and its contents right at Heather's face.

Silly of me to think you were alone.

Donovan had been listening all along on his phone. You kept a phone in your pocket, with an open line. He heard the lot. He burst in like a hero, while you were out cold on the floor. His fighting skills were less heroic though. Even for a stringy hipster he barely got a hand on me. I'm sure I broke his nose. I'd just reached for the knife block when the blue lights splashed the kitchen walls.

I'm not sure why I slashed myself across the face. Call it strategic thinking. I was going to make out he'd attacked us both. Knocked you out – with a kettle! You have to say, that was genius! – then came at me with the knife. So then I took it off him – as the story goes – then, in the middle of the fight, the knife got turned…

Too late. Cowardice kept Donovan alive. He ran around my kitchen counter like it was the Benny Hill show, shrieking like the bitch he is, even when the cops showed up. They were taken aback by the blood pouring out of my criss-crossed face, but took stock of the situation.

I suppose I *was* the one with the knife.

It made the papers. The big problem was the old bitch next door, of course. Cops only found out when they knocked on her door to find out if she'd seen anything suspicious. Irony of ironies.

The whole thing made quite a splash, it seems. There was even a TV documentary about it. Claimed I was a stalker, or obsessed. Some sort of personality disorder. Whatever.

I'll be out, though. Don't you worry. I can't write you letters. I can't send you postcards. I can't even send you the scalps I've taken in here, from the crackheads and maniacs I've put in the infirmary. But they can't keep me here forever.

I'm so looking forward to having a good catch-up, aren't you?

FRAGMENTS

Michael Connon

The nightmare came again last night. He burst awake with pounding heart amongst sodden sheets. And when the shaking and the nausea made their appearance, he curled into a ball and wished he was dead.

For most of us, even the most disturbing shadowplay acted out by the subconscious before our sleeping mind's eye can be mercifully shrugged off with the bedclothes or hosed away in the shower. But for Simon Doyle, dawn offered no respite because the image which intruded upon his every thought and action of the waking day carried with it the dread certainty of hard memory, of being there – of remembering it.

He remembered standing over the destroyed young woman. He remembered how brilliant white were the splinters of her skull; how they scraped and clung to the hammer's head as he drew it back from the deep lodgement of its final strike. He remembered too the visceral coating of the handle as it slipped through his fingers to the floor. And over all of that hung an overwhelming sense of guilt and self-loathing. All of this he remembered in its every sickening detail.

But the one aspect of it all which led him to question his tentative grip on sanity and to curse his very existence was that he'd only remembered it since last Tuesday.

Breakfast proved to be the silent, sullen affair it had become of late. He hugged himself tightly to curb the trembling and closed his eyes against his swimming vision while his stomach threatened to convulse itself right out of his body.

Jen eyed him discreetly over the untouched plates, not knowing what to say. She didn't understand either how a man can simply wake up one morning and remember he is a cold-blooded killer. But she didn't look at him like she would a murderer. Rather, she looked at him like a man losing his mind and he found himself wondering if that wasn't worse.

She was solid, dependable; the steadfast rock of their 12 years of marriage. Today though, the reassurances, the comfort, the 'give it time's, had run out. She drew her dressing gown together at her throat, her unmade-up face for the first time ever fraught with anguish, and regarded him with an unspoken concern that touched on pity. Tight-lipped, she reached over to gently squeeze his hand and when she did that – Jen the unshakable – he knew it was time.

'You've got to go back,' she spoke eventually. 'Go back and find out what they did to you.'

Going back meant an appointment at the unnervingly sparse offices of Libertas, a market leader among the slew of contenders in the burgeoning memory-removal sector. And also with its Post-Procedural Representative, a way-too-young executive well-schooled in the unctuous arts of public relations.

A man of slicked hair and impeccable suit, Nick Parker guided Simon from the company's reception across the floor of his vast, under-furnished office to a glass-topped, modernist desk. Turning smartly on his heel, he indicated to Simon to sit in the room's sole concession to comfort – a delicate-looking armchair. Simon lowered himself carefully into the leather cradle and clasped his hands tightly in his lap, swallowing hard on the bile that rose in this throat.

'So how can we help you, Mr Doyle?' Parker took his seat and smiled across the desk but everything about this man, this boy, suggested he would prove to be more of a barrier to answers than a gateway. Every movement, every word, seemed as carefully tailored as his smart suit to head off any threat of litigation.

'I had a removal here two weeks ago', Simon began, the words feeling oddly not his own, like he was taking the fact on trust, as indeed he was; he couldn't remember ever being here before.

Jen hadn't approved when he'd first come home with the

brochures. Of course she'd always known there was something; a dark something he couldn't tell even her about. She saw how he drifted off every now and then to another place, knew something terrible haunted him from beyond their marriage. So when he'd found the money to pay for it and insisted it was his one chance of peace, she'd relented.

'But something's gone wrong,' Simon continued over the other man's continual, professional nodding. 'I'm having a memory, a new one. One that's not mine… it can't be mine. And it's horrible. Horrible…'

'Do you want to tell me about it?' Parker asked softly.

'No,' Simon snapped. The blood, the whiteness of the bone fragments, the hammer slipping through his fingers? No, of course he didn't. 'Look, what I'm saying is – it's like I've got someone else's memory in my head.' He rubbed his face then pressed his fingers hard into his temples. 'In fact it doesn't even feel like my head anymore and I don't think I can cope with it.' At this point he stifled a sob and had to breathe deeply before he could go on. 'I need to know – is it possible – could someone else's memory have been implanted by mistake?'

Parker was shaking his head with as much reassurance as he could muster. 'Mr Doyle, I can assure you there is no way that can happen. We can't do anything like that. At least not yet. Maybe one day, who knows? But that would bring a whole host of ethical concerns.' He puffed out his cheeks briefly as if to say he had enough of those as it was, thank you very much. 'No, if the memory's there, then it's yours, I'm afraid.'

'So where's it come from?' Simon begged. 'Please tell me.'

'Mr Doyle, this industry is still in its infancy. Certainly, we know an awful lot more than we did a mere ten years ago, but our understanding of memory and the brain is still far from perfect. There are limitations to what we can do. And of course there are risks, which would have been explained to you before the procedure and to which you would have agreed.'

At this point he slid a slim document across the desk and tapped it lightly, allowing the gesture to hang in the air for a moment before continuing.

'When we operate, our technicians go as far along the neural pathways as possible to clear out all traces of the memory but our doctors tell me it's like rather like removing a tumour. You may get all of the main body but if it's metastasised, then sometimes it's possible to miss a far distant remnant of it. In short, I suspect you've been left with a fragment of the memory you had removed. I'm sorry.'

Simon stared back blankly as what little remained of his world began to crumble around him. 'You're telling me it's real? The m...' he stopped himself. 'I mean, the memory – it's real? It's mine? I was there?' He felt hysteria rising. 'Oh my God, no, I can't live with that. You have to remove it.'

Parker grimaced. 'All the research says not. No one's doing that – re-operating on the same area – it's simply not safe.'

'Well, then you have to tell me – what was the memory I had removed? I need to know.'

'Oh no, I'm sorry, but I couldn't tell you even if I knew. Only one or two people here would know your case and they're bound to confidentiality by severe penalties. We all are. Plus, it would be somewhat counterproductive after all the effort you've been to to remove it.'

'But there must be a way!' Simon stood and planted his hands on the desk, pleading.

'I'm afraid not,' Parker demurred. 'The service we provide is complete. After the procedure, not only are your case notes here destroyed, but we oversee the removal of any references to the memory from the internet, from databases, even down to local newspaper archives. It's like it never happened.'

'But it did! It's in here!' Simon stood, pounding his head as though he could expel the offending image by brute force. 'Don't you understand? I see it every minute of every day!' For an instant he wanted to grab this ridiculous man and make him see sense. And then he stopped. How could he blame him? How could he blame anyone? He was the one who had come here in the first place. To remove the memory of a crime he himself had committed. It was his fault and his alone. 'I'm sorry,' he muttered. 'I'm sorry, I just... I need to go.'

And with that, he walked slowly from the office.

Simon sat alone in the darkness of his study, the only light from the laptop screen before him. A search of UK female murder victims over the last 20 years had eventually yielded this:

Rachel Munro, 18, died of severe head injuries inflicted by a claw hammer in what Police described as a 'frenzied and horrifying attack'. The Birmingham University student had reported being followed by an unknown male in the months prior to her death. To date, no one has been charged with her murder.

The accompanying picture was the girl who haunted him, of that there was no doubt. But who was she? *Birmingham University student.* He'd left Birmingham for London the month after Rachel's death. But had he murdered a complete stranger? Her face meant nothing to him, roused no emotions; not now anyway, but it surely must have done at one time to lead to this. What could he possibly have had against this girl? He had no recollection of knowing her, of following her, of the killing itself, of the aftermath, the police investigation – nothing.

Frustratingly short, the article offered no more by way of detail and he could find very little else. Every attempt he made, at the bottom of the screen, resulted in the same dead end: *'Some search results have been removed in accordance with European law.'*

Which just left this one page; like the image in his head it stood alone, devoid of context, devoid of motive. They're editing the past, he thought. Cutting and pasting at will, excising whole chunks of reality with no regard for the surrounding narrative. Like a page torn from a novel. Which made the short life of this beautiful girl seem all the more meaningless because Rachel no longer had a story and stories are important. A story, a life, reduced to two fragments – an electrical impulse lurking down a neural pathway, tormenting him for the rest of his days and a scrap of reportage in a forgotten side road of the information superhighway.

So there it was. He'd obviously got away with it and this was his uniquely innovative, Dantean punishment. Well so be it, he deserved it. It was only right that the bastard who did that would have to live with the image of the destroyed face he had created. Forever. And then he began to wonder if he could.

Around the same time Simon Doyle was pondering his future, Nick Parker decided on a little research of his own. His visitor's behaviour had unsettled him and he needed to know exactly what could drive a man to fall apart like that.

He headed up the stairs to Information Management, knocked briskly and entered. Holly Morgan, who singularly made up the department in question, looked up from her screen. She was responsible for applications to websites and other holders of information to remove search results, links, articles and documents.

Parker perched himself as casually as he could on the corner of a desk and tried his best at a water cooler moment. 'I don't know, it's all go, isn't it?' he said, drawing a hand across his forehead in a laboured gesture. Such encounters did not come naturally to him.

'Just had a fellow in earlier with a fragment. Terrible business.' He shook his head forlornly before adding quickly, 'Don't worry, it's OK, we're covered.' Suppressing corporate instinct didn't come easily either. 'But you should have seen the state of him – completely in pieces – and it got me wondering, do you remember dealing with a Simon Doyle?'

Holly thought back for a moment but came up with nothing. So many cases.

'Tall fellow, blond hair?' he tried again. 'Birmingham, I'd say, from the accent. About two weeks ago?'

Holly gasped as realisation hit her. 'Oh! The murder case? God, that was horrible!' A hand flew to her mouth, an involuntary spasm, whether from the horror of the memory or the inadvertent lapse in professionalism, she didn't know.

'Go on,' Parker prompted, as gently as he could manage.

Holly hesitated.

'It's OK, I'm a director. It'll go no further. It can't.'

Holly reflected on this a moment, then nodded and parted with what she knew.

'He was only young, just in his teens – a student, I think. His girlfriend thought she was being stalked but he didn't believe her. She'd begged him not to leave her alone but he'd had to go somewhere, only for half an hour or so. When he got back, she'd been killed. Some maniac with a hammer – it was horrible. No one was caught but he blamed himself, couldn't cope with the guilt.' Holly bit her lip and went quiet for a moment. 'There was one thing, though, one detail I remember that stood out because it was so awful. When he got there he actually had to pull the hammer out of her head himself.' She looked away, sickened by the recollection.

Parker was stunned. The behaviour of his visitor made a grim kind of sense now.

For a long moment, the two of them sat in brooding silence.

'Do you think he'll ever find any peace?' Parker asked eventually.

'I don't know,' Holly shook her head. 'I guess something like that never leaves you.'

POWER TRIP

Emma Oxley

Ants, that's what they all reminded me of. A swarm of greedy ants bustling around my coffee table, picking at the food I'd set out for the evening, their voices one loud continuous drone. Hopelessly, I tried to shut out their relentless chatter as I stood with my back against the sideboard that ran along the far wall, attempting to stay as invisible as I possibly could. My eyes searched the faces of my milling party guests for what seemed like the thousandth time, as I desperately tried to seek out that familiar blonde head among all the others.

Where are you? I wondered, just as one of my hands knocked against the framed photograph that stood at my back and sent it tumbling off the sideboard to land with a thud at my feet. Taken three years earlier, it showed me and my husband Lewis on a day trip to the beach with our immediate neighbours, Mary and Alex. As I bent to pick it up, I realised that although I must have polished around the picture a hundred times during the past few years, I never took the time to really look at it. Lewis took centre stage in the shot, the hair around his smiling face lifted up by the breeze as he reached out a hand to take Alex's offering of a half-smoked cigarette. In the background, Mary was attempting to bury my legs in sand and I was laughing towards the camera, the freckles on my nose standing prominent in the light of the sun. How smug I had felt back then, with my new husband, new home, new friends and new life. When exactly had the cracks started to show? I wondered as I placed the frame back in its rightful place and took a step backwards, struggling to tear my eyes away. When had it all started to go wrong? I could barely believe that the carefree Lewis in the picture was the same one that I lived with now, the one who spent most of his time out of the house, returning late with no explanation as to where he had been, his body language closed off and guarded. A burst of emotion suddenly took a hold of me and I darted forward, roughly pushing the photograph over to land face down on the shelf before turning to face the room once more.

A flash of yellow cotton and tweed in my peripheral vision heralded the rapid approach of Jean and Clive Landon, who owned the house across the road. Pretending I hadn't seen them, I turned and scurried off in the opposite direction, noticing the bemused glances they exchanged with more than a touch of guilt. Usually, I'd go out of my way to speak to them but at that moment in time I just didn't have the strength to fend off their concern. They would have been the first to notice that I wasn't quite myself. As I carved my way through the barrier of chatting party guests, I wondered why they had never had any children of their own. The older couple had been quick to welcome Lewis and me when we had moved into this house and I had found myself firmly ensconced under Jean's wing before the last of the boxes had even been unpacked. She fussed over me like a mother hen and mostly that felt like a privilege to me, never having known the love of a parent. During times like this, as I tried to extract myself from her probing glances, it felt like oppression. I had to look busy, I decided. No one wants to bother a person who looks like they're busy. Plucking a half-empty wine bottle from the nearby ice bucket, I looked around for anyone in need of a top-up, feeling desperately in need of a top-up myself, despite the fact that I had probably glugged down more wine already than all of my guests combined. A headache was pressing at my temples and the sides of my mouth ached from the constant smile I was trying to keep up. I toyed with the idea of getting a lipstick out of my bag and painting one onto my lips like a clown. That really would give everyone something to talk about.

As my glances darted around the room, they landed on the double sliding glass doors that were set into the wall on the far side. Someone must have stepped out onto the patio, leaving one of them ajar. A thin wisp of smoke curled lazily through the opening, fanning outwards and quickly upwards towards the crystal chandelier that hung from the ceiling as if desperate to leave the darkness of the outside world behind. Hope unfurled like wings inside of my chest.

Thrusting the wine bottle into the hands of a passing guest, I made my way toward the opening, my eyes fixed on my own ghostly reflection heading towards me as I approached the glass. As I stepped outside into the grey damp air, letting the door fall closed behind me, the quietness of the garden seemed to fall over me like a glove. If anything, the fog that had kept us all indoors during this mild October night seemed to have gotten thicker still. As if through a film of dark grey gauze, I spotted the outline of a figure standing at the far end of the patio. Whoever it was seemed lost in thought as they gazed down towards the bottom of the garden.

As I drew close, I took a deep breath and the figure turned in my direction, the glow from the cigarette he held to his lips temporarily bringing to life the features of the man whose startled eyes met my own before the light dimmed once more at the end of his inhalation.

'Jenny.' Lewis's voice was almost bitter in its greeting. I watched the red tip of his cigarette take off into the air and disappear into the darkness to my left, and my disappointment turned into annoyance.

'I might have known you'd be out here instead of entertaining your guests.'

'Don't you mean our guests?' he asked. I heard the fence that separated the patio from the garden creak as he leaned his weight on it. Through the shroud of misty greyness I could make out his long angular body tilted at an angle, his arms crossed defensively at his chest. His face looked milky white, his eyes black holes against the skin, empty. I shivered.

'You invited the entire street over for a party, giving me less than eight hours' notice,' I told him, struggling to keep my voice from rising in pitch. 'And I don't even understand why. You hate social gatherings and always have.'

'You're always telling me I should make more of an effort with the neighbours,' he replied calmly, shrugging his shoulders. 'So I made an effort.'

I shook my head and turned away, resting my arms against the top of the buckling fence, feeling the pointed wooden panels pressing into my skin. In the otherworldly murkiness of the garden, the realness of the discomfort they caused was mildly reassuring. 'Maybe I did used to say that, a long time ago. You never took the slightest bit of notice back then.'

The fence shook violently under my arms as he took his weight away. 'You're wrong actually,' he said, in a voice so low it was almost lost in the wisps of fog that hung between us. I didn't turn to look at him, even when he took a step towards me and reached to run his hand across my cheek and through my hair, letting the thick, dark strands tumble through his fingers. 'Believe me in this, my love.' I felt his breath, hot against my ear. 'I always take notice.'

I forced myself not to pull away from him, focusing my gaze on the old Victorian asylum that loomed in the distance through a break in the fog at the end of the garden. Built 140 years ago here on the north western edge of Sheffield to house what the people of that era had thought of as lunatics, it spent over a hundred years in service before being left abandoned to brood and fall into disrepair for a while before the listed building had finally been sold and divided into apartments. To the right of the edifice, the spire of the old hospital church rose up out of the mist. Despite plans for the crumbling gothic structure, it still stood derelict. Ghost stories abounded of the spirits that were said to roam both buildings and the land around it, the most prevalent one concerning a Victorian nurse who had worked at the asylum before being murdered by a former patient just outside the grounds. Her spectre and an abundance of others were said to have been seen wandering the narrow corridors and stairwells of the asylum and the land surrounding. I loved being a part of this place and the myths and the legends came with it. I often spent hours sitting in the garden staring up at the old asylum, fascinated by its imposing presence and its mysterious history, knowing that whatever long forgotten secrets it may contain, it was going to continue keeping them firmly under wraps. Once again, all of the windows were inky black voids, but still their calming presence drew me in, giving me a chance to think about how best to handle this man who I had once thought I knew from the inside out but who had lately started to feel like little more than a stranger.

'Do you remember when we decided to move here?' I asked him, my eyes still fixed on the silent, imposing structure. 'Everyone told us we were mad.'

'You were so taken with this place,' Lewis answered, taking a step backwards and letting cool air rush in to fill the space between us. 'I just came to make you happy. But you were right when you said it had something about it. It's grown on me.'

My stomach twisted into a knot of unease. Lewis knew about my childhood, a blur of short term foster carers and an inevitable bi-monthly movement from one new home to another, every house unremarkable, transient and quickly forgotten. How I had always felt as though I stood on the outside of every family I ever stayed with, looking in. He also knew that it was only when we came here that I had finally felt I belonged. My neighbours had become like extended family to me, the only one I ever had. Lewis, having grown up in a stable loving family of his own, had never felt the same as I did. I knew that our home was only a house to him and yet if we were to divorce, Lewis could take everything. He was the one who made the mortgage payments, my wages being just a fraction of his earnings since he had taken over his father's business. I couldn't afford to buy him out and a small persistent voice inside my head told me he had thought of that very same thing. As I clenched my fists around the wooden fence panels, a splinter of wood slid under one of my nails and I forced my hands to relinquish their grip, trying not to wince as my fingertip pulsated around the sharp stabbing pinpoint. Our wedding vows may have been broken into a million jagged pieces but I had no plans to leave Lewis. Now I found myself wondering if my decision to carry on like everything was normal whilst assuming Lewis would do the same had been my downfall.

'I'm glad you're happy here.' I forced brightness into my voice. 'Well! I think we'd better get back to our guests.'

As I headed back towards the house, I told myself I was panicking over nothing. Lewis was making more of an effort because he wanted to try and make our marriage work and that was all there was to it. Nothing weird was going on.

I was almost at the sliding glass door before he called my name. My hand quivered in the air, just inches from the handle, the brightness and the rancour of the secluded world on the other side of the glass suddenly a very attractive prospect indeed.

'Yes?' I croaked.

'How did you know I'd be out here?'

I turned to look back towards where he still stood by the fence, a wavering shadow in the mist.

'I didn't,' I answered. 'I was looking for Mary, actually.'

Was it the movement of the drifting fog, my own imagination, or did his body flinch at the sound of her name? It was impossible to know. Everything seemed to be unravelling so quickly that I was finding it hard to keep up the charade. As I stepped through the door and back into the house, I noticed with relief that the party was winding down, most of our neighbours having already said their goodbyes and disappeared back to their own homes whilst I was outside with Lewis.

I hugged and air kissed my way through a few more farewells until finally there were only four of us left in the room, Jean and Clive Landon and Alex, who seemed perturbed to have returned from the off-licence with extra supplies to find the party almost over. Wearily, I picked up some empty glasses and made for the kitchen, conscious of Jean following along behind. The kitchen tiles were cold against my bare feet as I made my way to the sink. I deposited the glasses and then let my hands rest against the porcelain as I gazed down into the black depths of the drain. I heard her sigh as she entered the room, the click of the door closing.

'Jenny.' Her voice brooked no argument. 'I'd prefer not to say this to the back of your head.'

Slowly, I turned to face her, taking in the smallness of her stature, the lines on her face that were starting to show her age, the look in her eyes betraying just how much she really did care, and I felt myself beginning to soften. This woman was the closest thing I had ever had to a mother. I had a feeling that it worked the other way around too.

'Look…' She wrung her hands and I could see how hard she was struggling to find the words. Jean was a woman who always looked for the best in other people. 'I know how close you are to Mary…'

'She's my best friend,' I cut in.

'But can you trust her?' Jean went on as if I hadn't spoken.

'I'd trust her with anything,' I answered firmly.

Jean just gazed at me with one eyebrow raised. I stared right back at her. The rumours that had been floating around the crescent of late, about Mary and my husband, held no truth and I had to keep telling myself that.

'Somebody invented those rumours out of spite,' I told her. 'I'm sure of it.'

'Is Alex as certain of Mary's virtue as you are?' Jean asked me knowingly. 'Because he sure doesn't seem to be, if the frosty atmosphere that seemed to be between them when they arrived here tonight is anything to go by.'

'They'd had an argument,' I told her, recalling a moment earlier in the evening when Mary had been waiting for me as I entered the dining room with a plate of appetisers. 'I need to speak to you,' she had said, in a low tone of voice so that nobody else could hear. 'It's about me and Alex…' I had told her I would speak to her a little later. With a guilty pang I realised I had barely given her a thought since. 'It'll have been something and nothing,' I said to Jean. 'It always is with those two. I've been meaning to speak to her about it but she must have gone home in order to leave Alex to stew.'

Jean seemed to accept my words although she hardly looked convinced. I was aware that she, like a lot of people, found Mary hard to understand, with her flamboyant flirting, her short colourful skirts and five inch heels, but I knew that was just Mary's way and she meant no harm by it.

Side by side, we re-entered the living room to find it still empty apart from Alex and Clive.

'Jenny!' Alex called desperately when he saw me, quickly extricating himself from Clive's detailed narrative concerning his most recent fishing escapade. Never had a man encountered such a range of diverse characters and situations as Clive seemed to have come across on the banks of the Damflask reservoir. 'Have you seen Mary? I thought she'd be with you.'

'Sorry,' I replied, avoiding Jean's eye.

There was a loud clicking sound and the room was plunged into sudden darkness.

Nobody spoke for a moment. We all stood there blinking as our eyes tried to adjust, the only illumination available being the filmy grey moonlight that filtered through the windows.

'I think the power may have gone out,' I attempted a joke.

'Clive, where are you? I can't see a thing!' Jean's voice screeched from somewhere to my right, startling me with its pitch.

'I'm here, love!' Clive called back from elsewhere in the darkness. 'Jenny, have you got any candles knocking about? Jean doesn't like the dark.'

'Let's go through to the conservatory,' I said, gathering myself together and making my way across the room. 'We'll be able to see better in there with all the windows.'

They stumbled along behind me in the darkness as I led the way through the kitchen and pushed open the door that led into the conservatory. We found that it was only marginally less dim in there, although at least we could see each other better. Alex walked over to the doors that led outside and cupped his hands against the glass to peer out into the night, where the fog had all but drifted away, leaving a crisp blackness in its wake. 'I can't see even a trace of light out there,' he said as his hands fumbled for the door handle. 'No glow from the streetlights, not anything. So it isn't just a tripped switch here, it must be a power cut. If Mary's at home she'll be wondering what's going on. I'd better check she's OK.'

'The door should be unlocked,' I told him, feeling quite helpless with the situation. 'Be careful and let us know when you find her.'

The door clicked back into place behind him as he stepped out into the night.

Leaving Clive and Jean huddled together on a large wicker chair in the corner, I went to seek out something to provide some light in all of the darkness.

They were still in the same place when I stepped back into the room, although Jean released her grip on her husband's arm when I lit the candles I had gathered together and started placing them around the tiny room. 'You must think I'm such a scaredy-cat,' she laughed nervously.

'Of course I don't,' I assured her. 'Everyone's afraid of something.'

She turned to gaze at the impenetrable obscurity outside of the conservatory windows as the moon was lost behind a cloud.

'If you don't mind, we'll stay here until the power is restored,' she laughed nervously. 'I may be a superstitious old so and so, but if you ask me, there's something eerie in the air tonight.'

'You're welcome to stay as long as you like,' I told her, turning to place another candle on the last available surface by the open doorway leading into the kitchen. As I did so a large black shadow appeared in the door frame and I stepped backwards with a shriek.

'Calm down, it's only me,' Lewis said, stepping into the room and batting away the candlestick I was wielding defensively in his direction.

'Where have you been?' I demanded.

'I went for a walk to clear my head,' he answered, sounding

disorientated. 'I hadn't been out for long when the streetlights cut out so I came back.'

'A walk?' I repeated, my voice rising in annoyance. 'Lewis, we have guests here! What's the matter with you?'

He suddenly strode towards me, his eyes blazing in the candlelight. Despite myself, I flinched backwards. 'Do you really want to know, Jenny?' he asked menacingly.

I was about to reply when Clive cut in: 'You're back now, Lewis, safe and sound, that's the main thing,' he said firmly, rising from the wicker chair. 'Let's not let it descend into a fight. Now, I'm off to pay a visit.'

'Take a candle with you,' I told him, not taking my eyes away from Lewis's. Clive complied and left through the doorway to the kitchen.

No sooner had he gone than the door that led to the garden opened and Alex walked in. 'Mary isn't at home,' he stated. His eyes met my husband's. 'Have you seen her, Lewis?'

'No,' Lewis answered, shifting on his feet, just as the sound of pounding footsteps headed towards us from the kitchen. Clive appeared in the doorway, gasping for breath, his hair askew and his candle extinguished.

'It's Mary!' he cried.

'You've found her?' Alex asked impatiently, heading quickly towards him.

Clive held out a hand to stop him. 'Alex...' he said breathlessly. 'We need to call an ambulance. No,' he shook his head then, looking pitiable. 'Not an ambulance, the police. I'm sorry, Alex... But Mary's dead.'

We all sat in silence while the police sealed off the area at the bottom of the staircase where Mary had been found. I felt numb. None of us were allowed to speak to each other until we had made our statements and I was the last to be interviewed. The police were keen to talk to me about my husband's absence towards the end of the party. They wanted to know if I had reason to believe Mary had been having an affair with my husband and I wondered who had told them about the rumours, but then they were hardly a secret.

They enquired about the last time I had seen her. I told them it had been the beginning of the night when she had attempted to speak to me and I had told her I would catch up with her later.

'Do you have any idea what she might have wanted to speak to you about?' the young policeman asked and I shook my head. After that, I told him, I hadn't seen her again.

There didn't seem to be any doubt that Mary had been alive until the time of the fateful blackout. Until moments before it, people had been leaving the party, and would have passed within inches of her body had it already been lying in the place in which she took her last breath, since the street door opened onto the small space at the foot of the stairs. With the lights in working order at that point, there was no way that anyone could have failed to see her.

They arrested Lewis in the early hours of the morning, despite him protesting his innocence. People found it hard to believe that he hadn't noticed Mary lying there on coming back from his walk, despite the near darkness that the power cut threw us all into. There was speculation about whether he had even been out walking at all. And once Mary's lifeless fingers were found to be wrapped around a clump of human hair that could only be his, it seemed fairly certain that the police weren't going to look any further for their man. The tone of their questioning implied that they were going on the assumption that Lewis had never even left the house that evening and that he had been upstairs with Mary all along. People speculated afterwards that she must have threatened to tell me about their affair and there must have been some sort of struggle during the blackout, which concluded with him pushing her down the stairs before strolling into the conservatory like nothing had occurred, leaving our poor neighbour, Mr Landon, to find Mary's lifeless body on a trip to the bathroom. It was conceivable that none of us would have heard anything, the conservatory being a separate addition to the house.

As I watched them take my husband away, I hid my true feelings behind a veil of tears. Eventually Mary's body was taken away also, just as the sky was beginning to blaze into the orange glow of a new horizon. Alex and I stood on the doorstep and watched as her shrouded body was slid through the rear double doors of a silent ambulance.

'Those rumours, were they true?' he asked me quietly as we watched the vehicle roll slowly down the crescent, turn a corner and disappear from sight.

I didn't answer.

'She said my shirt stank of perfume yesterday,' he added and I turned to look at him, but his eyes were still fixed on the empty street. 'Not hers either. I felt like such an ass denying her accusations. She always seemed so righteous, so moral and good. Part of the reason I married her was in the hope that some of it would rub off on to me.' He glanced up at the lightening sky. 'What a right old laugh someone up there must be having at the lot of us.'

I watched him make his way over the grass to his own front door, turning away only when I felt Jean's hand take hold of my arm.

'If you need to talk, we're here, anytime,' she told me, pulling me against her chest. 'You don't have to go through any of this alone.'

When the Landons finally left, I closed my own front door behind me, leaned my back against it and smiled. For the first time in months, my head felt crystal clear. It had been a stroke of genius, planting some of my husband's hair inside Mary's lifeless hand. There was enough of it in the spikes of the comb he had left lying on the dressing table upstairs. I hope whoever reads my confession doesn't make any judgements against me. I do not consider myself a murderer. I always knew Mary would come a cropper eventually if she carried on going around in those ridiculous high heels. It's not like I planned any of it. When I had left the Landons in the conservatory the night before to go upstairs to find the matches I kept for my scented candles, I could hardly have known I would encounter Mary. Yet there she was, waiting for me on the landing when I came out of the bedroom, yawning, her hair stuck up around her head. She'd had an argument with Alex earlier on in the night, she told me. She had come upstairs to get out of his way and must have fallen asleep.

She'd also heard about a rumour that was doing the rounds and there was something that she wanted to say to me concerning it. I admit that I panicked, sure as I was that I wouldn't want to hear what she had to say. Nor did I want anyone else to hear it either. It wasn't that big of a push I gave her, mostly I just wanted to force her to get out of my way, but there's a section of carpet at the top of the stairs that doesn't fit properly and won't lie down. Her heel caught on it and suddenly she was falling. There was nothing I could have done to help her, even had I wanted to. It soon became obvious that she was beyond any help at all as I descended the stairs and saw her lying at the bottom like a broken and discarded doll with her head twisted at an impossible angle and her eyes wide open, glassy and uncomprehending. It was then that I realised that although I couldn't save her, she could still save me. I knew all about the rumours that were going around concerning her and my husband. I should, really, since I had started them myself. How better to deflect attention away from what I was up to with Alex? No one had ever suspected a thing, except Lewis, of course, but who would believe him now, a man accused of murder? As I walked into the kitchen at the beginning of that new autumn day and reached to switch on the kettle, I started to plan the rest of my life. With my husband in prison, I would be granted my divorce and the house would be mine. The neighbours would flock around me, the poor woman who had been left devastated by the actions of her husband. And if, over time, Alex and I started to get close, then who would hold it against us? We deserved a bit of happiness after all and it was only natural that we might turn to each other. Eventually, the seams that held the crescent together would slowly close themselves up again, and it would be like neither Lewis nor Mary had ever been there at all. I would live here with my new husband, Alex, someone else would move into the house next door and everything in the crescent could go on just as it had before, with all of us here, just one big happy family. That was all I had ever really wanted, after all.

INTRUDER

Danny Marshall

Yesterday was a bad day. As days go, it couldn't have been much worse – although it had actually started well. I try to write journal entries when something of note has happened in my life. Not like 'I bought a new TV' or even 'I got fired' – it's not a diary. It's a coping mechanism, my way of bringing order to the chaos. As it happens, it's not very full.

You're reading the entry for what was, without a doubt, the most terrifying night of my life. Up to this point, anyway; I've no idea what will happen between me writing this and you reading it. When I finish writing I'm going to hide this journal, for obvious reasons. Well, I suppose they'll be obvious when you finish reading.

Like I said, the day started well, but let's fast forward to the night – because it definitely wasn't the night I'd planned.

I'll start with me hiding in the wardrobe. I was in the spare room (Ruth's spare room, not mine – I was at her place) and I wasn't alone in the house. I was listening to the footsteps stalking down the hallway from her room. Except it wasn't Ruth – I knew that for a fact because the last time I'd seen her, she'd been lying face down on the bedroom floor with a kitchen knife sticking out of her neck. Her pyjamas had been sliced open, revealing gaping wounds across her back. The blood pooling on the floorboards had looked like an oil slick in the moonlight.

The spare room was dark, but a dim shaft of light fell across my hiding place. It was one of those old deco wardrobes that always smell like mothballs. I presume it was mothballs anyway, I've never actually used them myself. The pale light peeped through a gap as I peered out.

I realised I was still naked. Naked and completely unprotected. More footsteps in the hallway now, creeping closer. Whoever he was (I assumed it was a man), he was taking his time. The psycho was probably enjoying it, relishing the hunt. The floorboards just outside the bedroom door creaked.

Ruth's blood still glistened on my hands, from where I'd held her tenderly for the final time. I rubbed them against my thighs but blood is awful stuff. It just smears and gets stickier, and when it dries it's just as bad. Awful stuff.

The bedroom door opened with a groan and I shrank in fear. I watch plenty of horror films and I'm always the first person to shout at the screen:

'Don't get in the wardrobe, it's the first place he'll look!'

'Get a weapon!'

'Just get out of the house!'

Or my personal favourite: 'Attack them – they won't be expecting it!'

I reckon knife wielding maniacs stalking dark hallways don't expect you to jump out at them. I'm pretty sure it would scare the shit out of anyone, including them. But trust me, in the middle of the night, in the middle of nowhere, without a weapon and without clothes (somehow that makes it worse) I dare you to confront an unknown psycho. Instead I did what you'd do: I shrank into myself and watched that bedroom door slowly edge open.

He stepped into the room, a brute of a man. I'm no short-arse, a shade under six foot, but this guy must have been a good five or six inches taller. And twice as wide, if it wasn't a trick of the light. He'd still look big on a rugby pitch. His face was in shadow but it didn't make a difference, I'm sure I didn't know him. He wore some kind of combat pants and a dark T-shirt. Not much protection but I'd have given anything to be wearing something like that. He took another step forward and the moonlight glinted off a long blade. I held my breath as I recognised one of Ruth's kitchen knives.

His face flashed into the moonlight briefly as he bobbed under a beam, but not long enough for me to get a good look. Only the eyes, burning fiercely like a madman's, were visible in that second. He raised the knife and twirled it slowly in the moonlight, casting eerie flashes about the room. Suddenly he seemed to make his mind up about something and spun round, pounding out of the room and across the hallway.

I thought back to Ruth's coffee table – specifically, the front page of the newspaper sat on it. The headline flashed through my mind: *Serial Killer stalks Halifax*. I hadn't read the article; I didn't need to, it had been all over the news for the last couple of days. National news, probably international too. Every self-respecting horror nerd knows that two grisly murders does not make a serial killer, but what the media didn't yet know – and probably wouldn't find out for a while since the phone was dead (don't worry, I tested it) – was that this was the third night and now Ruth lay lifeless on her bedroom floor. That brought the total up to the required number. All killed in exactly the same way: remote cottage broken into in the early hours of the morning, attacked as they slept. Throat cut from ear to ear, stabbed in the back so deeply the spine was severed, and the eyes... missing.

No one expects a serial killer at large in their town. Maybe if you live in LA or New York – even London! But not round here, not really. To tell the truth there have been quite a few, but you'd have to look them up. If you did you'd also discover that most serial killers lure their victims somewhere – their car, their house, the deep dark woods – and to do that they have to gain your confidence first. Either that or they're the other kind, the kind that takes you by surprise. Running up behind you as you're strolling through said woods, or walking alone down that dark alleyway. Like most morbid kids, I'd read up on this stuff and knew that technically this was spree killing so far, but let's not split hairs: 'serial killer' is much more evocative. I also know that, unlike the movies, rare is the serial killer that silently breaks into your house to murder you in your bed whilst you're sleeping. And that's what made it so terrifying, such big news – and why everyone was talking about it.

At this point I know what you're thinking; if you're reading this then I must have written it down in my journal, therefore things must have turned out OK for me. I'll let you in on a secret – I'm not writing this from beyond the grave. But I digress...

A bang sounded from somewhere close by. I had no intention of ending up like Ruth. I knew I needed to get out of there.

I didn't know her place very well. It was the top house on a terrace of three, but next door were on holiday and the other end was being renovated, so it was just me and him. It was pitch black, but I knew there were three bedrooms and a bathroom on this floor. I pictured the layout in my head. This room was at the end of the house, overlooking the side garden. Ruth's bedroom and current resting place was next door. After that was a bathroom, then at the far side was another spare bedroom. A staircase led up to an attic, and another down to ground level. It seemed like the attic would take me further from safety, plus he could be up there, so I thought downstairs was a better option. This was my only chance to get out.

I eased open the door and gingerly stepped down onto the carpet. No one slashed my ankle so I pushed my head out. From here I could see out of the bedroom and straight down the hall. There was no one in sight.

There was a crash from one of the other rooms and I pulled my leg back in. I think it came from the other spare bedroom. Another crash, like someone tipping over furniture or boxes or something. Looking for me.

I stepped out again. I couldn't be sure where the ape-man was, but I knew it was my only chance to escape so I had to take it. I refocused my eyes in the darkness as I crept to the bedroom door. There was something on the landing. A dog? Ruth didn't have one. I prepared to run, but it didn't move. I realised I'd been holding my breath and let out a sigh – it was my own crumpled jeans. I dashed out in a crouch, sweeping them up into my arms as another smash echoed around the house; he was in the attic. I didn't have much time, he could be out any second and here was I, naked on the landing. I tiptoed down the stairs, the soft, deep carpet masking my steps. I swept up other items of clothing as I went, discarded in my earlier excitement.

I reached the bottom and glanced about. It was lighter down here; none of the curtains were closed. A warm breeze blew through the house, reminding me of my nakedness. I walked further into the lounge and looked to the open doorway which I knew led to the kitchen.

Pounding feet upstairs froze me to the spot, but thankfully they carried on into the end bedroom – the room I'd been hiding in not a minute before. A terrifying scream of rage followed by the splintering of wood could only mean he'd tipped the wardrobe over. He roared and thrashed around the room, presumably taking his anger out on the furniture.

I used the racket to mask my movements and ran to the kitchen, dropping my clothes to the floor. I hadn't been wearing pants – don't ask – so just threw my jeans on. Only one sock. I put it on anyway, making a mental note to find the other. I could still smell the chilli Ruth had cooked earlier. Plates and cutlery were stacked next to the sink and two empty wine glasses stood on the counter, surrounded by broken taco fragments. Bizarre reminders of normality, as if the house didn't care that there was a serial killer on the loose. I pulled my T-shirt over my head, and suddenly I didn't feel quite so vulnerable. Which was good, because the footsteps were pounding again. He knew I wasn't in any of the upstairs rooms so there was only one place he could be headed next. I fastened the buckle of my belt just as he reached the top of the stairs.

He paused, presumably pondering his next move. I didn't wait to find out. I tried the back door. Locked, and I had no idea where Ruth kept the key. I looked out the window to the garden beyond. I'd never wanted to be outside so much in my life; the garden represented safety. I patted my jeans and felt the reassuring presence of my car keys. I'd parked down the lane earlier that night as there wasn't room to turn round up here, but at least it meant that when I got out I had a means of getting away.

An ominous creak came from the stairs. I moved silently back to the kitchen doorway and poked my head round. It was one of those staircases common in these parts, open to the side and leading straight into the lounge. A dirty boot appeared from above. It hovered for a moment and then descended with a soft groan from the old timbers. A big heavy boot, but not workman's boots. Para boots, we used to call them. It was followed by another as the man did his best to creep down the stairs. I briefly wondered whether I should make a dash for the front door, but it was probably locked and I'd be left in the open. I slid up off the floor onto the kitchen worktop, backing up behind the kitchen door. I pushed myself against the wall and pulled the door right open so it rested against the cupboards. I figured he'd be dissuaded from looking behind. Not the most original hiding place but in the circumstances it would have to do.

A shuffling on the carpet signalled his arrival in the lounge. The sounds dragged closer, agonisingly slowly, until finally he stood in the kitchen doorway. A nightmarish shadow fell across the tiles, long legs and wide body bending up across the kitchen door just like in a horror film. I held my breath.

He didn't. I could hear him rasping on the other side of the door, with just an inch of plywood separating us. I willed my heart to stop in case the rapid beating gave me away. The familiar knife appeared round the door and a faint red smear streaked the wood. What an idiot I was. Twice in a row I'd forgotten rule number one of horror – grab a weapon. The knife block stood on the counter at the other end of the kitchen, well out of reach.

He whispered something. I can't remember exactly what it was, something like 'I'll cut your fucking eyes out.' I couldn't be sure, he muttered it so quietly in that deep hoarse voice but that was the gist of it.

He lurched into the kitchen. I pressed my back hard into the wall, tucking my knees right up under my chin and tilting my head down. If I couldn't see him, he wouldn't see me – children's logic. I could just about glimpse the back of his head now, long hair falling lankly across huge shoulders. The man really was a gorilla; there was no way I'd win in a straight fight, and on top of that he had a big fucking knife. He took another step forward, seeming to sniff the air like a dog. The shape seemed subhuman and ferine – an animal. I looked down. The knife glinted mere centimetres from my feet.

I realised I was fucked. He'd walked too far into the kitchen and any second now he'd turn to leave and see me cowering behind the door. I made a snap decision, and one that probably saved my life. I'm normally a coward but it was time to act.

I straightened my leg and thrust out my foot in one fluid motion, angling it upwards with the heel outstretched. I'm not blowing my own trumpet, but it was perfect. My heel struck him right at the base of his enormous skull, in that pit where your spine goes up into your brain. It hit just before my leg was fully outstretched, meaning I still had energy left to keep going, driving him forward across the kitchen. He flew at the door, reaching his arms out to steady himself. Unfortunately for him Ruth's back door was glazed and his hands disappeared through with a deafening smash. I jumped down off the counter and looked for the knife but couldn't see it. He staggered and swayed as if his body was deciding whether to lose consciousness. Taking the opportunity, I aimed a kick up into his belly and he slumped with a growl. As he did he dragged his arms down and back inside, smashing the glass further and slicing into the flesh of his forearms. He pushed against the door and tried to turn, thrashing wildly behind him. I knew better than to get within range of those arms; they were thicker than my legs. I backed away, feeling for the doorway behind me. He was already recovering so I needed to get out of the house – before I lost what little advantage I had. I turned and ran straight to the front door. Obviously it was locked. I looked for the key but it wasn't immediately visible. There was a shout from the kitchen. I can't recall what he said but let's just say he was assuring me that he certainly meant to kill me. I didn't have time to mess about looking for keys, so I ran into the dining room. The thin curtains over the patio doors billowed inwards, revealing a carpet littered with broken glass. I'd rather have gone out the front but this would have to do.

I dived for the door, squeezing through the gap. I sliced myself in the rush, but at least I was out and into the summer night air. I'd never been so happy to be outside. The lack of walls was liberating – I knew I could run in almost any direction if I needed to. I stood for a moment to get my breath back, planning my next move. The grass was already damp with morning dew, which reminded me that my feet were still bare. At the end of the garden a low fence separated me from the wooded hillside and the village below. Normally I'd be able to lose someone in there but not in the dark without shoes; I'd probably break a toe or slice my foot open before I got ten metres in. I looked back at the house. The shape by the door had moved; the kitchen was empty. The only evidence of his presence was thin trickles of blood on the doorframe, glistening black against the white painted wood. I needed to move fast.

I felt again for my car keys and sprinted for the corner of the house. I poked my head out and then ran to the next corner. I looked round and down the cobbled lane that ran past the houses. My car was parked at the bottom, a good 200 metres or so away. I hadn't run 200 metres for at least 20 years but I was willing to try. I realised I was delaying, and went for it.

My feet slapped on the worn cobbles as I ran across the front of the house. As I approached the front door an alarm triggered in my mind. Something was amiss, but it didn't register so I kept going. Too late I realised that where the front door should have been was black space. My momentum carried me on.

He launched out at me from the open doorway.

I managed to glimpse huge lips, bent into a furious snarl, before he slammed into me. We crashed to the ground, rolling across the cobbles and into the weeds. He landed on top of me but I managed to get a knee up and he came down hard onto it, driving the wind from his belly. He was far more powerful than me but I could tell he wasn't firing on all cylinders. Maybe he'd lost a lot of blood? I swung my right arm up and hooked my fist into his jaw, rocking him sideways. I tried to throw up my left arm but for some reason it refused to move. Getting to my car was no longer an option; I needed to finish this.

I swung again with my right fist and his nose exploded against my knuckles. He sat up, pulling both hands to his face. Blood streamed from between his fingers, mingling with the blood from his torn wrists before dripping onto my chest. I tried to move but he sat heavily on me, pushing his whole weight down. I strained to push him off, but again my left arm refused to move. I turned my head and gasped in shock. The kitchen knife – the same knife that had taken Ruth's life – was embedded deeply in my shoulder. He must have had it in his hand when he'd lunged.

He dropped his hands away from his face and grinned. The smears of blood made him look even more maniacal, if that were possible. His teeth glowed as he snarled down at me. It sounds cheesy, but I knew I was staring at my killer. He reached down, encircling my throat with his fat fingers, and squeezed. I struggled but he was just too big, too heavy. Even with his injuries he was twice as strong as I was.

I've never lost consciousness before but I came close. His teeth stopped glowing and my vision dimmed as if turned down by a dial. My world gained a fuzzy black border which crept inwards until all I could see was that savage grin. I could feel myself sliding away; little sparks exploding behind my eyes told me I had just seconds to live.

I reached across my chest and gripped the handle of the kitchen knife still embedded in my shoulder. He didn't care, I was no longer a threat. In one movement I slid the knife out of my shoulder, pulled it down to my stomach, and thrust upwards. I twisted my hand and the effect was instantaneous.

He roared in agony and rolled off me, clutching between his legs as if that would reattach things. I rolled on top of him and brought the knife in hard against his neck. The blackness receded and my vision returned. I sat on top of him catching my breath as he spluttered, losing his. Blood gurgled out from between his lips. I yanked the knife out of his neck and watched his life pump out across the ancient cobblestones of the path.

I closed my eyes and breathed deeply for what seemed like ages, but was probably only seconds. When I opened them the sky seemed brighter. In the last few minutes night had lost out to the dawn. Birds had started to wake and the trees were full of song. The air was thick with that warm damp smell of a summer morning. I'd survived!

I struggled to my feet and looked down at the figure spread out on the dirt. His huge beastly frame matched his enormous head, completely covered in blood. I had absolutely no idea who he was.

Which was odd, because I'd been watching Ruth's house most of the day. That's how I pick them – I make sure they're alone. I choose a nice remote house with no neighbours to hear them scream. I figure he was Ruth's boyfriend; he must have been in the bathroom when I'd killed her. I realised this was actually good – I'd taken on this guy and won. Maybe I don't need to stick to lone women anymore? Maybe when my arm's feeling better I'll branch out to a whole family.

But first I needed to find my other sock.

And then take the guy's eyes, like I did with the others. I would have to be quick; I didn't want the police seeing me.

The sky brightened over the trees. Yesterday was a bad day, but I have a feeling today is going to be better.

HONEYPOT

Sue Wilsea

The brilliant idea of stringing Jim up in the Folk Museum came later.
Obviously my first job was to kill him and God knows just deciding
how to do that occupied my mind for several weeks. But I'd read
and watched enough crime stuff to know that the key to success was
paying attention to detail and not rushing things.

Of course when I first found out I wanted to take the bread
knife and slit his throat with the serrated edge, preferably while the
great useless lump was dozing in front of the telly. I fantasised about
clubbing him over the head with the bread board while his back was
turned and hearing the satisfying crack when the hard wood met his
soft skull; or grabbing him by the scruff of his neck and forcing his
stupid face onto a hotplate, holding him there and watching his skin
bubble and blister. However, I sensibly bided my time, turning out
more bread cakes, doughnuts and loaves than The Yorkshire Pantry
could ever hope to sell, even if it had been high season. I pounded
that dough like you wouldn't believe, pulling, stretching and slapping
it onto the work surface from a height while imagining it was his
scrotum. The Sunday after learning the truth and when I'd been hard
at it since early morning, Jim came in and said he'd eat his dinner in
the front room. The kitchen was that hot it was like we were standing
inside one of the ovens.

'Suit yerself,' I said, punching the air out of a newly proved loaf,
'It's only tuna salad anyroad.'

Jim gave one of his deep sighs and ambled towards the hallway
but not before asking if I'd like the window opening.

'If I wanted it opening, I'd have done it meself!' I snapped.

Jim looked at me and made as if he was going to say something
but then obviously decided not to. I was suddenly aware that my face
must be like a beetroot and I probably had flour in my hair and all

over my face. Jim used to stroke my cheek with the back of his finger and say I had the softest skin in the Dales. That was after three pints of Theakstons, mind. A long time ago and a lot of water under the bridge since then. Now he sighed again, a timely reminder that I'd be giving myself away if I wasn't careful.

'I can do you a jacket spud if you like. When I've done this next batch.'

His face brightened, 'That would be grand, love. If it's not giving you too much trouble.'

Huh! He's a fine one to talk about giving trouble after what he did.

It's hard thinking about killing someone you've known since you were bairns. Jim and I were both Ridston born and bred. I wouldn't call us childhood sweethearts because for a long time we were more like brother and sister but we both went to the local primary, then the same high school in Richmond. Not the grammar, though unlike His Lordship, I passed the 11 Plus and could have tried for a place. But I didn't. I can't say I remember why but girls like me were expected to leave school at fifteen and get a job locally before getting wed so that's what I did, first of all working on the till in a fruit and veg shop in Richmond, then coming back to the village to serve at The Pantry, and eventually buying it from old Mrs Lowther after she tripped over the step at the back of the shop, breaking her hip and collarbone and subsequently decided to retire. Jim and me didn't start properly courting until he went off to technical college to do his joinery course and then we were engaged for nearly three years. Eventually I had to give him an ultimatum – name the date or sod off. His mum, always a nasty cow, urged him to take the sodding off option – she'd never liked me – but for once he stuck to his guns. The following June we were married at Ridston Parish Church with a reception at the Village Hall. I baked my own wedding cake and some said it were the best wedding cake they'd ever tasted. Jim and I had our moments but we were never what you might call a romantic couple. Jim's always been on the quiet side and after we'd been married for a couple of years it was always me who had to make the first move, if you know what I mean.

My mam still lives in the cottage where me and my two brothers were brought up, just the other side of the beck, while Jim's folks, a bit posher than my lot, lived in The Gables, a handsome double fronted house of Yorkshire stone next to the green whose downstairs was the post office and general store. Jim's dad passed away a couple of years back and his mum struggled to keep the place on but when the post office closed she threw in the towel. Anyhow, even before that she'd started going funny, some nights wandering round the village in her nightie or shouting at visitors from the upstairs window and chucking pillows at them. Turned out she had Alzheimer's or dementia. I'm not sure what the difference is to tell you the truth. But anyhow she went loopy. Jim had to put her in a home where she only lasted six months. Got a really nasty tummy bug. Mind, as I said to Jim after the funeral, it was a blessing in some ways. He didn't like that and that was one of the few times we had a real set to with him calling me all sorts once we were in the car driving home. Jim was an only child and his folks were getting on when they had him. Some might say he'd been spoilt. Anyroad, I made sure he paid for being so nasty to me. For several weeks after that there was no dinners cooked and he wasn't welcome in our bed but eventually he came crawling back with flowers and chocolates and apologies. Said he'd been 'traumatised' by his mum's death which was pathetic seeing as what an old bat she was.

We could have moved into The Gables: that's what a lot of folk expected but I had plans and those plans did not include spending the rest of my days being a skivvy in a big house. It had five bedrooms, would you believe! If there were grandkids, fair enough, but me and Jim would have rattled around somewhere like that. Property prices had gone ridiculous in the last few years and with money from the sale we could make ourselves a small fortune. For a start off, I had in mind one of those cruises to the Greek islands. I could just picture meself on the sun deck on one of them loungers, a cocktail in one hand and a saucy novel in the other. *Fifty Shades* of whatever it is. Then once back home a new car, nothing too flashy but something with a bit of style that would make people in the village sit up and take notice. I'd been reading about them gastric band thingies and wanted to get it done private and after that I'd need a whole new lot of clothes. It kept me awake at night wondering whether perhaps it would be better to have the op before the cruise.

But my big ambition, the one that made my pulse race and my hands itch with anticipation, was to give The Yorkshire Pantry a complete overhaul. It hadn't been doing well for some time now and it was no good Jim saying it was down to the recession when I knew it needed everything replacing, from the dirty old lino on the floor to the strip lighting to the old-fashioned glass display cabinets. But it would take money and that was not something we'd had much of during our married life. Jim took a bit of persuading and I had to be nice to him for weeks but eventually I got my way as I knew I would and a For Sale board went up outside The Gables. As soon as it did, I got started on my plans for The Pantry, ringing shop fitters and sign makers and getting quotations for the refit. I planned to get someone else to manage it on a day to day basis but the place would be mine and I dreamt that it would become known as the finest bakery in the area.

Looking back I see now that Jim had already started a campaign to rob me of The Pantry, winding me up by saying I didn't need to work so hard anymore and that we should both be thinking about retirement. I told him he could sit on his fat backside all day in front of daytime telly if he wanted but I wasn't ready to hang up my apron. The bakery is the only thing in my life I'm proud of. Six days of the week I fill it with lovely warm bread that I've made and shaped with my own hands and when I line up the loaves and set out the trays of breadcakes there's this thrill of pleasure that runs deep through me. But of course he never did understand that. How could he? If he had, he would never have done what he did.

Ridston is what you might call a honeypot. Meaning that it attracts a lot of visitors who park their cars in a cluster on the green and, having gazed at the view for a few minutes, then swarm over the village oohing and ahing as they poke their noses into, and I quote, *'this typical Dales village with stunning views'*. In fact we have two teashops, an ice-cream parlour, three gift shops (one consisting completely of imported tat), a pottery, and the Tourist Information Centre which boast an exhibition of local artistic talent – or rather lack of it. And the Folk Museum. The only good thing you can say about the visitors is that they do spend their brass. Then there's the walkers and cyclists, poncing about in their coloured cagoules and woolly hats with their stupid daysacks, feeling smug that they've not taken the easy option, even though a lot of them spend their lives polluting towns and cities with their 4x4s. That lot don't spend much, with the worst ones bringing their own food and sitting on the green unwrapping a foil packet of sandwiches and drinking tea from a flask. Bastards.

When we were courting me and Jim used to visit the Folk Museum when it was out of season which meant there'd hardly be any visitors with it being so hard to find. It's tucked away down a lane behind one of the tearooms and even in the summer, with a board on the green saying 'Ridston Folk Museum – Open Now' and a wobbly arrow pointing nowhere in particular you get people wandering round asking where it is. There used to be a handbell outside on the doorstep which you were meant to ring to say you're there but we'd ignore that and just go in. In our day the place was even more of a mess and it was easy to snuggle down in a corner. Course Jim was always trying to get into me knickers – I'd have been disappointed if he hadn't done – but by the same token he'd have been surprised if I'd let him. That's how it was in them days.

'Museum' is a grand word for what amounts to just three small rooms. Over the years people have donated bits and pieces and Maggie, who runs it with the help of volunteers, has done her best but basically it's a clutter of random junk: rusty old milking equipment, lumps of rock, maps, old photos of the village, crockery, teapots, piles of Yorkshire Tourist Board leaflets, old Mrs Binson's home made peg bags and knitted tea cosies, though I've never heard of any being sold. She's all but blind and her stitching is chronic. Some of the rubbish is labelled in glass cases but there are some wooden poles which have been propped against the wall for as long as I can remember and they could be anything.

Once I'd killed Jim getting the body there was going to be tricky but I planned on using a wheelbarrow – at night, of course. I've never been what you might call a small woman, even when I was a young lass, and now I'm what Mam calls 'well covered'. All my baking has given me strong arms and beneath the bracelets of fat around my wrists are tendons that are as strong and elastic as dough. I'd got a key for the place – another clever move on my part. I'd heard that Maggie was going on holiday and so I offered to keep an eye on things and give it a bit of a clean too. Maggie was ever so grateful.

I wanted everyone to see him there. Three weeks ago, *The Darlington and Stockton Times* had run a front page article about how Yorkshire Cultural Heritage was considering a grant for The Museum which would provide interactive portals (whatever those might be when they're at home), a gift shop, a café, toilets and a proper reception desk – all those things which organisations like that consider essential for a visitor attraction. Local people were invited along to look at plans and offer their views on the proposed development. So what better visitor attraction could there be than Jim, mounted on the wall, as an example to all husbands who consider double crossing their wives?

Jim's betrayal was simple and brutal: he agreed to sell The Gables to someone he knew was planning to use it as a bakery. Of course I didn't know anything about that until the deal was agreed and on finding out I thought I would explode with rage.

'But she's giving us a good price!' he protested when at last I'd recovered enough to take him to task.

'So? Money's not everything!'

'I seem to remember it was you who wanted to sell up and make money.'

'It's not too late to back out, Jim! Please!'

'I don't want to back out.'

It was the only time I'd begged him for something and the only time he was stubborn as a bloody mule. There was no shifting him. Later, I could never work out whether this had all been a cunning plan on Jim's part to put The Pantry out of business, thus robbing me of the only thing I could truly call mine, or whether the physical assets of Sylvia Mannington, the buyer, had blinded his judgement. A divorcee in her thirties from London, she was blonde (by choice) and had breasts which continually looked like they were trying to escape from the snug fitting and low cut tops she always wore. Her bum was better contained but seemed to move separately from the rest of her body. I wasn't surprised Jim fell for her – in a strange way I'd have been disappointed if he hadn't. And in all probability he didn't think the whole thing through. Sometimes Jim could be as thick as clotted cream.

When Sylvia visited at weekends, I made a point of befriending her so that I could find out about her strategy. She was only too willing to tell me. Apparently her bakery would only use the very finest of organic flour to produce loaves with names like gruyere and red onion focaccia, produced in a collective near Manchester and delivered fresh every morning; she would also stock speciality chutneys, olives and oils and have baskets of free range eggs and fresh herbs on the counter. Possibly local cheeses too but that would come later. She explained in detail to me how she planned to give it a rustic feel with scrubbed boards and details of special offers written on blackboards. She wasn't my type, of course, and she was

229

never going to be anyone other than what we call round here an offcumden or incomer and I wondered what would happen if she had an accident. Those high heels she tottered around in could be deadly. But at the end of the day it wasn't Sylvia I had a quarrel with. She was even nice enough to say that she hoped we wouldn't be in competition with one another. No, I agreed, there certainly wasn't going to be any competition. What I didn't say was that I knew that she would win. A posh bakery would go down a bomb.

Once I'd got Jim's body into the museum and mounted it I planned to label it as 'Traitor'. Black letters on white card. And I intended to stuff a bread roll in his mouth. Not nice, I know, but I've never claimed to be nice. I used to wonder if having children would have made me nice – it does some women. But as the years rolled by and nothing happened I eventually stopped wondering and just got on with making my bread. It's funny but whenever I get the chance to cuddle a baby I press my nose into its neck and inhale because a baby's neck smells warm and yeasty, just like bread fresh from the oven.

It never happened, of course, the killing and Jim becoming a museum exhibit. I should have known he would find a way of thwarting my plans just like he always did. He had a fatal heart attack in the solicitor's office, just after having signed the final papers for the sale of The Gables, so denying me the chance to tell him how I really felt. Or to explain about his mother: how the freshly baked breadcake filled with ham and mushroom that I brought in for her the week before she died was never intended to do her any good. I'm a country girl which means that I know all about which mushrooms to pick and which to avoid.

So, I've got the money and the world's my oyster as they say, but I haven't done anything yet. I closed The Pantry on the day of Jim's funeral and don't see any point in re-opening. The 'R' and the 'Y' have fallen off the sign and some teenage yobs have chalked an 'S' in the gap. Village life goes on, Sylvia's doing good business and the

Museum is closing very shortly for its revamp.

Sometimes I think I might do some baking. I get out the flour and mix up the yeast and start mixing but it never seems to hold together well.

DOG DAY AFTER LUNCH

Adrian Fayter

There's an old joke that goes 'A man walks into a bar [pause for sound effect]... *It was an iron bar.*' It's not a great joke, but believe me, it's even less funny when it happens in real life.

'Poor Max,' they were saying at the customer service counter, 'Poor Max, found out back in Smokers' Alley, lying in the gutter with his head smashed in...'

'Poor Max,' whispered the box clerks upstairs. 'Did you hear? In a coma, fighting for his life!'

'Poor Max,' echoed the New Claims Advisers. 'Who'd be a security guard, eh? And we thought *our* job was difficult...'

'Poor Max,' I said, as I walked into the saloon bar of the Duke of Wellington and sat down next to my old friend Paul Wodehouse. I needed a drink: it was 6.55pm on a Monday evening and I had only just managed to leave the office. Paul, I guessed, would be going back to work through the night. 'Poor Max. What are the chances, d'you think?'

'Of him pulling through?'

'No, of you buggers catching the attacker.'

'Larry, I won't lie to you.' Detective Sergeant Paul Gerald Wodehouse took a deep pull at his pint of bitter. 'I called your Regional Director this afternoon, and the first thing he said was "Max who?" It seemed to sum up the whole investigation so far.'

The next day Paul and I went to visit Max's wife. Since our Centre Manager was on his eighth month of sick leave, naturally all his duties were falling on the next most senior member of staff: that is, God help us, *me*.

So here I was on my way to give my own – and the Department's – condolences to a woman I had met once at the last Christmas do, in the company of a police officer who would be asking whether her husband had any enemies, and could she confirm her own whereabouts on the afternoon of his death? It wasn't the sort of morning I could ever have imagined back when I first started working in a Jobcentre; it wasn't even the sort of morning I would imagine nowadays, with all my experience of the oddness of human nature and the absurdity of working life. I wasn't at my most confident, I have to admit. But then, who needs confidence, after all, so long as your own skull is still intact?

The door was opened by a tall blonde with immaculate make-up, skin-tight stretch denim jeans and a shimmering, silvery blouse. A king-sized cigarette smouldered between the fingers of her left hand. She smiled at us, sadly.

'Mrs Straker? Larry Di Palma. We spoke on the phone. And we met…'

'I remember. I trod on your foot, didn't I?'

I attempted my best rueful smile. 'Twice. This is Detective Sergeant Wodehouse.'

Paul extended his hand. 'I'm very sorry. A difficult time for you.'

'Thank you.' She closed her eyes for a second or two. 'Please come in.'

There was a carafe of strong Italian blend coffee waiting. I told her how well thought of her husband had been amongst our employees and I gave her an edited version of comments from our customers. I explained the Civil Service policy regarding *Insurance Benefits in case of Death in the Workplace*, and I said that our trade union steward had already notified his Branch Office of Max's entitlements from that quarter. I assured her that any members of staff wishing to attend the funeral would be able to be released from duty with no loss of earnings. I even promised that the investigation in process might well help ensure that this sort of tragedy would never happen again. I addressed her as Mrs Straker three times, and she told me to call her Helen twice. I thanked her for the coffee and said it was delicious.

Paul said, 'Do you own a dog of any sort, Mrs Straker?'

'I'm sorry?'

'A dog. Do you have one?'

'No. We... I... No. I'm allergic; we couldn't have pets. Why? Is it important?'

Paul gave a sort of non-committal shrug. 'Can you think of anyone who would have wished to harm him?'

'No.'

'You're sure?'

'Of course I'm sure. I've been awake all last night wondering about it. I think I'd have some ideas by now, wouldn't I? If there was anybody...'

'He did work in security.'

'Then you should ask his workmates, shouldn't you?' She gave me a rather pained look and I scratched my ear in embarrassment.

'And he worked as a bouncer at Dixie's Nightclub, as well as for the Department of Work and Pensions during the day.'

'Sergeant, Max didn't talk about work when he came home. He didn't talk about anything, to be honest, except football, what was for dinner, and...' Mrs Straker – Helen – screwed up her eyes again and took a deep breath, 'and did I want to look for a new dress in the sales...' She took a tissue from a little box on the coffee table. 'Since he was made redundant and he started work as a security guard, he talked less and less as time went by. There's nothing I can say that will help you. I wish I could, but I can't.'

'And what did he do before he was made redundant?'

Helen looked down into her lap and didn't answer. I cleared my throat and said quietly, 'He was a salesman. In the pet food industry. He signed on as unemployed until we offered him the security job.'

'If he hadn't been made redundant in the first place,' she sobbed, 'none of this would have happened.'

'The SOCOs found a number of hairs all over his jacket,' Paul explained as we drove away. 'Dog hairs.'

'You think the attacker had a dog with him?'

'Not particularly. It's more likely that a dog came sniffing around while he was lying there. There were no bite marks on the body. A dog would join in if its owner was in a fight, wouldn't it? But we have to check all angles.'

I nodded. 'The dog hairs are a bit of a dead end, then.'

'We're appealing for witnesses, so I suppose we can add "*Were you out walking your dog?*" to the wording. But it's a bit of a long shot. It would be too much to hope that someone was going by, with their dog off the lead, at the exact time that our perp was out on the street. The dog was probably lost anyway, or let out on its own because the owner couldn't be arsed walking it.'

'Can forensics tell you the exact breed of dog?'

'Oh, yes. Believe it or not, there are several experts in animal identification and matching. Breed, likely age, state of dog's health and so on will all be available soon. But it doesn't help us, does it?' Paul turned and smiled wryly. 'Without the owner being there, I mean. It's not as if Counsel can cross examine a whippet.'

Paul dropped me back at the office where I still had a mountain of benefit fraud cases to work through, never mind filling in for WJ Bell, BA (Hons), our absent Centre Manager. But I couldn't really concentrate: my mind kept drifting back to Max, kept reviewing the evidence… Or such evidence as I had in my possession. Paul Wodehouse was a professional police officer; there was a limit to what he was prepared to share.

Smoker's Alley, though. What a place to go. An old-fashioned snicket full of rubbish and covered in graffiti, stinking of piss and worse, a short cut between the Three Tuns and the All Nite Discount Booze Store. Although two Jobcentre fire exits opened onto the alley, no one ever used them during fire drills, and it was only the hardened nicotine addicts who ventured out there, smoking out front now being a disciplinary offence.

According to Paul, the position of the body indicated a short struggle, during which Max had been pushed violently back, had slipped in the wet and smashed his head on the short end of an iron bar, that is a piece of half-broken balustrade from the building's original, now rust-eaten fire escape steps. Surely then, this was an opportunistic attack. No weapon had been used against him, and it seemed unlikely that anyone would know the exact time he would be going outside for a smoke. Our own staff might see him go, but who would want to pick a fight with Max? The whole reason we employ him is that we're all afraid of violence.

You could see Paul Wodehouse's problem. The seriousness of Max's condition was quite possibly an unintended consequence of a brief scuffle, and the guilty party could be any Jobcentre claimant with a grudge, or anyone he had thrown out of Dixie's on a Saturday night, or just some lowlife chancing his arm for a few extra quid to spend at the booze store. There appeared to be no witnesses, and the crime scene was dirty and contaminated. Paul had promised that we would all do our very best to catch the assailant, but really, in the words of another very old joke punchline, the Police had nothing to go on.

Paul was back on the Thursday morning to check on the constables who had been interviewing our staff and cross-referencing any mention of Jobcentre clients with a PV sticker on their paperwork. PV stands for 'Potentially Violent', but there are no clear rules about who should fall into this category; it's an odd convention from 30 or more years ago, and one which no doubt now contravenes both Human Rights guidelines and the Data Protection Act. There are red dots plastered over quite a number of our customers' claim files, mainly those of perfectly normal individuals who just happen to have banged the desk and shouted a few obscenities at one time or another. I would guess that finding a murderer amongst them would be highly unlikely, but any PV clients who had attended the office on the day of Max's death would already have been visited at home by the police. Those without an alibi would not be able to leave town without a Detective Inspector's permission, not for a funeral, wedding, christening or even a job interview. And if they had any sort of past criminal record, their fingerprints would be painstakingly matched against all the smeary half-visible dusts from the alley. All of which seemed to me to be clutching at straws, but then, if a man's in a coma, I suppose someone has to do *something* to help reassure the public.

I said this to Paul and he rubbed his chin thoughtfully. 'Maybe I should just arrest *you*, Larry,' he said. 'You claimed to be on a fraud investigation visit, but you had over an hour without an alibi after you left the DoggieBest factory...'

'You know I always have a cigarette in the park afterwards!'

'And you were dancing with the victim's wife at the Christmas party.'

'Yes, and obviously I spiked Max's drink so he spent the whole night throwing up in the gents while I moved in on her.'

'By which time you were already working on a plan to get him out of the way permanently. And there's another thing.'

'Oh, yes?'

'Years ago you told me that before you dropped out of university, you were a member of the karate club.'

'Alright, Miss Marple,' I admonished him. 'I also told you that I lasted exactly one term. I asked out a total of four girls who were also club members, and after they had all turned me down, I stopped going.'

Paul Wodehouse sighed deeply. 'This investigation is just going nowhere,' he complained. 'None of your staff have given us any real leads. We've had five death threats reported to us, and not one of them is anything more than an unwise comment by someone whose money got stopped by mistake. Isn't there anyone else we could talk to?'

'No. Only Diane, and she's been off sick all week.'

'Alibi?'

'The doctor was at her house on Monday. And her husband said she was in bed all day. On the plus side, she's supposed to be coming back to work tomorrow, so you could interrogate her if you like. Just for the sake of completeness.'

'Yeah, maybe.'

'Of course, some people said she had gone sick because she had a shouting match with a client the Friday before. But that isn't Di's style. She can cope with angry clients more than most of the clerks can. She'd make a much better security guard than Max.'

Paul stood up and brushed biscuit crumbs from his suit. 'OK, I'm off to the Discount Booze Store.'

'Bit early, isn't it? Even for you?'

'Idiot. It's right by the far end of the alleyway. We have to check if they saw anything suspicious. And I need some beer for the weekend, too. I'm seeing the DCI on Monday morning; I'll need something to keep me positive until then.'

It was a relief to see the back of the police for a little while, and especially on a Friday morning, when our homeless clients come in to sign on. Friday is *Personal Issue* day: those without an address, and therefore without a bank account, can come and collect their giro cheques in person.

Traditionally, no other clients attend at this time. It's like we're embarrassed about the homeless, and we want them in and out quickly and anonymously so that we don't have to dwell on the reasons for their situation, or how little help we can really offer them. We don't treat them like our other clients. We don't sit them down and go through the vacancy lists; we don't stop their money if they haven't applied for any jobs. Some are obliged to sign on weekly instead of fortnightly, but even that sanction is to stop them spending two weeks money on one big bag of smack. We see them as unemployable, we've given up on them, we are scared of them, we can't even look them in the eye. We just want them to take their giros and go. We, like everyone else, fail them.

And they make the office smell too.

Don't ask me why I was hanging around the signing point on a Friday morning: some stupid compulsion to show that I could be a more hands-on manager than Will ever was, or some need – now our security guard was in a coma – to be protective of the younger women on the customer service desks. It wasn't necessary, was it? Diane, looking great despite four days off with the flu, was paying out swiftly and with friendly, professional aplomb, and the other desks, as usual on a Friday morning, were temporarily unavailable.

'Mr Smith. How's your leg today? I'm so sorry. But you know very well that the doctor comes to the hostel every week…'

'Mr Ross. Everything's fine, my love. You cash this as usual and then go to the chemist for your prescription. I shouldn't need to remind you; you know what you'll be like if you miss it.'

'Mr Brown. Just slip that lager can into your pocket, will you? I don't want our junior staff getting ideas…'

'Mr Simpson. And how's that little dog of yours? What d'you mean? Why wouldn't I be sorry? Now don't start again or I'll have to call security…'

'Mr Watson! No smoking in this office!'

From the corner of my eye I saw Ravi, our brightest casual box clerk, hovering for my attention, and John B waving a phone receiver at me and mouthing 'Call for you.' I turned away as Mr Simpson made a quick exit – perhaps he was the only person here who didn't know there was no longer anyone who could give him the bum's rush – and I smiled at Rav as I answered the phone. It was Ray Model, General Manager of the dog biscuit factory. The man I had been visiting when Max was attacked.

'I've thought about what you said,' Ray told me, 'and I'm willing to help. You can check the staff National Insurance numbers with my HR clerks, and if any of them match your unemployed clients, then, well, as you said, it's evidence of a fraudulent benefit claim.'

'Thank you, Mr Model,' I said. 'What changed your mind?'

'To be honest, Larry, I need to cut down my wages bill again. And anyone I can sack for misconduct will save money on redundancy payments.'

'It's a mean old world.'

'I was sorry to hear about Max Straker,' Model said. 'He used to work for us, you know.'

'I know.' I thought for a moment and then asked, 'I don't suppose you know if he had any enemies, do you?'

Ray laughed. 'What, apart from me for sacking him? Well, you could consider the whole sales force. He used to fiddle his figures and claim bonuses that should have gone to other people. They were relieved to see him go.'

'Really? You know, I would never have guessed. But no wonder he needed two jobs to keep him going after that...' I was about to thank Ray and hang up, when one final question occurred to me. 'Was anyone else made redundant at the same time?'

'Yes, one other salesman. James Stuart MacIntyre: another deadbeat, to be honest, but at least he wasn't a cheat. Larry, I have to go. Call HR and arrange an appointment to do your checks. Be seeing you.'

I put down the phone and looked at Ravi. He opened his mouth to ask whatever question he had for me and I interrupted to ask him if we had a live claim for a James MacIntyre. It turned out that we did. And that he came in to sign as unemployed on Mondays. He had signed on at 12.45pm the Monday just gone, about 15 minutes before Max would have been due to take his lunch break.

I called Paul Wodehouse. He said, 'We're looking for a...' and I said, 'James Stuart MacIntyre' at exactly the same time as Paul finished 'red lumberjack coat.' Then we both said 'What?' simultaneously. Ravi stood beside me, still forlornly holding whatever paperwork it was that he'd wanted me to authorise.

'What?' I said again.

'Forensics came back with more fabric sample results. And the assistant at the off-licence remembered a customer acting oddly that lunchtime. Wearing a dirty old lumberjack-style coat. What's this about a MacIntyre?'

'Hang on.' I put my palm over the receiver and said to Ravi, 'This MacIntyre. Does he wear a red lumberjack coat?'

'What?'

'You know, a padded jacket, with a sort of tartan or check pattern, but mainly red?'

'Mr MacIntyre always wears a dark blue suit.'

'Oh, bollocks.'

'I'll tell you who does wear one though. One of the PIs. I don't know his name. One of the ones who signed on this morning. He didn't have the jacket on today, but he definitely wears one, you know, when the weather's a bit cooler...'

I stared at him. I could hear the tinny voice of Detective Sergeant Wodehouse coming through the earpiece, asking me if I was still there, and if I was, what the fuck was I playing at? I said to Ravi, 'Where's Di?' and he said, 'Well, she's closed the desk, so she's probably gone out for a fag' and I shoved the phone receiver into his hands and ran as fast as I could to the fire escape.

We closed the Jobcentre early so I could go with Diane down to the police station, but of course we had ages to wait before Paul arrived back from the homeless hostel. The squad cars had caused quite a stir, and the liberal-minded key workers were thinking of making an official complaint, but they didn't really have a leg to stand on: Max hadn't woken up yet, and it was looking more and more like the case would be one of manslaughter, or worse.

'Thanks for coming out to find me,' Diane said. 'I'm touched that you thought I might be in danger.'

'You're worth it,' I said. 'Imagine if you got bashed on the head too? Who could deal with our difficult clients then?'

Paul's suit was crumpled, his collar undone and his hair awry, which is a look he sometimes creates to impress junior solicitors, but today might just have been genuine. Certainly, there was a bulge under his armpit that was shaped more like a flask than a firearm, and when the blonde WPC brought us tea, he asked for black coffee and extra sugar. I sympathised: as a Fraud Supervisor, I know that trying to close a case is the most nerve-wracking time of all…

'So,' he said, patting a white cotton handkerchief against his brow, 'Mr Brown is an incurable alcoholic. Mr Watson flouts the rules for kicks. Mr Ross is unreliable when he comes to taking his medication. And Mr Simpson…' He sighed, tiredly.

Di gave me a worried glance, and then turned back to face Paul. 'I'm sorry, you don't seem very happy. Have I done something wrong?'

'No, no, not at all,' said Paul. 'It's me that got it wrong. If I'd talked to you as soon as you got back to work, or if I'd visited you at home, we might have got the answer sooner.'

'Told you so,' I joked, and Paul curled his lip. 'Tell me about the argument,' he said.

'There's really nothing to it,' Diane told him. 'He was angry and upset. Who wouldn't be? It only happened on Sunday night. He's lost his pet, his companion, his minder when he's on the street… Did you know that homeless people are forty per cent more likely to be mugged than ordinary members of the public? He's lost the one thing that would keep him warm in the winter. It's not a problem; he left as soon as I mentioned calling security…'

'I don't mean the argument *today*,' said Paul, taking out his handkerchief again. 'I mean the one last week. Last Friday, just before you were off work with the flu. The last day you were in work before coming back today.'

And, I thought to myself, the last working day before Max took a fall onto an iron balustrade…

I took DS Wodehouse to the Iron Duke again because we both needed a drink, and because only one of us would have to be up early in the morning to deal with the overwhelming bureaucracy of an early arrest. It was times like these when I thought I had been lucky after all to have failed the police recruitment selection procedure. At least in a nine-to-five job you know exactly what time you can lock up your desk and put everything, however briefly, out of your mind.

'Pull yourself together,' I told him. 'You've solved the case.'

'It's such an obvious mistake,' he complained. 'We assumed that if it was a Jobcentre signer who attacked him, then it would be one who had signed on that same morning. Not one from the Friday before.'

'Well, it's a reasonable assumption. Most people avoid coming anywhere near the place unless they have to.'

'Or unless they just happen to be passing by after a trip to the cheap booze store.'

'But you had no way of knowing about the bust-up on Friday until you spoke to Diane. Why would you suspect a Friday client at all? You weren't to know that the other clerks all take a long tea break to avoid the PIs, so that no one else heard the argument. Your guys spoke to all our staff, but there were only two who knew about the argument: one was in bed with flu and the other with… brain damage. And even so you've got an arrest within a week! I can't understand why you're so miserable.'

Paul took another sip of bitter, fiddled with a beer mat for a moment or two, and then drank again, more deeply. 'You know what?' he said. 'It's because we've got the collar that I'm miserable. I must be going soft in my old age, but I actually feel sorry for Simpson.'

I got a couple of whisky chasers and said, 'Now we come to the curious incident of the dog in the afternoon.'

'Ha bloody ha.'

'Come on, you're not entering into the spirit of things!'

'The dog did nothing in the afternoon,' said Detective Sergeant Wodehouse, gloomily. 'Because it was already dead.'

'I hope you're not going to get annoyed again about not guessing what really happened.'

'Let's just say that we investigators can learn from this. Don't just go with the obvious. Dog hairs don't only come from the dog. They come from anyone who has been in close contact with the dog. And they stick very nicely to threadbare brushed cotton.'

'Such as a lumberjack coat.'

'Exactly. The sort of coat that is perfect as a blanket for a sick dog.'

The truth is that crime is very rarely committed by selfish, isolated individuals who are only in it for their own material gain, or their own pleasure. You learn this quickly if you work in benefit fraud. Most of my cases involve small amounts of money claimed by people who just want to provide a few extra luxuries for their partner or children. They do a bit of cash-in-hand work and end up getting found out. (I prefer tracking down the major fraudsters and the bent employers, but such opportunities are few and far between.)

So it wasn't hard to join Paul in feeling sorry for Mr Simpson. That first Friday he had begged, cajoled, threatened and abused because he hoped for an extra emergency payment so he could afford to pay the vet's fee. He was unstable enough for Di – our expert on difficult clients, remember – to call for Max's support. You don't have to condone his actions to understand the strength of feeling involved.

And as for what happened on the Monday, well, drunk and grief-stricken, he had lashed out, and started a fight that ended badly. Of course we're all desperately anxious about Max; he was unconscious for a week; they're still assessing how much permanent damage has been done. But Simpson claims he had no idea how badly hurt Max was; he had just run off as fast as he could. Which might explain why he legged it on the second Friday when Di said she would call security. He thought Max would be on his way downstairs to carry on the fight.

Still, there are some positive outcomes from all this. Paul told me their Clinical Psychologist had recommended bereavement counselling for Simpson. I thought he was joking, but it turned out it wasn't so much about the dog as the circumstances that had put him onto the streets in the first place. And Max's wife is there for him every day, reassuring him that it's not about the salary or the job description or the dresses, but it's about something else altogether.

All of which is a big relief to me. I mean, I'm still acting as office manager and running all the fraud investigations, and, since we still have no proper security backup in the office, I'm on call for that as well. So at the end of a busy day's work, I feel I deserve to relax. I don't want to be worrying about my staff or my clients, and I don't want to be reminded about crime and violence each time I walk into a bar. I just want to have a drink and a joke instead.

ABOUT THE WRITERS

KARON ALDERMAN grew up on Anglesey but studied English at Newcastle, where she now lives and works. *The Millionaire's Wife* is her second published short story, following *The Golden Fur* (*The Journal*, 2011). Currently writing a crime novel, Karon has also written four children's novels, including *The Story Thief* (Frances Lincoln Diverse Voices Fiction Award runner-up, 2010) and *For Keeps* (second in the same award 2011 and Northern Promise Award 2012).

PAT BLACK is a journalist and author who lives in West Yorkshire. His short stories have been published in several anthologies and have won prizes including the *Daily Telegraph*'s Ghost Stories competition. He has also been shortlisted for the Red Cross International Prize and the Bridport Prize (twice), and longlisted for the Fish Short Story prize. His most recent work will appear in the Momaya yearly anthology, and *Chase The Moon* magazine. He finished in second place in the prestigious Bloody Scotland international short story competition in 2014, and was longlisted for the William Hazlitt essay prize for 2015. He is currently working on a crime novel, *I'm The One*.

LYNNE M BLACKWELL writes crime fiction, set in atmospheric Yorkshire/Derbyshire locations. She was brought up by Ilkley Moor, close to disused tunnels, mossy remains of bleaching mills, and ponds. After a stint in the Special Constabulary, she moved into a Victorian mansion on the edge of the peak district to begin nurse training. Lynne has worked mainly in acute general and psychiatric hospitals. She co-ordinated day-care for people with dementia before attending an Arvon course to pursue a writing career. She has a BA in Social Policy from Sheffield Hallam University, where she studied Psychology, Sociology, Politics and Criminology.

BEN BORLAND was born in Blackpool and grew up in Chorley, Lancashire, where he learned the correct term for a bread roll (barmcake) and inherited a love of crime fiction from his dad. He later chose to go down the mean streets of journalism (although he is not himself mean) and pursued a career in newspapers in Sheffield, Congleton, Blackpool, Edinburgh, Glasgow and Manchester. He has written a spoof walking guide, *Britain's Worst Walks*, and self-published two crime novels, *Sharko* and *LA 3-Way*. Ben is married with two children, aged seven and 10.

MICHAEL CONNON hails from Wallsend and while having lived in London and Ireland amongst other places, currently resides in his native North East. His short fiction has won several competitions and awards, including Most Highly Commended in the 2013 John Howard Short Story Competition, and been published in the 2014 anthology, *Speak!* Michael has also written for stage, TV and radio and is currently looking to develop some of his stories for TV while working on a novel.

ADRIAN P FAYTER is the author of the *Larry Di Palma* series of crime novels. *Death Benefit* was published in August 2013, and further titles are in production. Larry short stories feature online in the *Words from a Bench* joint project between writers in York and Reykjavik. Adrian is a graduate of the MA in Creative Writing at York St John University. As well as the *Larry* series, he writes poetry and short stories and has been published in online magazine *Indigo Rising UK*. Working for the Employment Service Jobcentres in the 1990s, he was described by his boss as 'the best damn box clerk ever,' and the experience has allowed him to create an authentic setting for the *Larry* stories. Adrian is married, with two grown up children. Find him at http://crimebooks.wordpress.com.

BRADLEY LANGHAM grew up in Haltwhistle on a heady cocktail of movies and Bruce Springsteen, and started writing from a young age. He went on to receive a BA in Media Production and an MA in Creative Writing from Northumbria University and has since developed his writing for a number of different mediums including short stories, film and biographies. This is his first published work and it's a pretty big deal for him.

DANNY MARSHALL lives in Halifax, where he was born and raised. He has been an avid reader since pre-school age, but didn't start writing until 2014. He enjoys writing crime fiction with elements of horror – and is currently working on two mystery thrillers. His debut horror novel, *Ferine*, is out in early 2016. He works for a bank, and spends any free time (when not writing) tinkering with old cars, walking with his dogs in the nearby countryside, or trying in vain to keep his old house weatherproof.

KATH MCKAY's publications include two poetry collections: *Collision Forces* (Wrecking Ball, 2015) and *Anyone Left Standing* (Smith Doorstop 1998); one pamphlet, *Telling the Bees* (Smiths Knoll, 2014); and a novel, *Waiting for the Morning* (The Women's Press, 1991). Stories feature on www.cutalongstory.com, in anthologies *Migration Stories* (Crocus), *Light Transports* (Route), *Mountains of Mars* (Fish), and *Arc Short Stories*; and in magazines such as *Red Ink*, www.pulp.net, *Moving Worlds* and *Metropolitan*, and have been broadcast on Radio 4.

TOM MOODY lives in a village in rural Northumberland. He was born on Tyneside, but lived for some years in the high Pennines. As a Registered Nurse, he had articles, and short stories published in the nursing press. He has written a prize-winning script for BBC local radio and had poems published in literary journals. He is currently studying for an MA in Creative Writing at Newcastle University.

EMMA OXLEY lives in Sheffield with her husband and daughter. After leaving college, Emma worked in sales. A storyteller at heart however, she would spend her weekends eagerly scribbling down her ideas. After the arrival of her first child, she decided to stay at home to devote her days to writing and has not looked back since. When she is not working on her first novel, Emma divides her time between taking care of her daughter and studying psychology at the Open University.

PAM PLUMB was inspired to write *Memento Mori*, her short story in this anthology, after attending the 2014 Crime Story weekend held at Northumbria University. Some of her other work, in the form of short stories and flash fiction, has been published both traditionally in anthologies and on a variety of websites and online magazines. Recently Pam won the Cockermouth Crime Short Story competition which was judged by crime writer Mark Billingham.

BASIL RANSOME-DAVIES has been writing and publishing for over 40 years, along with teaching American Literature & Film Studies. A regular winner of *New Statesman* and *Spectator* literary competitions, he has published widely (short prose and verse) in various collections and magazines as well as critical works on fiction and film, but crime fiction is his primary interest. Winner of the Newcastle Lit & Phil crime story competition 2007, and shortlisted for Moth's Northern Crime Competition 2012, Basil was born in Metroland and lives in Lancaster with a wife and two cats.

ALEX REECE ABBOTT is an award-winning writer, working across genre and form. Her short work has been nominated for writing.ie Short Story of the Year and is regularly published around the world. Alex's stories have been shortlisted internationally in competitions including Fish, Mslexia, Lorian Hemingway, and the Bridport Prize. Her first three novels have won or have been shortlisted for prizes and her latest crime novel, *Last of the Lucky Country*, was shortlisted for the 2015 Northern Crime Awards. She barely blogs at www.alexreeceabbott.info.

MARTIN ROBINS grew up in rural North Yorkshire and currently resides in Gateshead with his wife and two small children. He spent several years as a freelance music journalist and photographer, reviewing and shooting acts as diverse and Arctic Monkeys, Eels, and Snoop Dogg, published in music blog theregoesthefear.com and Newcastle-based zine *NARC*. He is guitarist, singer and songwriter for rock band Ten Degrees Of Pitch. *May Tricks* is his first published work of fiction.

NICK TRIPLOW is the author of the crime novel *Frank's Wild Years* and social history books *Family Ties, The Women They Left Behind, Distant Water* and *Pattie Slappers*. Originally from London, now living in Barton upon Humber, Nick has recently completed his biography of Brit-noir pioneer Ted Lewis, whose landmark 1970 novel, *Jack's Return Home*, was filmed as *Get Carter*. He is also working on a sequel to *Frank's Wild Years*, provisionally titled *The China Hall*.

BETTY WEINER has focused on writing since her retirement from social work. She has had a short memoir published and her stories have appeared in small press anthologies, on the net, in the *Newcastle Journal* and read on BBC 4. Two full-length plays have been runners-up in competitions and a short comedy performed. One of her plays will be performed next March by the amateur theatre group at The Theatre Royal.

BELINDA WEIR is a leadership development consultant, an academic teacher and researcher (at the Universities of Birmingham and Lancaster) and a writer. The first prize she won for writing was in 1970 – 10 shillings from Puffin Post, presented by Alan Garner. 25 years later she was a winner in a national children's short story competition and she continues to write short stories, blogs and magazine articles as well as research papers. She lives in Lancaster with her husband and has two grown-up children.

MJ WESOLOWSKI is a horror writer from Newcastle upon Tyne. His first ever book, written and illustrated at age 11, was entitled *Attack of the Killer Flytraps* and whilst his writing style has possibly matured since then, his themes and content almost certainly haven't. His short fiction has appeared in a number of UK and US horror anthologies and his debut novella, *The Black Land*, set in the Northumberland countryside was published by Blood Bound Books in 2013. Matt blogs about horror, the supernatural, books and other strange things at https://mjwesolowskiauthor.wordpress.com/. You can follow him on twitter @ ConcreteKraken.

SUE WILSEA retired early from teaching to write and in 2010 was selected by Arvon as one of nine New and Gifted Writers. In 2012 Valley Press published her short story collection, *Staying Afloat*. Sue also performs as part of a spoken word duo. She teaches part-time at Hull University and recently completed an MA in Creative Writing at Newcastle. For the last 20 years Sue has lived on the banks of The Humber.